BILLY WHEELER'S
SPACE-TIME TOURNAMENT

BILLY WHEELER'S
SPACE-TIME TOURNAMENT

Matthew Bucknole

ISBN 9798834567189

To my family and friends,
for your never-ending support and encouragement.
We got there in the end.

1

The letterbox slapped shut and a small, heavy box thumped to the floor. Dressed in a full-length black raincoat and wide brimmed hat, the man delivering the parcel walked away. He hadn't knocked, he hadn't waited to see if anyone was home. Unseen, he'd simply left.

***

The early morning sun wrapped its warm arms around him as he sat in his cosy kitchen. He was eating breakfast on autopilot and in a typical daydream when the noise of the letterbox interrupted him. *Was that the postman?* he thought. *On a Sunday?* It wasn't of course, but the apparent early arrival of post was too out of the ordinary not to raise interest.

He crept into the hallway and spotted the small black box on the doormat. His heart began to thump. This wasn't expected, not today. Picking it up, memories came flooding back. The colour, the name printed on the front, the embossed design that traced its corners. They were more than enough for excitement to take hold.

Retreating to his bedroom he opened it up and peered inside. He expected to find a tournament Insignia. But he didn't. Instead, it was something far more valuable!

'A Memory Trace,' he said, surprising himself by speaking aloud. Not wanting to wake his parents, he fell silent and into secret thought. *Why have they sent me a Trace? What would I want with someone else's memories?* Unable to resist the temptation of knowing whose memories he held, he set the Trace on his VR-Wall and pressed play.

Flickering into existence, the life of a boy began to surround him as if he were living his life and seeing it through his eyes, but then he wasn't experiencing someone else's memories after all. He watched in silence. No words would ever do.

***

Billy Wheeler was sitting in the back of the car when a holographic advert popped up, replacing a dull, ordinary road sign. It was triggered by a traffic jam that had lasted no longer than five minutes. It seemed that even in the year 2102, while technology had changed everything, it hadn't solved the problem of there being too many cars. The Time Travel Lottery was being advertised yet again and Billy was watching it, yet again!

'Oh, not this flippin' advert,' he groaned. 'Everybody knows time travel is a waste of … time,' he coughed, in a comedy laugh. 'If I ever win the lottery, I'm going to head back to when it was invented and un-invent it.' He knew this was all but impossible on the basis that people like him couldn't afford Time Tickets, but he liked the idea all the same. 'Is it really true that time travel is useless?' he asked.

'Nobody really knows,' his mum replied. 'Lots of important people have tried to change the past and failed. At least that's what they think, because nothing seems to have changed and nobody's ever come back to say otherwise.'

It was common knowledge that time travel appeared to be a one-way ticket, but Billy had ignored this largely on the basis that being a time-traveller would be 'the coolest thing ever!'

'I'd still go for a spin,' he said, with complete honesty. Then, thinking better of his earlier comment, 'but I think I'd go back and high five Marty McFly.'

Billy spent the next five minutes contemplating this thought, when much to his relief, the traffic jam had gone.

***

Billy Wheeler isn't the kind of boy that you could ever call average. For starters, he owns the messiest head of ginger hair. It often has the appearance of being cut with a pair of garden shears such are the stark angles it achieves. Despite the effort of his parents who send him to school looking tidy in his hand-me-down clothes, you can be sure that by morning break he has the air of ragged and rough that everyone knows him for. To complement his comical appearance, his red and grey school jumper always looks one size too small – something that Billy says will make him more aerodynamic – and grey trousers that are always a bit too baggy – something that he quite sincerely claims will stop him being too aerodynamic.

For most boys Billy's age, you might expect them to be noisy and energetic or forgetful and clumsy. But with Billy, it would be more accurate to describe him as dangerous. Not that he isn't good, because he is. In fact, he's very good. The trouble with Billy, is that he's very good at doing dangerous things. So, in the middle of morning break, it wasn't a great surprise when Miss Cravity spotted him hurtling around the school yard with one foot in a Dynoblade and the other on a Hoverboard.

Billy's physics teacher is about as slim as a pencil and most notably has a sharp and pointy nose. It's the perfect match to her sharp and pointy character. As a matter of fact, Billy often comments on how aerodynamic she must be with her pointy body, skinny pencil skirt and tight-fitting blazer.

'Billy Wheeler, you stop that at once!' she shouted. 'You're going to break something!'

Billy looked up to see his teacher cutting through the maze of energetic school kids. 'Don't worry Miss. I've got this!' he declared confidently. Billy should have known better. No sooner had the words left his mouth when his legs began to do the splits and travel in opposite directions. Powerless to stop himself, he watched in horror as an incoming rose bush shot between his legs and hooked firmly into his trousers. Latched on like cat's claws, it followed him until tipping over and smashing its terracotta home into a thousand pieces.

'Nice one Billy,' came a shout from behind. It was Katie Jack, his best friend. 'You're showing your cheeks again!'

Billy leapt off the Hoverboard and came to an abrupt stop, sheepishly trying to cover the brand-new hole in his trousers whilst his freckled face flushed plum red. 'No way!' he complained, looking at the smashed pot. 'I am dead when I get home!'

It might have been the first time he'd reckless enough to damage school property, but it wasn't the first time he'd ripped his trousers; Billy was in trouble and he knew it.

'Maybe you're not going to get that bike for your birthday after all,' Katie said.

'What d'you have to say that for?' Billy complained. He'd been asking for a new bike for ages, but his parents knew all too well that while you could often describe him as dangerous, he had no regard for what the word meant. That alone was a good enough reason not to buy him one. Well, that and their disastrous bank balance, anyway.

Distracted by Katie and awkwardly trying to cover his backside, Billy had failed to notice that Miss Cravity was now standing right behind him.

'Right then, Mr Wheeler,' she said, her voice sounding every bit as sharp as her nose looked. 'You might possess the talent to perform an endless supply of tricks, but you're certainly lacking the ability to explain yourself to Mr Crankworth this time.' Her delighted tone suggested that Billy had gotten away with things a little too easily before. 'Headmaster's office,' she ordered. 'Right now!' Without waiting for a reply, she turned away and scurried off in search of her next victim.

2

Billy spent the remainder of his break-time staring at the heavy wooden door of Mr Crankworth's office. It was the kind of door that shouting did not travel through very easily. After a long wait, he'd started to hope the Headmaster wasn't in the office after all. But then the door creaked open, and a voice came rumbling from behind it.

Mr Crankworth's office is a familiar place to Billy. An old looking room panelled in blackened wood, it reminds him of the local library, but instead of being covered with books, every wall is home to a collection of sparkling trophies. Billy liked to see the one he'd earned for playing Dynoblade Hockey, but it had always been overshadowed by another. Sitting next to his own, was a dull and odd-looking thing that was shaped like a large egg-timer. On each visit to the office, he'd tried to investigate its identity but had only managed to read the letters S and T on the base. All the others had been rubbed away. Once again, whilst daydreaming about its owner, he found himself interrupted.

'Now then, Billy. Have I not told you enough times about putting an end to this nonsense rivalry with Dean Tuffnell?'

'It isn't really a rival—'

'Stop right there,' Mr Crankworth demanded.

In Billy's opinion Mr Crankworth was as old as the moon, but he still had a deep and powerful voice that would stop you in your tracks. Despite the undeniable authority his voice gave him, he'd often seemed to soften when telling Billy off.

'I know you have the talent for these tricks. I've been watching you long enough to know that. But school is not the place to prove what you can do!' He glanced around the room and sort of hunched over like he was going to share a secret. 'If you're going to insist on outdoing Mr Tuffnell in the future, then I suggest you choose wisely. You can enjoy a fifteen-minute detention after school for interrupting my morning. Now, before I change my mind about your punishment, get yourself off to class.'

Billy left the office barely minutes after walking in, once again feeling a little confused. Why did Mr Crankworth tell him that school was not the place to prove himself and then offer strange advice? And why did he always seem to give such insignificant punishments? Although when Billy thought about it, being given an after-school detention on the last day of term didn't feel insignificant after all.

Back in class at his favourite subject, and despite sitting next to Katie, Billy spent most of the time daydreaming about his imminent birthday and the reducing possibility of owning a new bike.

'Billy,' Katie whispered. 'Have you heard what Dean's been saying?'

'No,' he replied, dismissively. He didn't want to think about Dean. Dean was the sixteen-year-old who made him look like an idiot whenever he got the chance. The boy who Mr Crankworth had referred to only half an hour ago when telling him to stop their nonsense rivalry.

Despite Billy's lack of interest, Katie shuffled closer. 'He's been saying that his dad was in the tournament.'

'What tournament?' asked Billy, with slightly increased interest.

'Are you for real? Katie replied. 'The Space-Time Tournament!'

Billy burst out laughing. 'You're having me on,' he said, jabbing her in the ribs. 'How could Dean's dad possibly have anything to do with that?'

Katie put a finger up to her lips. 'Shush,' she said, trying to keep their conversation quiet. 'I didn't say I believed it. But if he's telling the truth, because then Dean could—'

'No offence K,' Billy said, butting in as though trying to protect his precious tournament. 'But if Dean's dad has anything to do with that, then you're good at telling jokes!'

Billy had been obsessed with the tournament from the moment he'd read the story of Casey McGrips – the most talented contestant ever. She'd activated an ice-pick wheel Gadget on her Magbike to land an outrageous jump and win the Everest event. Billy had re-told the story countless times, always insisting it would be the most awesome thing to do, but Katie wasn't so sure; being infinitely too sensible was a hard habit to break.

'Do you really think he was in it? Dean's dad,' Billy asked, thinking about the tournament yet again.

'I think Dean would say anything if he thought it made him look impressive,' Katie replied. 'Especially now you're always competing.'

When Billy had started at Peregrine Heights – a very expensive school where he and his family didn't seem to belong – Dean hadn't noticed him at all. But then he'd overheard Billy's surname, and everything changed. From that point on, Dean had made Billy his target and hunted him daily.

After months of torment, Billy's redemption came in the form of a borrowed hoverboard. After his many schoolyard tumbles and tricks, some of the kids had labelled him Wheeler-the-fearless. It became a sort of reputation that Dean ended up wanting for himself, and so began the rivalry. From that point on they'd been battling it out, one ridiculous challenge at a time. Unfortunately for Billy, he'd often end up covered in mud … or worse. There were moments during their antics however, where Billy's remarkable talent began to show, and to the Spotter at least, it hadn't gone un-noticed.

For the last fifteen minutes of class, Katie and Billy whispered back and forth, discussing what a ridiculous idea it was that Dean's dad could have been in the tournament. If they were certain of anything, it was that Dean Tuffnell must be a complete idiot if he thought anyone would believe such a thing.

3

Billy couldn't shake the thought of Dean's foolish lie as he trudged through after-school detention. But brightening his mood, he found Katie waiting at the school gate.

'What are you doing here?' he asked, with delighted surprise.

'Waiting for you, Billy-boy. I thought I'd walk back with you.'

'Umm … Okay,' he said, fixing her with a suspicious stare; Katie's house was in the opposite direction to his own. She never walked home with him unless she was coming over.

She held up her Holo-Phone and showed him the screen. 'I got my credits. Let's get some sweets.' Before Billy could ask any questions, she began to walk away. 'We can share,' she said, reading his mind; he rarely had any credits for sweets.

Halfway back to his house, Billy couldn't stand it anymore. 'K, why are you walking home with me?'

Katie stopped dead. 'Why not?' she asked defiantly, with that hands-on-hips look of hers.

'Well, it's not that I don't want you to but—' Billy fell silent; Katie had stopped looking at him and was staring over his shoulder.

'What?' he asked, suddenly feeling very uncomfortable. He turned around to see what had grabbed her attention and understood what she'd been up to; she was looking out for him. Further up the road, two boys were walking towards them. Two boys who had no business being on his route home: Dean Tuffnell and Harry Conram.

'I overheard them talking earlier,' Katie explained. 'Dean wants to make sure you don't try and pass the blame to him for smashing the plant pot at school. I think he might have some Turd Bombs.'

Billy spotted a hole in a hedge than ran along the path and ducked through it like a scared rabbit being chased by a fox. 'Let's go, K,' he whispered from the other side. 'Ripping my trousers is bad enough let alone stinking like some rotten cow turd.'

'Where are you off to?' Dean shouted, from further up the road.

'Where *are* we going?' Katie asked, realising Dean had a point.

'This field leads to Worthy Park, doesn't it?

'Yeah, of course it does. But we'll have to cross Whitelake River. We can't get over it.'

'We can! There's a rope swing,' Billy replied defiantly – hopefully.

Billy arrived at the riverbank expecting to grab the rope, but all was not well. 'No way!' he complained. 'It's not tied to the bank.'

Katie arrived and quickly realised they were faced with two bad choices: Get soaking wet or face up to Dean and the possibility of his Turd Bombs. She pointed at the green water. 'I'm not swinging over that! Dean can be a bit scary, but I'd rather give him an arm wrestle than fall in there!'

'I can get it,' Billy mumbled. Already off in his own world.

Despite her resolve to confront Dean, the thought of how Billy was going to reach the swing suddenly became more important. 'How are you going to do that?'

'Do what?' asked Billy.

'The swing. How are you going to get it?'

'I'm gonna jump.' He walked to the edge of the bank and kicked the tree stump that the swing was normally tied to. 'It sounds alright to me!' he said. The hollow thud it created suggested otherwise. Rotting inside, it was not a great launch platform! Seemingly satisfied, he took several lunge-like steps back. Looking like an athlete at the start of a race, he crouched down and pressed his hands into the dirt.

'Oi, Weeweeler! Where d'you think you're going?' Dean was half-way across the field. 'I just want to talk.'

The realisation that Dean was nearly upon them triggered Billy into action. He thrust himself forwards, quickly running flat out. Despite kicking up dust with every step, Katie could hardly hear a sound.

'You won't make it!' she shouted.

When Billy's foot hit the stump, Katie heard a dull crunch that suggested if she got to jump, she should avoid it at all costs. Lost in his own world, Billy paid no attention and launched himself skyward from the dead wood. Remarkably, he flew – seeming to ignore gravity itself – until his hands grabbed the swing.

Katie looked on, barely able to believe her eyes. 'How did?' she muttered. 'You can't …'

Hanging onto the rope, Billy swung in a giant arc. He had no right to have made the jump, but there was something special about Billy. Something very few other people could claim they shared with him.

'Get Ready K,' Billy shouted, mid-swing across the river. 'When I let go, it's coming back. You've got to grab it and then jump. Okay?'

'No Billy, it's not okay. I don't want to fall in.'

'You'll be fine. I'll catch you. I promise!'

She watched Billy let go of the swing and land in a puff of dust on the other bank. Then, taking all her nerve to do something so not sensible, when it arrived she grabbed the rope, closed her eyes, and jumped.

When Dean reached the river he promptly fell into fits of laughter. On the opposite side, Katie was clinging to the rope and Billy had her by the belt. She was hanging precariously over the water and screaming at him not to let her fall in.

'Why don't you let go, Weeweeler?' he taunted. 'Go on. I dare you.'

'Why don't you come and make him?' Katie screeched.

Billy looked at her with shocked eyes, but Katie wasn't stupid. She knew exactly what she was doing.

'Come on! Or aren't you big enough?' she taunted.

Goaded into action, Dean was obliged to act. 'Go on, Harry. Get them! Get over there!'

Dean's long-term sidekick wasn't foolish enough to say no and quickly jumped into action. He took a few steps back and timing it as best he could, ran flat out at the swing. In stark contrast to Billy his feet slapped heavily on the dirt, throwing stones and dust everywhere. Reaching the rotten stump, his foot sank deep into the wood. The sound that came from his mouth reminded Dean of a whimpering dog, and instead of launching himself skyward, Harry tumbled down the riverbank head-first into the river.

For the second time in two minutes Dean fell about laughing without a hint of guilt. Sidekick or not, Harry received no sympathy. 'Get out of there you idiot!' he shouted. Momentarily distracted, by the time he looked back to Billy and Katie, all he found was an empty riverbank. 'There's always next time, Weeweeler … next time.'

4

Having made Katie promise to go home a different way, Billy crept through his front door, hoping to sneak upstairs before anyone knew he was home. But then in a way that only mum's can, she magically appeared from the kitchen.

'Where have you been?'

Owing to his diversion across Whitelake river, Billy had forgotten all about his detention; she'd been expecting him a long time ago.

'Well?' she said, noticing her son's guilty expression.

Billy's mind worked overtime, racing to find an excuse for being late. 'Blading … wasn't me … Miss Cravity ripped my trousers.'

'Oh Billy, not another pair of trousers. I've told you a hundred times, we can't afford new ones. You know how difficult things have been since your dad's accident.'

Billy didn't know exactly what happened with his dad's accident; it had happened long before he was born. But he only had to look around his home to know she was right. They were far from well off.

'I was blading, and Miss Cravity made me fall over.'

'Don't tell lies, Billy.'

'But Mum,' he begged.' She shouted at me while I was proving I could blade and Hover—'

'Up to your room, Billy. I've told you time and time again about trying to out-do that Dean Tuffnell. In fact, I'll be talking to your dad about it when he wakes up. I don't think you're ready for this—' she trailed off abruptly, realising what she was about to say. In a poor attempt to brush over her mistake, she simply turned away. 'Go on, up to your room.'

***

As expected, Billy's dad had told him off. Not just for tearing his trousers and damaging their already poor bank balance. And not just for mashing the plant pot. But for drawing attention to his ongoing feud with Dean Tuffnell. Billy didn't get why he'd made such a fuss about that part, but make a fuss he had. A lot!

Now beyond his threshold for boredom, Billy decided to go to bed. He crossed his room, reached the door, and stopped. His parents were talking downstairs. Not talking, arguing.

'I know he's in trouble again Sue, but we can't ignore it, the invite arrived. I know he's not old enough, but they chose him.'

'He's not sensible enough either,' she argued.

Old enough for what? Billy thought. *Who are they?*

He crept onto the landing, but a creaky floorboard betrayed him and gave him away. His parents fell silent before the lounge door clicked shut. An hour later he fell asleep with a single thought looping round and round in his head: *Old enough for what? Who are they?*

5

Billy's eyes popped open with his heart pounding wildly in his chest. Not because he'd woken up from a nightmare, and not because he was excited about it being his birthday. But because in his dream he'd nailed the perfect trick and beaten Dean. In his mind's eye he could see Dean sporting an expression that he'd normally call the massive grump, but other less enthusiastic people might describe as angry.

'Happy birthday!' came bellowing through the door as his mum walked in. 'Breakfast in bed.'

A second and slightly quieter happy birthday came from his dad downstairs. 'I'll see you after breakfast,' he promised.

Billy sat in bed looking typically Billy-like. With his bed-head hair achieving impossible angles he really was an amusing sight.

'Slow down Billy. You'll give yourself gut-rot,' his mum pleaded, watching Billy trough his breakfast.

'Mum!' he groaned, 'I am quite old now. I'll be fine.'

'Ooh, a grown up,' she teased.

Billy smiled at her a touch guiltily. He might have been a year older, but he was still her Billy and always would be.

Sue knew there wasn't much point in telling him to slow down. It was only yesterday that she'd heavily suggested a new bike was waiting for him – which strictly speaking there wasn't – so aside from seeing his dad, surely all he wanted to do was get downstairs and look at his present. Lost in his breakfast daydream, he'd totally forgotten about the conversation his parents were having when he fell asleep last night.

Old enough … who are they?

Breakfast finished, Billy rushed into the bathroom and stood at the mirror. He briefly contemplated what the life of a fourteen-year-old might be like, quickly deciding it couldn't be all that different to being thirteen. But then he didn't know what his parents knew, and he couldn't see into the future very well. If he could, he'd think differently!

Brushing his teeth, he moved the brush so fast that it flicked toothpaste foam everywhere. It was something he practiced twice a day just to prove he didn't need any flash electric toothbrush. He splashed water on his face and considered himself done. Instead of using the towel – which would take far too long – he simply ran to his bedroom. Wind dried!

Billy's room, as his mum would say, 'could be used in the English dictionary to describe the word chaos.' So, it was quite remarkable that he managed to appear downstairs not five minutes later – even if he was wearing just one sock and sporting a hairstyle more scarecrow-like than ever before!

Sitting in his wheelchair and waiting for Billy to arrive had frustrated Tom Wheeler no end. But that feeling evaporated the moment he saw his son.

'Billy Wheeler, you really are a sight,' he remarked. 'How on earth did you forget to put a sock on?'

Billy didn't answer. He was busy looking around the room, oblivious to anything that was being said. There were a quite a lot of presents, but there weren't any new-bike-sized presents. Travelling quickly from excitement to disappointment, his heart sank. He would have gladly swapped all the presents in the world for a bike.

'Come here Billy-boy,' Tom said. Despite his son's best attempt to hide it, he couldn't help but see the look on Billy's face. 'How about giving me that hug I've been waiting for?'

Patience was something that Tom Wheeler had needed lots of since his accident. Before it happened, he'd had it all figured out: winning the tournament and joining the Space Exploration Programme. But then it hadn't worked out as he'd planned at all. He hated to see Billy's disappointment yet again; it was something he'd seen far too often however hard Billy tried had to hide it. Although this time things were going to be different, so he'd just have to ignore it. For now …

'Come on then,' Tom said, cheerily. 'Get opening. You've got a big day in front of you.'

Billy couldn't help but wish for a bike to be sitting in the corner of the room, but he did believe in how lucky he was. Despite that his dad couldn't work much, his parents did their best and that was enough.

6

Half an hour later and surrounded by a pile of scrap paper, Billy finished opening his gifts. He'd received a box of Pop Rocket sweets; a bumper pack of Glow Candy – which he would share with Katie later – and a huge hand-held X-Ray glass from his nan. But the best gift of all was a collection of nearly new Space-Time Tournament magazines, his favourite being Casey McGrips and the Lunatic Leap. Much to his mum's disapproval, Katie had given him a vintage science kit from the year 2068. It wasn't all that difficult for her to imagine hearing a loud bang before finding Billy sitting in cloud of purple smoke.

In 'typical Billy' style – a phrase his parents would frequently use to describe his actions – he leapt off the ground, sending wrapping paper flying everywhere.

'Thank you,' he said, smiling broadly. 'They're great, I love—'

'Hold on, Billy,' Tom interrupted, snatching a ball of wrapping paper out of the air. 'There's just one more thing.'

Billy stared at his dad in admiration. 'Awesome catch, Dad!'

Despite his need for a wheelchair, it didn't stop Tom having the odd moment of speed and dexterity that Billy himself was jealous of.

'The old boy still got it!' Tom replied, handing Billy a small box. 'Happy birthday Billy-boy.'

Billy gazed at the box sitting in his hand. Printed on the front was a large silver hourglass half-filled with tiny tumbling stars. On the back, a single howling wolf took centre stage. Beneath that, the letters S.T.T. shimmered brightly. When Billy saw them, it felt like something was poking at his brain; something like a memory that he couldn't quite identify. A grey foggy image began to take shape in his mind. But then his dad interrupted his thoughts, and the image was gone.

'Open it up then,' Tom said, impatiently.

'What is it?' Billy asked, staring at the small box. He'd never known anything to feel or look like this before. It felt like a strange cold metal but was almost weightless in his hands.

'Come on, Billy-boy. What are you waiting for?' Asked Tom, his voice sounding rushed like a five-year-old desperate for the loo.

Billy peeled open a magnetic seal before pulling out what appeared to be a faceless watch. On the outside of the wristband his name shimmered brightly in a tiny LED matrix. On the inside, a small disc was engraved with the letters S.T.T. When he moved it, the letters shimmered in the background. Although he'd never seen one for real, Billy knew what it was immediately.

'You got me a Profiler?' he asked, looking at his parents for an explanation.

'I think maybe you missed something,' his dad said, urging Billy to look in the box again.

Sure enough, when Billy checked again, he found a Black Insignia. The moment picked it up, a Holographic image appeared from the top and shimmered like a weightless letter hovering in the air.

Event: Space-Time Tournament – 2102.
Contestant: Mr Billy Wheeler.
Date of birth: 10-07-2088.
Category: 16+
Qualifying criteria: Classified.
Events to be contested: Kielder Forest; Grand Canyon; Everest.
Date of issue: 01-07-2102.
Authority: President C.

Dear Billy, a paragraph began, but the words dropped away as Billy's hand fell to his side. His dad was smiling from ear-to-ear and his eyes were sparkling brightly with excitement. His mum however, looked anything but excited; her expression was more like fear and concern. Her lack of a smile didn't change when she spoke.

'Turn the Insignia around, Billy. I want you to read it all.'

'Feeling a bit old, Mum?' Billy joked. 'How am I supposed to read the other side of something that isn't there?' He felt quite stupid when he turned it over and found a completely different letter floating in front of him. 'Um … sorry,' he said, with a sheepish smile.

What Billy could then see was a giant list of the smallest small print he'd ever seen. Although some of the words, like risk, and danger, pulsed back and forth as if demanding to be read first.

'Oh, don't worry about all that mumbo jumbo,' Tom remarked, before Billy could read too much. 'We can look at that later. It's not that important really. Besides, it's your birthday.'

Tom and Sue became locked in a stare-off.

'I don't like this one bit,' her eyes said.

'Everything will be fine,' his eyes replied.

'I don't understand,' Billy said. 'How can I be in the Space-Time Tournament? I thought you only got an invite if you had a parent who'd competed. Either that or you've got to be rich.'

'Turn it over and read the letter,' Tom told him.

Reluctantly and despite the numerous questions filling his head, Billy flipped the Insignia and began to read once more.

7

Dear Billy,

I am delighted to write to you about the Space-Time Tournament. For many years it has been our goal to find the incredible talent necessary to continue our work at the Space Exploration programme and Time Travel Initiative. As such, the tournament has become the finest method of finding the best young people to join our team.

It is with great pleasure that I am offering you an invite to compete. Should you accept, you will take part in three events, each designed to test your mind, body, and bravery; just some of the characteristics we look for in our new recruits.

I have taken the liberty of issuing a tournament Profiler as this will guarantee access to all tournament areas, provide you with a Kinetic suit, your Gadgets and basic travel needs. Unfortunately, I have not been able to offer Advanced Travel funding. In time you will understand why this decision has been made. I cannot wait to tell you about it.

I expect you will have many questions, and I am confident that with the help of your family you will find the answers. I presume that until now, you believed being a Wheeler meant you could never enter the tournament. But let me assure you, it is because you are a Wheeler that you have a place. Your father was a worthy contestant, and I have been assured that despite your age, you also possess his talent. Of course, it is not compulsory for you to accept our invitation, the tournament can be daunting even for our older contestants. But like you, they are our greatest source of skill and youthful bravery. Please take your time and choose wisely. I would imagine you could do rather well.

President C.

Billy stood in the middle of the room with the recent explosion of wrapping paper sitting as motionless as he was. His heart was beating heavily, and his mind was rushing with thoughts. The first one being that he didn't know whether to believe if this was real or not. The tournament was something he'd grown up with, frequently hearing stories that his dad had told him, and of course, watching the contestants he'd idolised. He would stare in awe as competitors raced amongst mountains, explored the depths of long abandoned mines, and turned seemingly impossible tasks into minor obstacles. Watching the tournament was almost a right-of-passage for the teenagers of his time. Most wanted to take part, but only few ever got the chance. Astonishingly, Billy was now faced with the thought that he could be a contestant himself.

'Aren't you going to say anything?' Tom asked.

'I can't do it,' Billy blurted out. 'I can't … I mean … I'm not even old enough!'

Tom responded in a voice so flat and so determined that the knot of fear in Billy's stomach began to shrink like a deflating balloon.

'I don't know how you ended up being entered in the tournament, because you shouldn't have been. Not because of your age, or because we don't have the money, but because we didn't apply for you. Listen Billy, there are thousands of teenagers who would give anything to get a Black Insignia, but you've ended up with one. You deserve the chance. You might think you can't do it, but you can. You're Wheeler-the-fearless.'

Billy wondered how his dad knew about that nickname; it had only ever been used at school. But crucially and regardless of his question, the knot of fear had disappeared. He was Wheeler-the-fearless, and he could do anything if he tried hard enough. At least he thought so. He leapt up and started jumping around the room, kicking the once silent wrapping paper into the air yet again.

'No way!' he shouted. 'I can't believe it. I'm going to compete in the tournament!'

'I presume that means you're going to accept and put the Profiler on?' asked Tom. 'You won't be able to take it off if you do.'

'Am I ever!' As if to make it happen before anybody could change his mind, Billy stretched the wristband open and thrust his hand through it before it shrank onto his wrist and locked tight.

'I guess that's that then,' Sue said, trying to hide her frustration. Although she wouldn't be able to continue that for very long and she knew it.

Billy's dad watched him with a mixture of both pride and happiness, but he couldn't quite shake that little niggle of jealousy at the recurring thought: *it was taken from me.*

As for Billy, it hadn't even crossed his mind to ask why they didn't tell him his dad was a contestant. If he had, Tom might have needed to tell his first white lie. He didn't want Billy to be asking those questions just yet; there was more history to his own tournament than he cared to remember.

8

Katie answered her Holo-Phone. 'What can I do for you, Billy-boy?' she asked, enthusiastically.

He held a box of sweets up to the camera. 'You can come over and eat Pop Rockets with me if you want to?'

'Awesome, you got some! I heard about those from Flick. She says they're wicked. Apparently, if you find a red one, you're dead lucky. They're super rare!'

Both Billy and Katie had wanted to try Pop Rockets since they'd seen the advert on TV. 'Pop Rockets, the world's first self-propelled sweets! Just put them on the floor and light the fuse.'

'Let's do it!' Katie said. 'Although I can't come over till tomorrow. Mum went and invited my aunt over. Is that okay?'

'That'll be … Sweeeet,' Billy joked, thinking it gave him time to figure out how to tell her that he'd received a Black Insignia.

'Oh, Billy-boy, that's terrible,' Katie replied, unable to hide a smile. *Typical Billy*, she thought, affectionately. 'Ooh, Happy Birthday by the way. Have you had a good day?'

'Oh, you know, it's been okay,' he replied, not wanting to give away the fact that he might well be the next Casey McGrips. 'By the way, I love the science kit. I don't know how you found one so old.'

'It's amazing what you can find on ye'oldieBay,' she said, warbling her voice in a grandma-like manner.

'Not bad, K. That was almost funny,' Billy teased.

'Ooh, thanks,' she said, sarcastically. 'Enjoy the rest of your day!'

'I will,' he replied. Any day that didn't involve Dean Tuffnell was a good day.

***

Dean Tuffnell isn't exactly short for a sixteen-year-old, but he isn't quite average height either. He could gain an inch or so with a different hairstyle, but he likes to look tough, so a buzz-cut it remains. The short cut takes a bit of the blackness away from his hair too, making it look a bit grey, but he doesn't mind; he thinks it looks menacing.

His dad, by comparison to most, is well off – especially compared to that pauper Weeweeler – so it's really no surprise that Dean owns all the technology that 2102 can offer. Taking pride of place in his bedroom is his brand-new VR-Wall. He's had a lot of fun with it recently, scaring the life out of his friends with the Amazon leopard attack. In fact, it was so convincing that one of them even cried; Dean teased him for weeks.

Another part of Dean that he's sure to show off, is his clothing. Designer names such as Viper fill his wardrobe. The futuristic T-shirts impress with their active shape, magically changing size to fit. Dean hardly cares that he has ten! He even owns a pair of Xenon shoes. Filled with rare gas, they both look awesome and have the propelling properties of Ion-thrusters. You can jump incredibly high if you want to!

Dean likes it that way, having lots of expensive things, it makes him think he's better than anyone else. If there's one thing that Dean Tuffnell likes, it's to be better than others. Living with his ill-tempered Dad taught him to think like that a long time ago. He's had to learn some hard lessons along the way, but now he can teach them to others. The one boy he's happy to teach more than any other, is Billy.

9

Sitting in his hi-tech kitchen, Dean offered a sarcastic and false smile.

'Finally letting me have it then. I've known about it for ages, but you made me wait 'til that idiot Weeweeler got his! How did he even get an Insignia anyway? He's not even sixteen!'

Even in the presence of his dad, Dean called Billy, Weeweeler. Almost certainly because that's where he'd heard it first.

'I've already told you, boy. Space-Time Industries knows when the Insignias are activated. Today was the earliest you could open it no matter when I gave it to you!'

'Well, it's stupid!' Dean argued. 'I hate waiting! Anyway, I've got the Insignia, so I want to go to Peddleton's and get my suit!'

'Okay, stop going on,' Kurt replied, quickly becoming annoyed. 'We can go later, but I've got to talk to the owner first.'

Kurt isn't a patient man, but he used to be, much more so than now. But when Tom Wheeler's life had changed all those years ago, so had his own. What he hadn't bothered telling Dean, was that the last time he'd been to Peddleton's he'd had a fight with the owner and got himself kicked out. But then why should he? It wasn't his fault, was it! At least that's what he kept telling himself. The problem was that nobody seemed to believe him when he tried to explain things. So, none of it was really his fault at all.

Kurt and Dean have lived on their own since Dean was two years old; this was around the time that Kurt had given up and changed. There was only so long you could deal with people looking at you in disappointment before it made you resent them. It's what drove Dean's mum away. Sometimes he thought that he could have handled things a bit better, that he might've had a tiny part to play in it. But everybody was at fault in some way.

There was one person, however. One person who'd always looked like they'd suffered the most when the reality was that it was his fault more than anyone's. That person really was the bad guy in all this. Not Kurt, not Dean, but him!

**

Harvey Peddleton had been enjoying an easy morning in his shop when the bell rang over the door. There were newer methods of alerting you to new customers, but Harvey thought of himself as old-fashioned, so the old bell remained. He kept things traditional where he could, 'engineered by man, not by machine' was his favourite saying. It's why he's remained one of the favourite suppliers of tournament equipment across the country.

He watched from the counter as a man sauntered across his store. The hat he was wearing had been set visor down, obscuring his face. It was rather un-nerving.

'Hello old friend,' Kurt said, from beneath the visor. He tapped the side of his head and the visor slid away.

'YOU!' Harvey replied, somewhat shocked. 'You have no business in here. Get out!'

'Oh Harvey, don't be like that,' Kurt replied coolly. 'After all these years I thought, maybe you'd manage to forgive and forget. Besides, Dean received a Black Insignia, so it turns I do have business here.'

'I hope you haven't forgotten! I can guarantee no-one else has.'

'Don't I know it!' Kurt retaliated, his voice becoming notably louder. 'You've all made sure of that, haven't you!' Kurt could feel a prickling heat building on his skin – anger, it appeared, did that to him. 'Anyway, we both know how this works. Dean got a Black Insignia and you're his choice! There's no point making this harder than it needs to be. He's waiting outside while we get through this, how shall I say, reunion. So, if you don't mind, let's just get on with it, shall we?'

'The sooner the better,' Harvey muttered under his breath. 'I've got another appointment at three, so you better be gone by then.'

'Oh, don't worry yourself,' Kurt replied sarcastically. 'The less time I'm here the better. Although you're going to have to get used to it. We'll be coming back for Gadgets.' Turning his back, Kurt opened his Holo-Phone. 'Get in here, boy.'

At 2pm, Dean Tuffnell walked into Peddleton's shop, brimming with confidence that whatever the problem was with Mr Peddleton, it had been sorted. As 2:45pm approached, Harvey was becoming increasingly nervous; if his next appointment arrived early, Kurt would come face to face with the woman who'd threatened his life the last time they'd met. Frankly, it didn't bear thinking about.

10

After Billy's surprise at receiving the tournament invitation had faded, Tom tried to explain everything that needed to happen. But the moment he'd said that Billy could choose a suit on his actual birthday, he'd shot out the door like a greyhound out of the traps. On the plus side, he'd totally forgotten about wanting a new bike, and Tom's sadness at seeing Billy's repeated disappointment could finally fade away.

'Where's Billy?' asked Tom, as Sue helped with his coat.

'He's already in the car. Couldn't wait a moment longer. You know how much he's loved the tournament ever since he was old enough to listen to your stories. I'm surprised you're not out there with him!'

Tom gave her a look that tried to suggest she was completely wrong. But of course, they both knew that she was completely right.

When Sue closed the front door behind them, Tom could see it was just as she'd said. Billy was sat waiting in the back of the car with his seatbelt on. When he spotted them, he huffed on the window before writing hurry up into the misty glass.

'Come on, come on!' he shouted. Although he'd been waiting a few minutes, it truly felt like time had fallen asleep.

'Clunk-click always does the trick,' Tom said, putting his seatbelt on.

'Don't forget to shout if you're going to fall out,' Billy replied, finishing the rhyme.

There were lots of sayings within the Wheeler household, all linked to an event of some sort. This one had been brought about by Tom almost falling out of the junior pirate ship when he was riding it with Billy; being in a wheelchair could often be a much smaller obstacle when you were as determined as he was.

They were only ten minutes into their journey when it struck Billy that everybody who owned a car must be taking an afternoon drive.

'Anyone who drives so slowly cannot possibly own a Ferrari,' he declared, reading a bumper sticker that claimed otherwise. 'Are we nearly there yet?' he asked. 'Why don't you just tell me where we're going?'

'It's a surprise,' Sue replied. 'And no, we're not there yet. We weren't the last five times you mentioned it, either!'

Finally, at 2:58pm, family Wheeler pulled into a car park.

'Have we come to the right place?' Billy asked, looking out the window. 'This is Peddleton's. There can't be anything we need here!'

'Oh yes there is,' Tom replied. 'But tournament equipment isn't just for anyone. You need to be rather lucky to see that kind of stuff. Come on, I'll show you.'

From the moment they left the car, Tom and Billy took turns leading the way. First, Billy strode ahead, then Tom gave a push on his wheels and took the lead himself.

'Hey, that's cheating,' Tom complained when Billy pulled the brake on his chair. He swerved sideways and forced Billy to trip over the front wheel. 'That'll teach you!' he said, bursting out laughing.

Harvey watched them making their way across the car park and breathed a sigh of relief; Kurt and Dean had left only five minutes ago. He only had to look at the somewhat forgotten figure of Sue Wheeler walking behind them to know that things would not have gone well.

11

'Hello Billy,' said a kind looking man as they approached the counter. Billy had to look up and almost stand on tiptoes to meet the man's eyes. He was very tall and slim – aerodynamic as Billy would say – and a bit frail looking. The man held out his hand which Billy shook willingly. Nobody had ever done such a thing before; it made him feel quite important.

'My name is Harvey Peddleton. It's nice to see you here to do something other than look at bikes. I've been waiting quite a long time for this moment.'

'Have you?' asked Billy, surprised.

'You bet,' Mr Peddleton replied, as he and Billy's dad tipped each other a nod. 'So, let's not waste any more of it shall we. I just need to see your Insignia.'

Drifting into thought, it occurred to Billy that he'd never spoken to this man before, yet he knew his name. How was that possible? And now that he thought about it, there was the invitation for the tournament too. It had simply called him Billy and spoke as they'd known him for years. Just how many people knew who he was and had been waiting for his tournament to begin?

'So … your Profiler?' Mr Peddleton prompted.

'Oh no!' Billy cried, filling with panic. 'I've forgotten my Profiler.' In an instant, he was full of dread that his tournament would be over before it even began.

'Um, Billy,' Sue said with a smirk on her face. 'It's on your wrist.'

He looked down before offering a sheepish smile. 'Ha! I knew that. I was just testing you.'

'Ah, very good. It pays to keep them on their toes,' Mr Peddleton said, giving Billy a wink. 'So, shall we go then?'

Behind the shop counter, a large display held a variety of every-day bike parts; Elasto Tubes; Brake Binders and Ion-chain drives made up the impressive display. There were even Magbike stickers that you could put on your own bike.

'Dad, look' Billy said, tugging on his sleeve. 'Magbike stickers. I always wanted one of those.'

Billy had asked a hundred times about getting a sticker for his bedroom wall, but however much he'd asked, they'd never reached the 'next time' that came after 'maybe'. Today was different though; he no longer needed a sticker. Soon enough he'd be riding a real Magbike.

Much to Billy's surprise, instead of walking to the door at the end of the counter, Mr Peddleton turned around to face the display and simply walked straight towards it. Billy winced, expecting to hear the loud clatter of bike parts falling to the floor, but instead, he simply walked right through it.

'Come on through,' Mr Peddleton called, from the other side. 'It's just a Hologram to stop any inquisitive people stumbling into the exciting stuff. Nothing to worry about.'

'That is epic!' Billy declared. Without need for further prompting, he dashed around the counter and leapt through the Hologram. It would have been fine, had he not kicked the real display with his foot. The loud clatter of parts that he'd expected Mr Peddleton to create, was of his own – typical Billy – making. 'Sorry,' he said, hunching his shoulders and wincing.

'Don't worry, Harvey. I'll sort this lot out,' Sue said, from other side. 'We'll catch you up.'

Mr Peddleton, totally unfazed by the incident, produced a smile and gave Billy a 'these things happen' kind of shrug before continuing.

They walked along a dimly lit corridor that was lined with sketches displaying all manner of Kinetic suit and Magbike designs. Above each one, an hourglass shaped lamp shone down on it like an important piece of artwork.

'Did you draw these, Mr Peddleton?' Billy asked.

'A few of them, yes. But the clever ones, the designs that I do wish were mine, they'll be Saddleton. You won't find many better than a Saddleton, Billy.'

Reaching the end of the corridor, Mr Peddleton stopped at a steel door. Beside it, a silver box projected a red Holographic F into the air.

'Right then. This is what we call a Focus. Think of it a bit like the world's largest computer; it knows everything. If you have a Profiler and you want to go anywhere, like Porting on holiday, or opening a locked door, you need to link to a Focus. It's the same for the tournament. You can't access tournament areas without linking your Profiler to a Focus. Okay?'

Mr Peddleton might have looked frail, but the authority in his voice was strong. Billy suddenly felt rather nervous without the support of his parents, and the best he could manage was a rather timid nod.

'I trust you know how to use your Profiler?' Mr Peddleton asked.

Again, Billy could only manage a small nod.

'Excellent! Well, here's your first chance to use it. Link your Profiler to the Focus and we can carry on.'

When Billy's wrist neared the Focus, he gave his wrist a flick. Immediately, the red F flashed green. Without delay, a series of mechanical clicks followed, accompanied by the sound of large gears turning inside the door. With a final puff of air, the door swung open.

'What do you think,' Mr Peddleton asked, smiling.

'I think it's the most epic thing I've ever seen!' Billy replied.

12

A large round room dazzled Billy. Taking pride of place around the wall, tournament Insignias were brought to life in hologram form. Mount Everest's snow-capped peaks collected fresh dunes of snow, whilst the howling wolf of Kielder Forest called to the moon. Even more impressive, was the vast array of Kinetic suits. Waiting patiently for their next occupant, they surveyed the room like guards on duty.

'Is that the one a Saddleton?' asked Billy, looking at a particularly shiny gold and silver suit. But before Mr Peddleton could reply, Billy was already dashing across the room, 'Gadgets!' he said, excitedly. 'No Way! Those are the Ice-Pick wheels that Casey McGrips used.'

'You certainly know your stuff,' Mr Peddleton said, approvingly.

'World's biggest tournament geek!' Billy replied proudly. 'Hold on, is that what I think it is?' He walked across the showroom and picked up a large metal glove.

'I'd be surprised if you didn't know what that was. Parker Rockworth used that to defeat Stoneman and his Gravel-gun in the movie Granite Wars. It's an—'

'Airshield 2.0!' Billy finished, his stomach turning over. Billy had known about the tournament forever, but he'd not expected to feel like this at all. Despite reading the disclaimer only this morning, with the words: 'risk' and 'danger' pulsing within it he'd not really thought beyond the excitement of being a competitor. But now, when faced with the reality of it, he felt completely overwhelmed.

He'd frozen to the spot, as rigid as a steel girder, when his dad touched his arm.

'D … Dad,' he stuttered, 'How am I going to choose the right suit? And how am I going to choose a Gadget? And what if I can't control it, and …'

'Calm down Billy, it's okay.' Tom looked at him, beaming from ear-to-ear. 'There's no need to worry. I remember the first time I came here, and I know how you're feeling, but it's okay. Just look at them all. Aren't they incredible!'

Like some sort of miracle medicine, Tom's calm enthusiasm helped Billy immensely. Despite his nerves, some of the youthful bravery the Space-Time president had mentioned in the invite, returned. Slowly and deliberately, he walked around the room. The longer he looked, the more youthful bravery he found. He was well qualified, after all. Being aerodynamic for one, and Wheeler-the-fearless for another.

'I don't know where to start,' he said, finally.

'Why not choose like your mum does and start with the colour,' Tom said, joking.

'Duh! That won't help!' Billy replied, with fake sarcasm.

'Yeah, I know, sorry. But listen, just trust your instincts. No matter what you decide, I'm sure you'll choose wisely.'

Billy had a vague flash of Déjà vu. It wasn't the first time he'd heard those two words put together recently. Was it just simple coincidence, or was there more to it? The number of questions in his mind was growing by the hour. In time they would be answered. But for now, they'd have to wait.

13

Billy, his dad, and mum – who, without raising suspicion had been remarkably quiet all along – spent an over an hour looking at all the different suits.

'You can't rush the decision,' he'd told them sincerely after looking at them all twice.

The problem was, there were so many things to consider: Would it fit the right Gadgets? Was it light and fast, but fragile? Was it strong and heavy, but slow? He even had to consider how good it was at magnetic bonding – whatever that meant.

'I'm think I'm ready to give up,' he said, having travelled from worried, to calm, and finishing at frustrated

'Have you considered your old suit, Tom?' Harvey asked. 'I'm told he's good enough.'

Sue's thought process was immediate and powerful: *Not that one, any suit but that one. When Tom wore that suit, he nearly*—

'Dad? Are you okay?' asked Billy, suddenly concerned.

'I'm not sure that's a good idea,' Tom replied.

For the first time since they'd arrived, Billy could see that some of the enthusiastic sparkle had left his dad's eyes. More than that, he'd gone a bit pale.

'Come on, Tom,' Harvey whispered. 'In the right hands it's nearly perfect. Can't harm to take a little look, can it?'

'Well, I suppose not,' Tom replied, not looking at Sue.

Harvey led them across the room and through an inconspicuous looking door. They entered what appeared to be a store cupboard.

'How about this one? he said, looking at the suit admiringly. 'It's a Saddleton Mimic.' He pointed to the showroom filled with modern suits. 'It's not like any of those out there. It's, oh how can I say it? It's like it feels what you're doing and enhances your movement. It's genius! Although, there is a downside.' He touched his chin and looked up as if searching for the words. 'You know what it's like when sometimes you shiver, or maybe sneeze and flinch? Well, the suit still listens, and it responds. It's um … a bit tricky.'

Harvey was utterly convinced that the idea behind the suit was perfect, but it had only ever been remembered for that one incident a long, long time ago.

Having second thoughts yet again, Tom piped up. 'I don't think it's the right one, Billy. There are much easier suits to use.'

Tom's words fell on deaf ears. Billy was lost in thought. There was something about the suit that made it hard to take his eyes from it. To most people it just looked like a tired old thing – dull and lifeless. But to Billy it looked almost magical.

Saying nothing, he reached out and touched it. A tingling sensation scurried up his arm before the suit shivered in response. 'This is it,' he whispered. 'This is the one.'

14

On the other side of the Atlantic, one of Billy's future problems was nearing the end of her journey. Louise Kelley was a rather short girl – short enough to have benefited from a booster seat during her flight, perhaps. She'd left Heathrow Travel Station under a black cloud of annoyance that had darkened her mood from the moment she'd learned they were going to America

Her normally bright and polite manner that complemented her gentle green eyes had quickly switched to the moody darkness of her black hair. She hadn't wanted to go to America because she had more important things to be doing at home. More important things such as studying, because she'd always been told that she needed to. Or working hard, because she'd always been told that she needed to. Or indeed, being an achiever, because, well, that's what her dad expected of her. He was hard on her, but he did it 'because people who achieve matter, and those that don't, do not!' It was a good job for all concerned that Louise Kelley was one determined girl.

By the time she'd landed at JFK Travel Station her determination had a new focus all together. The Black Insignia that landed on her tray table had given her a different outlook on the trip. It had given her hope that she could finally make her dad proud. So, she would take hold of the opportunity with both hands (whether one was robotic or not) and be that achiever. More significantly, she'd do whatever it took to succeed.

'I've arranged for a chauffeur to meet us outside,' her dad said, gloating. 'We don't use taxis. We're different to them.' He sneered at the other passengers; better was what he thought.

Duncan Kelley had no doubts about what kind of person he was. He was an achiever through and through – his success in the Space-

Time Tournament was proof of that. Thanks to his friend Fletch, his daughter would soon be an achiever too. It was about time!

'Who did you say we've come to see?' Louise asked.

'A man who knows how to achieve, my girl. There'll be no doubt about us winning the tournament with him on our side.'

'But why did we have to come all the way to America? Couldn't he have come to us?'

He appeared to contemplate what he should say next, or perhaps how he should say it. 'Well, it's a little delicate,' he began, sounding unsure of his words. 'Let's just say he had a … difficult patch a few years ago. He was a skilled contestant and doing very well, but there was a family disagreement or something like that. So, he left the tournament and came to America to forget about it. At least that's what he told me, anyway.'

At this point, Duncan felt he'd probably said enough. Despite being a wealthy man, wearing fancy designer suits, and owning several sports cars, it did nothing for his ability to know when he should or shouldn't say something. 'But we don't need to concern ourselves with that!' he added. 'What's important is that he'll get us what we want. Besides, he supplies the best Kinetic suits available. Much better than you'll find in the likes of Peddleton's.'

Louise conceded that getting what she – her dad – wanted, was all that mattered. *I need to be an achiever,* she thought. No need to ask any more questions about the difficult patch.

***

'Come inside, quickly, quickly,' Fletch said, ushering Louise and her dad into Worthies Bike Outlet. It seemed that a friendly greeting was an un-necessary delay when he simply wanted them out of sight.

'Where is this tournament winning Gadget then?' Duncan asked, looking around the showroom with disappointment. 'These suits and Gadgets don't look anything special to me.'

'It's not up here,' Fletch replied, sharply. 'And watch what you say. You never know who's listening. Now, follow me.' He crossed the showroom and stopped at what appeared to be a plain wall before swiping his hand across a picture. A hidden door then slid open beside him. 'It's in here.'

The three of them descended a staircase and walked into a stark looking basement room. It was brightly lit and impossibly clean like an operating theatre. An array of tools and magnifying cameras were precisely placed over a workbench where the inside workings of a small robotic arm rested.

Fletch approached the remarkable device. 'I believe this is what you're looking for. It's called a Disruptor. I had to make it small enough to fit in her existing arm, so I could only fit one charge cell.' He looked at Louise directly. 'You'll only get one shot, after that it'll need to be recharged. I suggest you're careful how you us it.'

'What if I get caught,' Louise asked, looking at her dad.

'Don't be silly, Louise. It'll be hidden in your arm. The stewards might check your suit, but they won't check your arm.'

It was against his better judgement that Fletch was doing business with Duncan Kelley; the man was a fool. But the truth was that he paid handsomely. Sometimes, when you were short on money and had a score to settle, you didn't have a choice.

***

An hour later and having chosen her suit, Louise Kelley left Worthies safe in the knowledge that Fletch's addition would carry her to certain victory. He'd shown her how to use the Disruptor and had been surprisingly helpful when she'd asked him for a favour; she'd waited until her dad used the bathroom before making *that* particular request. She wasn't sure if Fletch would be willing to help, but the result had been very pleasing. All she had to do now was figure out when to use the Disruptor; if she happened to choose badly, it could be devastating.

15

Just around the time that Louise Kelley had left Worthies Bike Outlet, Billy was starting to think about his favourite part of the tournament: Gadgets. Loved by fans and competitors alike, Gadgets allowed competitors to do things which would otherwise be impossible. If someone was having trouble scrambling to the top of a tree. A Hyper-wind grappling hook would come to the rescue. Or if a competitor had to tackle white water rapids. Turbine Boots would save the day. Billy would often daydream about winning the school cross-country whilst wearing his favourite Gadget: a pair of Instinct Claws. There wouldn't be a climb too steep or mud track too slippery for him to conquer.

Despite being excited about seeing the Gadgets in person, Billy had become increasingly aware of the uneasy feeling surrounding his dad. From the point Mr Peddleton had suggested the Mimic suit, things had felt different. His dad had become quieter and lost the excitement he'd shown racing Billy across the car park. Was there something wrong with the suit? Something that bad enough that he should choose another one. He'd barely considered if he should ask what was wrong when his mum appeared beside him.

'We need to talk,' she said, solemnly.

Billy's dad had made himself scarce. Despite trying to hide his emotions, his son had still noticed the change in his mood. Only this morning he'd hoped they wouldn't have to face this thorny issue quite so soon. But then he hadn't expected Billy to choose the Mimic. If his son was going to wear it, then more than ever, he deserved to know the truth about why his dad needed a chair.

'Several years ago,' Sue began, 'long before you were born, your dad was competing in the tournament. He was one of the best contestants they'd ever seen! He'd entered a few months after his sixteenth birthday and ended up in a three-way battle to win it. But then during the Everest event, something very bad happened.'

'He had an accident?' asked Billy, interrupting her. He thought he already knew the answer – that his dad made a mistake and hurt himself badly enough to have ended up in his wheelchair – but he was wrong. Soon enough he would know the hurtful truth, and for the first time in his life he would be angry!

'I want you to watch this Memory Trace,' she told him, holding out a small device that looked like a wafer. 'We don't have a Holo-Tab, so you can't watch it at home, but I'll take you to the library and you can watch it there.'

Billy suddenly felt apprehensive. 'What's on it?'

'It's from your dad's tournament when he had his accident.'

Billy was completely stuck for words. His mood had switched from utter joy – the sort he got when he was spending time with Katie – to complete dismay, as if he'd been told he'd never get to see her again!

He'd learned about Traces in school. Sometimes they were used to fight crime, other times – mainly for people rich enough to have VR-Walls – they were used in the same way you would use a video camera; you could live parts of your life all over again. As was the case with Tom Wheeler, they were used by organisations like Space-Time Industries.

***

Sue parked the car opposite the library and waited for Billy to get out. Instead, he sat motionless and stared at the Trace in his hand.

'Do I have to watch it?' he asked.

'I think it's best if you do. It's too complicated to explain everything properly. And your dad doesn't like to talk about it even after all this time. Do you want me sit with you? Or wait for you?'

'No, I'll be okay. I was going to call on Katie anyway.'

Sue offered a tentative smile. 'Are you sure?'

'Yeah, I'll be fine. I'll see you when I get home.'

Billy got out of the car and looked up at the old library. Surrounded by the new buildings in his town, the aged and worn stonework was a hint of the buildings that used to be commonplace. Now he only got to see them on ancient history school trips.

He climbed the stone steps and circled through a wooden rotating door. Inside the library, he once again made that link to Mr Crankworth's office; the dark wooden panels on the walls, the old but lovely smell of real paper, and the volumes of priceless books that filled the shelves. Beyond their ancient, printed pages filled with words, lay a more familiar world of technology.

Finding a quiet desk away from anyone else, Billy sat down and picked up one of the new VR Holo-Bands. At first, he hesitated, unsure if he wanted to know what the Trace might reveal. But then decided he should watch it, otherwise his mum wouldn't have asked him to.

Like a scared child trying to poke a spider with his finger, he activated the band. Seconds later, in a virtual world of his own, he began to live a life seen through his dad's sixteen-year-old eyes.

16

Tom Wheeler sat in his tournament Demountable trying to relax before a critically important event. Beyond the open door in front of him, snow danced back and forth in the wind like a shaken snow-globe. He'd just completed his pre-race checks with Harvey – who Billy recognised as a young Mr Peddleton – to make sure the Magbike was ready.

'Tom? You've got a red message,' Harvey shouted, seeing the text pop up on his Holo-Tab. 'We're going to have to visit the stewards.'

Tom joined him in the back room and sighed with frustration; red messages were only sent if something was wrong. 'A message? This close to the start of the race. What's does it say?' he asked.

"Mr Tom Wheeler and Mr Harvey Peddleton are requested to attend the steward's office immediately," Harvey read aloud. "Further details will be discussed at the meeting."

'I guess we don't have a choice then,' Tom said, stepping out through the door. 'Let's go and be done with it.'

***

Ten minutes after arriving, Harvey and Tom were still sitting outside the empty steward's office.

'This is getting silly,' Tom complained. 'I need to be getting ready, not sitting here.' He stared at his watch anxiously. 'Come on! Where's the steward?' Negative thoughts began to pester his mind. If he didn't make the start, Kurt would streak off into the lead. Fletch wasn't a problem, he was four Credits behind on the points table. He could still win the tournament, but he wasn't really a concern. Kurt, however, was a different story. He'd been battling fiercely at every event and was becoming a genuine concern. 'I don't need this just before the race,' Tom complained, standing up. 'Can you wait here for me? I need to prepare!'

'Of course,' Harvey replied, reading the red message once again. 'If it's really important I'll come and get—' He looked up and stopped mid-sentence. Tom had already disappeared into the swirling snow.

***

Even from a distance Tom could see the door to his Demountable was slightly open. He could have sworn it was closed when they'd left, but then both he and Harvey could be forgetful from time to time. And with the wind blowing as strongly it was, it had probably just blown open.

Back inside the Demountable, his suit was just as he'd left it, standing there in a frozen in a star jump and ready to put on.

'Would all competitors for the Mount Everest Challenge make their way to the starting grid,' a voice boomed across the stadium. 'I repeat, all competitors to the starting grid.'

Tom began to panic. He'd wasted so much time waiting for the steward to no-show that he wasn't even dressed. He stepped into position ready for his suit to assemble around him. That's when noticed the power pack. It was on the floor. When they'd left to visit the steward, it *was* connected, at least he thought so. In a panic he grabbed the pack and shoved in into the suit, but it wouldn't connect. 'What's wrong with you?' he said, frustrated at the connectors. 'I've got to go!' Running out of time, he rammed the pack into place. It clicked home – nearly.

Tom left the safety of his garage and stepped into the whirlwind of snow outside. The thermal sensors inside his suit lit up: Fifteen degrees below zero, they shouted. Within his suit, Tom only felt the temperature drop to ten. It was cold enough to make him shiver, but the energy cell was full, and everything was working perfectly.

The five competitors walked side by side to the starting grid. Their Magbikes were waiting for them in silence, powerful sleeping beasts waiting to be awoken. Reaching the start, Fletch and Tom turned to one another and bumped fists.

'Good luck Fletch,' Tom said.

Fletch smiled. 'Yeah, you too.'

He turned to Kurt. 'Good luck Kurt. May the best—'

'I don't think so Wheeler,' Kurt replied, cutting him off. 'I won't be needing any luck! Although you should be careful out there. It Looks dangerous.' He offered a false smile that didn't reach his eyes.

Tom could hear a deliberate venom in Kurt's voice; the advice was not well meant. He turned away and sat on his bike before closing his eyes and visualising the race. His sixteen-year-old heart was thumping against his ribcage. He was far from calm, but he was in control. Opening his eyes again he gave Kurt one last look. He was sitting right alongside and frankly, looked as if he didn't have a care in the world.

How can you be so calm when there's so much at stake? Tom thought. *It's almost like you're not in a race at all.*

Mount Everest was renowned for its dangerous mixture of deep chasms and granite peaks. And whilst a deep blanket of snow covered the ground making it look soft and inviting, grey craggy rocks poked through at threatening angles, waiting to claim their first casualty.

With the first red light, the Magbikes awoke. A storm of Ion-powered snow blasted through the contestants like an avalanche. Glowing red lights became amber, then go, green lights started the race.

Tom's bike thrust forwards, challenging his grip with the sheer force of its acceleration. His snow-track Gadget ripped at the icy surface like powerful claws, throwing clouds of snow into air and smothering his opponents. Immediately taking the lead, Tom checked his mirror and watched Fletch disappear behind – out of sight, he was no longer threat. Beside him, Kurt swerved in and out of view. One moment he'd be right there, the next, there wouldn't be anything but a plume of snow.

Spotting the edge of the first chasm jump, Tom readied himself. Gripping the handlebars, he threw his weight back and pulled upwards heavily, lifting the front wheel from the ground. But then out of the whirling snow, Kurt veered into view. His face displayed a grim smile – a knowing smile.

Within the blink of an eye, Tom's heart sank. It was as if his body had felt the problem before his mind could catch up. The display in his suit flashed a terrible warning that would change everything: Power pack FAIL! Gadget FAIL! Just like that, the suit shut down.

Tom arrived at the chasm's edge in first place, but he didn't jump. Instead, he simply dropped out of sight.

***

It was an agonisingly long wait before the first rescuer's voice escaped the chasm. They'd found him nearly twenty meters below the cliff on an impossibly narrow ledge. His Kinetic suit had fired the body-brace, but with a damaged power pack it hadn't worked properly. He should have been saved from serious injury, but he wasn't.

Tom knew nothing of the next few hours, or indeed anything about the week that followed. He wouldn't know that Kurt went on to win the Everest event, and he wouldn't know that he'd also go on to be crowned Space-Time champion. The first thing that Tom would know, was that he'd never walk again.

17

Billy walked home with the Memory Trace hanging limply in his hand. He was so stunned by the experience that he even forgot to call on Katie.

'Your dad's sleeping,' Sue whispered, having caught sight of Billy and opening the front door to meet him. 'He needed the rest. Are you okay?' Billy was far from okay. He was furious and she could see it in his eyes. Although she didn't regret giving him the Trace; she'd done it for good reason. 'I wanted you to watch it because I don't want you to take part in the tournament. The suit wasn't faulty, someone had tampered with it.'

'Kurt?' asked Billy.

'He denied anything to do with it. He claimed it must have been someone else. Or a fault with the suit. But we all know what he'd said to your dad just before the race and that's just about as good as a confession, to me. He still maintains that he wasn't involved. Rather conveniently, his Trace was damaged in transition, so while we know he did it, we've never been able to prove it. Or more accurately, he's not been able to prove that he didn't!'

'How can anyone let that happen and not do anything about it?' asked Billy, angrily. 'Surely somebody can do something?'

'No. We tried everything, including going to the tournament president. He was the one who gave us your dad's Trace. He confirmed that Kurt's was damaged too. There was nothing to do except move on. But now that's become impossible, because it's all come back. The fact that you're competing is half the problem. The other half is that boy you're always in competition with at school … Dean Tuffnell … Kurt's son.'

Billy hadn't made the obvious link between Kurt and Dean; father and son, team Tuffnell, life wreckers. Although how could he? Watching a Memory Trace was like being the person and living their life. It didn't give you a list of names. Billy had just lived a part of his dad's life – he'd literally walked in his shoes; something that his dad would never do again.

Both Kurt and Dean had a lot to answer for. Dean's dad was the reason his own father was in a wheelchair. As for Dean, now he knew why the boy had always been so mean … like father like son!

'I'm sorry Mum, but I have to compete. I've got to try and win for Dad. I could get a Time Ticket, which means we could sell it and have enough money to buy a house that Dad can actually move around in.'

He stood there expectantly and waited for his mum's approval while his mind flooded with images of all the things they could do with the money. He simply wanted her to say what a great plan it was and tell him it was the best idea he'd ever had. But instead, she was silent. He gave her the kind of smile that asks for forgiveness after giving bad news, hoping it would soften her mood. He was wrong.

'How can you smile after watching the Trace and seeing what happened to your dad in the suit that you've chosen to use?'

Billy's expression changed in surprise. 'But Mum, we could—'

'I don't want to talk about it anymore,' she said, turning away from him. 'Not another word!'

Knowing there was nothing more to be said, Billy slouched off to his room.

***

Sitting alone in his room that night, Billy's anger at Dean and Kurt had all but gone. He knew his mum didn't want him to compete and he'd come close to telling her he wouldn't, but then he'd had his big idea. An idea far better than the one about selling his Time Ticket. From that point on, all he could think about was the moment he'd tell them about his great plan. After all, what was the one thing he could do with time travel?

He could change the past!

18

The morning after his birthday, Billy walked into a silent kitchen and found his parents eating breakfast. He knew they'd been talking because he'd heard them whispering as he'd walked down the stairs. He shivered with the chill; even in the mornings of early summer the kitchen was often cold. Winter didn't bear thinking about!

'You look tired,' Tom said, breaking the silence.

'Oh, I'm alright. It was a long day yesterday.' He offered the weak excuse as a diversion; he didn't want to admit that he been awake half the night.

'Actually, I wanted to talk to you about that,' Tom replied. 'I wasn't keen at first, but your mum convinced me that letting you watch my Trace made sense. That it would help you understand what you're letting yourself in for. But I don't want you to go doing anything stupid as a result, okay? It happened in the past. You know that don't you?'

Billy's pulse began to rise. It hadn't occurred to him to do anything to Dean or Kurt, but his big idea, the one that kept him awake half the night, that wasn't stupid at all! In the darkness of his room, he'd decided not to tell his parents about it. But the one thing he didn't want to do was lie. Lying was for people like Dean and his dad. He didn't think he was anything like them at all.

'Billy?' his dad said, pursuing him for an answer. 'You're not going to get any silly ideas, are you?'

Billy didn't want to sit there looking at his dad and tell a total lie – not even one pale enough to be see-through. But it was beginning to look like he didn't have a choice.

'Well … I was thinking that—'

A loud knock at the front door interrupted him. He leapt off his chair and ran from the room to find Katie peering through the glass.

'Billy-boy,' she sang. 'How's the life of a fourteen-year—'

He grabbed her hand and pulled her through the door with such enthusiasm that she almost fell on top of him. 'Come with me,' he whispered. He pulled her along the hallway to the stairs. 'I've got something to tell you.'

'Hi Mrs Wheeler,' Katie called, waving cheerily as they spotted each other during her northward flight.

It wasn't unusual for Billy's parents to see them together. Despite being boy and girl, they were best of friends and couldn't have looked less boyfriend-girlfriend-like if they tried. Sue liked to think that Katie's exaggerated amount of common sense would rub off on Billy. Who knows what he'd get up to if she weren't there to be the voice of reason!

Arriving in his room, Billy faced her. 'Close your eyes K. Hold your hands out!'

'I don't think so, Billy-boy. The last time you asked me to close my eyes you sprayed water in my face and pretended to sneeze!'

'Trust me?' he asked. 'Please.'

Compelled by his expression, Katie closed her eyes. She felt him place an object in the palm of her hand.

'Now, open your eyes.'

'Oh, ha-ha,' she said, 'very funny. You got a Black Insignia for your birthday. I totally believe you Billy-boy. You got me.'

'It's not a joke K. That's a real Black Insignia. My Black Insignia.'

'You're having me on' She replied, staring accusingly into his eyes.

'Not this time,' he said, almost in a squeal. 'That's as real as they get. I'm only gonna be in the bloody Space-Time Tournament!' He did a comical jig around his room, utterly unable to contain his excitement.

It was only then that Katie knew he wasn't trying to prank her. As hard as it was to believe – because surely this kind of thing just doesn't happen to boys like Billy – her best friend was going to be a Space-Time contestant. She grabbed hold of him and gave him a hug.

'Billy Wheeler, you lucky git! You wait 'til Dean hears about this.' She took his hands and began to spin around the room. He joined in, delighted in her happiness. He'd think about Dean some other day. And he'd tell her about his big idea in a little while. But right now, dancing around his bedroom with his best friend was perfect.

'Dance 'til you drop,' he said, as they laughed together, and danced.

19

With dizziness taking hold of her, Katie slumped to the floor.

Billy touched her shoulder. 'Listen K, I need to tell you something.'

'You better not tell me that thing's fake!' she stated, pointing at the Insignia on his bed.

'No, I promise, that's real. But the thing I want to talk about. I can't tell you here.' He jumped up. 'Come on, let's go out.'

Two minutes later, they were at the front door. 'Were going to the park, Mum. I'll be back later.'

They'd barely reached the garden gate when Katie began to hassle him. 'Come on then Billy-boy, what's the big secret?'

'Not yet, K. Wait till we get to the park.'

'Run then, Hedgehog boy,' she said, shoving him into a bush. Even the super-sensible Katie Jack had moments of prankster within her.

***

Much to his surprise and for the first time he could remember, Billy arrived at a completely empty park. It wouldn't have been if they'd arrived a few minutes later, but they'd been spotted just in time. For now, at least, it was theirs and theirs alone. He dashed across the field pulling Katie along behind.

'Quick, let's get on the AirTube. It's hardly ever free.'

'Oh, you know I can't ride that thing,' she complained. 'It's too hard. I can't do it.'

'Don't be a wuss. You just need to practice. Tell you what, I'll hold your hand if you want me to?' He smiled at her teasingly, secretly hoping that was exactly what she wanted. 'Besides, if you don't, I can't tell you about my big idea.'

Katie stared at the large clear cylinder that reached high above the ground – high enough to see over the treetops if you were brave enough. Surrounded by a collection of smaller tubes that were connected to the body, it looked like a giant clear Octopus.

'Ok, fine! I'll have a go.'

Stepping into the tower, a cyclone of air lifted them skyward. Side tubes puffed at Katie whenever she flew towards the wall, saving her from painful bruises. Billy laughed with delight whenever she shrieked in fear, but reluctantly and very awkwardly, she managed a short and simple belly flight. Fearless Wheeler, as you might expect, had mastered belly flight and back flight, and was now experimenting with head-down madness.

'Stop it, Billy. You're going to make me puke,' Katie said, after he spun her around several times like a human whirlwind. 'If you don't stop it, I'll leave!'

Ten exhilarating minutes later, Katie was exhausted. Billy thought she'd screamed a little bit too much to be genuine, but they'd stopped flying anyway. As for their unseen observer, he'd preferred to have learned a little more.

Katie found the nearest pop-up sofa and slumped into it. 'Want some?' she asked in a high-pitched voice, producing a can of sherbet liquorice Heliyumm.

'Do I ever!' Billy agreed. 'I love that stuff!'

It wasn't long before the pair of them were in fits of laughter, fully into a Heliyumm-fuelled conversation. It was a considerable amount time before Billy was calm enough to tell his story.

'Mum said she doesn't want me to compete,' he began. 'But I told her I need to. I was thinking that if I win, then I'd get a Time Ticket, and I could sell it. I thought we'd finally be able to get a house that Dad can move around in. Maybe we could even get one of those new Hoverchairs. But then in the middle of the night, I had my big idea,' he told her, proudly.

'Go on,' Katie said, with a nervous tingle fluttering in her stomach.

As if the flood gates had opened, the words tumbled out of Billy's mouth in one unstoppable flow. Katie listened patiently and didn't interrupt throughout the entire story. But when he finally did fall silent, she still struggled to find the words. She stared at him blankly, before trying to make a joke.

'But if you go back and change things, who's homework will I copy? You'll disappear, and I'll fail my exams.' This was poor even by Katie's standards; it was Billy who frequently copied her homework.

'What do you mean, disappear?'

'I mean, Billy-boy,' she said, animatedly, 'if you go back in time and change the past, then nothing would be the same. We're friends because your dad had that accident. You already told me it was the only reason your parents met. If you change the past and stop the accident from happening, then they won't meet, and you'll disappear … from me!'

Katie's eyes glazed with tears filling Billy's heart with fresh guilt. Not only did he have the problem of whether time travel was a one-way ticket – because he along with thousands of others didn't want to believe that – but because whether it was true or not, if he changed the past to stop what happened to his dad, he'd lose the only true friend he'd ever had.

'Well, well,' a sarcastic voice said, from behind them. 'If it's not Weeweeler and his little sad-kick.'

Dean Tuffnell and his own sidekick Harry Conram had seen Billy and Katie arrive just before they'd walked into the park themselves. He secretly knew that a skydive was planned for Everest and he'd gone to practice in the AirTube. He'd thought about how much fun it would be to kick them off. But catching some flying hints from Billy was worth more.

'Don't get carried away, Weeweeler,' Dean said. 'You don't need to worry about time travel. You've got no chance of winning the tournament even if you can AirTube.'

'What makes you think that?' Katie asked, defensively.

'Because I'm not going to let him.'

'You can't do anything about it,' she replied. 'You're not even in the tournament.'

'Oh, but I am.'

Billy looked at the floor dejectedly, remembering the conversation he'd had with Katie a few days ago. 'He's right. His dad was in the tournament, so he qualifies too.'

'That's right, Weeweeler. I am, because I deserve to be. But you? You don't deserve to be in it at all. The fact that you're not old enough is a joke. But I don't really care about that. What I want to know is who paid for it, because it certainly wasn't your dad.' He sniggered teasingly, knowing just how poor the Wheelers were. Becoming bored, he turned to walk away and laughed. 'See you in the forest,' he said over his shoulder. 'And enjoy your train ride. I think I might Port.'

'He is so horrible,' Katie whispered angrily. 'Why is he always so mean to you?'

Billy didn't think that now was the time to tell her Dean's dad had caused his own dad's accident. She'd probably go running after Dean and cause all sorts of trouble.

'Our parents are enemies,' he said, limiting the truth. 'They fell out during the tournament years ago.'

'Well, that's not your fault.'

'I know, but Dean doesn't care about that.' He got up to leave. 'Come on. Let's go.'

Katie grabbed hold of his hand. 'Wait, I've got an idea.'

Un-known to Dean, he'd as good as told them that a skydive was going to be in the tournament. Katie, observant as ever, had spotted it. 'You've got no chance of winning the tournament even if you can AirTube,' he'd teased.

'Time for more skydiving practice,' she said.

Billy looked at her, one eyebrow raised. 'You want to fly again?'

'Beats homework,' she replied.

The AirTube lifted them skyward and their encounter with Dean quickly became a distant memory. Best friends, they flew together until the park had filled with children.

20

In the two weeks that followed, every contestant did their best to prepare. Alisha May spent her time surfing in Newquay while wearing her Kinetic suit. Unsurprisingly, this was only ever at night to avoid unwanted attention, although reports from the public claiming to see lights hovering over the sea increased ten-fold. During her second week, and not without considerable effort, Alisha mastered Nimble-balance.

Anderson Toms had the luxury of practicing white water diving in a Tumble Tank. His dad's connections to the Deep-Sea Agency meant that Anderson could swim whenever he wanted. Despite being disgusting at the time, being sick inside his helmet had taught him what to expect and how to cope.

Louise Kelley, by contrast, didn't focus on any one skill. When she practiced, her dad constantly reminded her that being an achiever meant you had to work hard on everything. His wealth meant that her week was spent not only swimming in a Tumble Tank and tackling indoor skydiving but doing plenty of Nimble training too. He didn't really think his daughter would need any of the skills; they had Fletch's Disruptor hidden in her arm. But why leave anything to chance?

As for Billy, his training wasn't about cheating or Nimble practice. It wasn't about experiencing the Tumble Tank or any other such expensive activity. All he had, was honesty, hard work, and the sometimes very busy AirTube.

***

'Billy?' Sue whispered. Looking at her son sleeping peacefully in his bed. She almost felt guilty about waking him up – almost.

Beyond giving a small grunt, Billy didn't respond. Not even the slightest hint of waking up.

'Billy?' she repeated, not so quietly. She marvelled at how her once energetic son was so utterly exhausted. It was probably from the weeks of practice Katie had made him do on the AirTube.

'Sorry Billy, it's going to be the quilt-snatch.' She gripped the corners of his quilt and whipped it away.

'QUILT SNATCHED!' Billy shouted, thrashing around on his bed. 'So cold … So freeeezinnng,' he complained.

'There's my Billy-boy,' Sue said, laughing. 'It's time to get up. You're getting your suit fitted today.'

'Today?' asked Billy, seeing his mum through the foggy vision of sleepy eyes. 'Like today, today?'

'Yes Billy. Today.'

'Wicked!' he shouted, far too loudly. He leapt off the bed and stood up like a pro surfer hitting the waves. 'I can't wait to try it on. It's gonna be so cool!'

From that moment on, the morning became a mirror image of his birthday. The shocking bed-hair, the speed brushing of teeth and the running from bathroom to bedroom – wind dried. It was like watching an action-replay. The one difference that did occur arrived about half an hour later, when instead of it being just Billy sitting in the car, it was both an over-excited son and an over-excited father that waited for Sue to leave the house.

***

The three of them arrived at Peddleton's bike shop just after 11am. Unlike their previous visit, Sue didn't trail behind like a child who didn't want to be there. Instead, they walked across the car park together. Her concerns were still apparent, but after Harvey had offered to mentor Billy, it became a little easier for her to think of him competing in the tournament even if he was wearing the Mimic suit; lightning was hardly going to strike twice, was it!

The heavy metal door to Harvey's showroom had barely swung open when Billy spotted the Mimic taking pride of place in the centre. It was resting on a raised platform in a frozen star jump.

'Is that mine?' he asked.

Mr Peddleton smiled. 'It sure is.'

'Can I put it on?' Billy asked, excitedly. 'Can I?' Not even waiting for an answer, he rushed across the room and began to undress. 'This is gonna be wicked!'

'Billy!' Sue shouted. 'What are you doing? Use the changing room!'

'No way! That would take way too long.' Unlike when he'd ripped his trousers at school, he didn't mind anyone seeing his underwear this time.

'I'm sorry, Billy,' Mr Peddleton said, interrupting the rushed de-clothing. 'I'm afraid you don't have a choice. Your Skinsuit is in the changing room already.'

Billy paused one leg in and one leg out of his jeans.

'You didn't think you'd just jump in wearing nothing but your underwear, did you?'

Billy offered Mr Peddleton a sheepish look, suggesting that was exactly what he'd thought.

***

'I look like I'm wearing one of those ridiculous Onesies,' Billy remarked, emerging from the changing room wearing what looked like a silver overall. 'But check this out. Super stretchy.' He proceeded to do several exaggerated lunges across the room.

'Like father, like son,' Harvey remarked, trying to stifle a smile.

'Are you sure about this?' Sue asked as she and Tom sat watching their son take his first steps in the tournament.

Tom focussed on Billy who was chatting with his own old mentor. He could already see that the bond that he'd shared with Harvey was growing with Billy too. It both comforted and saddened him. The comfort came in the form of his old friend Harvey. But the sadness that lingered came to the surface when he remembered what had happened to him. What life he'd been forced to live because of his own tournament and Kurt Tuffnell. If Billy could better Dean in this tournament, it wouldn't be revenge, but it would sure feel good. He considered Sue's question for a moment and the answer came easily.

'Yes,' he said, taking hold of her hand. 'I'm sure.'

21

'Okay Billy. You need to come over and link your Profiler.'

Doing as he was asked, Billy joined Mr Peddleton by the Mimic. He held his wrist out and hovered it over the chest. Immediately, little puffs of air whistled from the joints as the legs and arms pulled away from the body. The small metallic scales that formed its skin shrank into themselves, making impossibly small tubes at each hand and foot.

'Okay, it's time to climb in.'

'Check it out Dad. Star jump, tournament style.' Billy crouched under the body of the suit and proceeded to do a full-on star jump, punching his hands and feet into the empty gloves and shoes.

'Well, would you look at that,' Sue remarked, with a comical grin.

'What?' Billy asked. 'What's so funny?'

Tom faked covering his eyes. 'At least you put underwear on.'

'Oh, not again!' Billy said, looking down at the hole in his skinsuit, his own skin turning pink once more.

Mr Peddleton, ever the gentleman, was quick to act. 'Stay still whilst it re-assembles,' he said, hovering his Profiler over Billy's chest.

Billy stood utterly motionless and watched as each limb of the suit extended over his own arms and legs before linking to the body with a reassuring hiss of air.

'This is the last piece of the jigsaw,' Mr Peddleton said, picking up the helmet and placing it over Billy's head. 'Remember what to do?'

'Do I ever! I've always wanted to do this. ACTIVATE!'

Without delay, the inside of the suit expanded, squeezing his body like a strange inflatable body armour. A display then lit up in front of his eyes showing his heart rate, the outside temperature and the suit's power pack level.

'It feels like I'm not even wearing anything.'

'That's what you get when you choose a Saddleton Mimic,' Mr Peddleton said, proudly. 'Have a walk about and see how you get on.'

'A walk about?' Billy asked. 'No way! I'm going to Jump.' Before anyone could react, he left the floor like a coiled spring and leapt high into the air. 'This is so cool!' he declared, floating for what appeared to be far too long.

Mr Peddleton closed his eyes in dread, expecting to hear a heavy crash when Billy came down, but there wasn't one. Instead, he landed with the gentleness of a feather. He looked at Tom. 'How did he do that?' he mouthed, silently.

Tom merely held his hands out and shrugged.

'Did you see that?' asked Billy, elated. 'Best tuck jump, EVER!'

'That would be what you call a Shadow Fall,' Tom said. Pretty much nobody else will ever make a landing like that no matter how much they try. You know what, Billy? I think we might know what your talent is. You're a Whisperer.'

'A Whisperer?' asked Billy, sounding disappointed.

'Yes, a Whisperer,' Tom replied. 'You weren't likely to be a Mighty… you're too aerodynamic,' he added with a wink. 'Maybe you could have been a Heed, or a Nimble, but I'd say being a Whisperer is excellent. It means you're quiet.'

'Quiet?' Billy repeated. 'I don't want to be quiet. What use is that?'

With the last word leaving his mouth, Billy felt a firm push from behind, forcing him to take a swift step forward. Despite reacting instinctively, he still made no noise at all.

'That's what use being a Whisperer is,' Sue said. She'd crept up behind him without giving a hint of being there. 'You can move without making a sound. You know when that will make a difference, don't you?'

Billy racked his brain for the answer, trying to unlock a memory from all the events he'd seen in the past. Then, just like that, it popped into his head, flipping his disappointment into instant approval.

'The Hunters! They won't hear me.'

Billy's mum smiled and put her hand in the air ready for a high five. When Billy swung his arm, she pulled her hand away and ran it through her hair like a comb.

'Ahh,' she said, smugly. 'Too slow.'

Billy's eyes shot between his hand and hers. The comical expression on his face made her laugh and she was quickly joined by Billy himself.

Tom looked on, delighted in their laughter. A hint of where Billy got his sense of humour from had returned to Sue; she'd been worrying far too much. 'I think we should probably check out some Gadgets,' he suggested. 'Wouldn't you agree Harvey?'

'Absolutely. I've had a few ideas for that already.'

'Don't you think you should take the suit off?' Sue asked Billy when he started to move.

'No way! I'd rather eat sprouts dipped in chocolate than take this off.' He looked at Mr Peddleton, pleadingly. 'Seriously, I hate sprouts.'

'I don't mind. Keep it on if you like. But really … sprouts?'

Sue went to Tom and kissed his forehead. 'I'm going to do some shopping while you boys finish up.' She smiled with a glint of mischief in her eyes; 'I'll get something nice for Tea.'

Mr Peddleton joined Billy and Tom at the Gadgets 'I thought maybe this would be a good idea,' he said, settling in front of a set of Finger Beams.'

'I do pick my nose without thinking about it,' Billy replied.

'Oh, perhaps that's not a good choice then. Lasers and nose-picking probably don't work well together. How about an Ion Backthruster? Tom, what do you think?'

Tom looked at Billy. 'Fancy being a flying squirrel?'

Billy thought about the flying practice he'd done with Katie and considered the option for a few moments. But then he found his own imagination planting him head-first into a tree hollow and winced.

'No, I thought not.'

'You could try a Thermal Visor,' Mr Peddleton suggested, holding a mirror-like curved screen. 'It can be foggy in the Kielder Forest. It might help see things that others can't.'

Billy took hold of the visor. 'That's a brilliant idea. I love it!'

'Okay, that's settled then, a Thermal Visor it is. I think you're just about ready. Except for taking the suit off, that is.'

Billy looked horrified at the suggestion. 'I'd rather eat—'

'Some of these?' Sue said, cutting in.

Billy whipped around to see his mum holding a bag of sprouts.

'Get me out of this thing,' he demanded. 'Sprouts are gross!'

Five minutes later and after taking one final look at his suit, Team Wheeler were on their way. Billy's first event had all but arrived.

22

'Tell me then,' Katie demanded. What are you going to be doing in Kielder Forest?'

'Uh, I don't really know. Going to find checkpoints or something. Dad said we'll know more when we get there.'

'Checkpoints? What, like navigating checkpoints?' It wasn't all that difficult for Katie to see that Billy looked worried. 'I tell you what. Let's get some Heliyumm and go to the park?'

Billy's eyes lit up. 'Okay!'

'Excellent! We'll work on your navigation skills whilst we're out. Remember how you kept getting lost when you first moved here?'

'No I didn't!' Billy stated, certain he'd only gotten lost twice.

Katie did that hands-on-hips thing of hers that he loved so much before she grabbed him by the hand. 'Yeah right, whatever you say, Billy-boy.'

***

For a full week, Billy and Katie had been almost inseparable – mostly trying to avoid seeing Dean at the park. Katie had managed to get him to practice navigating as much as possible, which was a good thing; he was useless. More than once she'd had to go looking for him, only to find him sitting under a tree, blowing a grass whistle like a distress call. That said, the last time she'd left him somewhere near Worthy Park and said to meet her at home, he'd turned up just five minutes late. It wasn't perfect, but it would have to do; he was out of time.

***

The blurry vision of recent sleep returned once again as Billy sat up in bed. He closed his eyes, rubbed them, and yawned loudly.

'Billy-boy,' Katie sang, extending her usual greeting from the door.

Billy half jumped out of bed in shock. 'K? What are you doing here?' He grabbed at the quilt and pulled it up to his chin.

'I thought I'd come and see you off. Your mum said it'd be okay to come up but I didn't think you'd still be in bed!'

'She wanted me to sleep in. She says you're meaner than Miss Cravity, making me do all that AirTube and navigation practice.'

Katie's mouth dropped open in comedy shock. 'Meaner than Miss Cravity? I'll make you screw-up another trick that rips your pants again! Then we'll see who's mean.'

'Don't you mean trousers?' a smug Billy replied.

Katie pursed her lips, giving him that disapproving look. 'I need to tell you something before you go.' Her tone was more urgent than she'd intended it to be.

'Okay ...' Billy replied tentatively. 'What's up?'

'Right then ... the thing is ... that ... well ... Dean—'

'Spit it out Mumble Mary.'

Like a volcanic eruption, the words rushed out of her in one long, breathless flow.

'Dean and his dad are going to be at the station when you are and I know what happened to your dad and I'm worried that you'll see them and what might happen and—'

'What do you know about my dad and Dean's dad?' asked Billy.

Katie looked at the floor sheepishly. 'I don't know anything really. I just put two and two together. I know Dean's dad was shamed out of the Space-Time programme because he had something to do with the accident. And I know how horrible Dean's always been to you. It just kind of made sense. And now I'm worried you'll all bump into each other.'

'There's no need to worry,' Sue said, walking into his room; she'd been waiting nearby, having noticed Katie's worried expression. 'Tom and I have already talked about it. The port terminal and train station are in the same building, so we've always known that we might bump into them.'

'Sorry Mrs Wheeler. I didn't mean to interfere.'

'You don't need to apologise Katie. I'm pleased Billy has such a thoughtful friend. If it makes you feel any better, you can come with us if you like?'

'I'd love to,' Katie whispered.

'Great, I'll see you downstairs. It's half an hour till we leave.'

'Thanks K,' Billy said. 'You're the best. Although I do still have one question.'

Katie fidgeted anxiously. She was expecting an awkward enquiry about her knowledge of his dad's tournament, and she wouldn't lie to him if he asked her, but she'd rather he didn't know that she was up to just yet.

Billy's smile began at his lips and quickly joined his eyes. He took his hand from behind his back and produced a box that was shaped like a miniature launch pad.

'Who fancies Pop-Rockets?'

Katie stepped back in surprise. 'No way! Have you've been saving those all this time?'

Billy tilted his head and looked at her in that way. She'd never tell him how it made her feel; he didn't seem to think of her in that way.

'Of course I have,' he said. 'I told you I would.'

'Well in that case, how about you carry on saving them for when we have something big to celebrate? You know, like a win.'

Billy wondered if he'd ever get to eat them if they did that. But then she clearly believed in him, and his parents did too!

He put them on his bedside table and smiled. 'It's a deal!'

***

Billy arrived downstairs to find Katie talking to his dad in the kitchen. They were looking at his copy of Casey McGrips and the lunatic leap, discussing the finer points of male versus female contestants. When Sue walked into the kitchen five minutes later, she found them all having a passionate discussion about the pros and cons of Ice-pick tyres.

'Time to go, kids,' she joked, including Tom in her remark.

Responding to the deadline, Billy's heart started to thump, and his stomach developed sudden cramps; he was thankful Katie had suggested they save the Pop-Rockets for another time, otherwise they might have been popping back up.

'What if I forget something? he asked, holding his lurching stomach. 'What if we haven't done something we need to?'

Tom watched the colour fade from Billy's face. He was paler than a flour-bomb. 'Don't worry, Billy. Everything's going to be fine. Katie's taking care of your bag and she's more sensible than the two of us put together! Mr Peddleton is already waiting at Kielder Forest, and everything else has been checked. All we need to do is get there'

Katie touched his hand and smiled. 'You've got this, Billy-boy.'

Billy didn't know if it was Katie's touch or if he'd only imagined the sickly feeling. But the knot of fear that was filling his stomach quickly shrank to nothing.

'Team Wheeler huddle,' he said, stepping up beside his dad.

They crowded into a circle and huddled up.

'Air-biscuit,' he whispered, before he farted and fell about laughing.

'Oh, you beast,' Sue complained, stepping back in surprise.

With Team Wheeler dashing out of the kitchen and heading towards the front door, Billy's Space-Time Tournament had finally begun.

23

Dean Tuffnell stood in the entrance of the local Travel Station and surveyed the steady flow of people. He didn't know if any were travelling to Kielder Forest, but wherever they were going, he was certain not all would be Porting; only people like him could afford such luxuries.

'Here you go,' Kurt said, interrupting his son's self-importance and handing him a packet of Glow Candy. 'I don't know why you like that stuff. It doesn't taste of anything.'

'That's exactly why I like it,' Dean responded.

Kurt surveyed his son. 'Why are you waiting here anyway?'

'Oh, I just thought I'd wish Weeweeler a safe journey on the train.'

'Right … well, as fun as that might be, I don't think I can be bothered with the hassle. Maybe you should save it for during the event and have your fun there?'

'I've already got that sorted,' Dean replied. 'Besides … it's too late!' He pointed into the crowd having spotted Billy and his parents approaching. 'This'll be fun.'

Sue and Katie climbed the steps while Billy and his dad took to the ramp. Pre-occupied with one another and trying to reach the entrance in first place, they'd both failed to notice that Dean was waiting in the doorway. But then Billy turned the final corner and came face to face with him. He was standing there with his arms folded across his chest looking all-important.

'Hi Dean,' Tom said, brightly. 'Couldn't your dad make it?'

Dean turned abruptly to find an empty space where his dad had should have been standing.

'What?' he barked, snapping back to Tom. 'Oh … well, he's obviously busy doing something important.'

'Oh, I see,' Tom replied. Just like he and Sue had agreed, his words were steady and deliberate. 'Well, you have a good journey now, we've got to run along.' He offered another generous smile before they moved away, leaving Dean standing there alone, and wordless.

Dean felt embarrassed and annoyed; his attempt to humiliate them hadn't gone to plan. But then they hadn't seen the little pack of Glow Candy he was holding, had they! He might have looked annoyed, but inside he was secretly smiling, and scheming. Determined not to let them get the better of him, he left to find his mysteriously absent dad.

24

Katie gave Billy a hug. 'I'll be watching you on the broadcast.'

'Look out for the hair,' he said, pointing to the remarkable thatch of ginger on his head.

'I can't you muppet. You'll be wearing the suit.'

Billy gave a sheepish smirk. 'Um … I'll give you a wave?'

She did that hands-on-hips thing she was so fond of using, making that feeling visit him once again. If only she thought of him in that way. He wanted to ask her if she did. Had done for ages!

'See you later,' he said, bailing out and getting on the train.

'Um, Billy-boy. Your bag?' She held it up, smiling smugly.

'What would I do without you?' he asked, as the train pulled away.

'You'd be eternally miserable.'

He looked back at her in that way, deciding she could well be right.

***

Billy sat in the window seat of their carriage and stared out at the lush green countryside of the Lake District. He'd never seen so much water in one place.

'Are we nearly there yet?' he asked his reflection, half hoping it would reply and say yes.

He'd been sat for nearly three hours and was bored beyond belief. More annoyingly, his home in Pilton felt like a million miles away and the homesick feeling that niggled at his stomach was refusing to leave. He'd repeatedly complained how annoying it was that Relaxers were first class only. If only he had one for himself, then perhaps he could sleep the sickness away.

Several carriages down, Anderson Toms was not suffering the same frustrating journey. He'd boarded the train in Worcester and was lucky enough to be sleeping in one of the famous Relaxers. He'd been oblivious to the journey for at least an hour and was deep into a vivid dream about winning his own Space-Time Tournament. His goal of becoming an explorer with Space-Time Industries would soon come to fruition. Just not in the way he'd expect.

He didn't know Billy yet. But he would soon enough.

***

'Thank goodness for that,' Sue said, wheeling Tom down the exit ramp and away from the train. 'After that journey, Porting seems far more appealing.'

'Dad, look,' Billy said, pointing excitedly. 'That man has a sign with the Space-Time logo on it.'

Tom looked over and spotted a tournament official with a sign that welcomed the contestants and their companions. When he moved around, the sign being projected from his backpack turned and swayed with him.

'Would all contestants of the Space-Time Tournament please have your Profilers ready for linking,' he shouted, through a voice-volumizer. Large green arrows in the sign above his head flashed brightly, pointing in the same direction as his hands. 'Contestants queue here,' he said, pointing to his left. 'Companions, please queue to the right.'

Billy had never liked the brash sound that voice-volumizers created. Miss Cravity used one several times a day at school. It was very effective: you had no choice but to listen wherever you were trying to hide.

'The tournament coach will be leaving in twenty minutes,' the man continued. 'Please have your Profiler ready.'

'We won't come on the coach,' Tom said, gesturing to his wheelchair. 'Bit of an oversight. We'll see you at the stadium.' He watched the colour flush out of Billy once again. 'Don't worry Billy-boy, we'll be there when you arrive. you'll be fine.'

Saying goodbye, Billy shared a brief hug with his parents. He strained a smile that didn't quite reach his eyes before joining his own queue – despite being with the other contestants, he felt utterly alone.

He shuffled along uneasily, looking down and kicking at his feet, when somewhat out of the blue he found himself at the front.

'Name?' The man asked, stiffly.

Billy held his Profiler out to show the official. 'Billy Wheeler,' he said, nervously.

The man's eyes narrowed slightly. He looked Billy up and downy suspiciously. 'Don't you think you're a little too young to be wearing one of those?'

Billy found himself stumped for words. He knew he was officially too young, but the Space-Time president had invited him personally. What was he supposed to say now? He began to feel hot and uneasy; the man was just staring at him with narrow eyes. Without adult words to help, all Billy could do was offer his Profiler again and try to smile.

'You don't talk much, do you!' the man stated.

Billy just shook his head. He was utterly tongue-tied.

'Well, I suppose you are wearing the Profiler … Come on then, give it here.'

Much to Billy's relief, the man gave up his questioning and swept a handheld Focus over Billy's wrist. A flood of relief washed over him. As soon as the Focus did its thing and flashed, he'd be in the clear.

It didn't respond … No beeps, no flashes … Just nothing.

Billy's skin began to prickle with heat. It felt like time itself had slowed to a crawl while he waited for the Focus to react. Then, as if saving him from some terrible fate, the green flash rescued him.

'Thought you might have been in trouble there, boy,' the man teased. 'Billy Wheeler eh. I think I'll keep an eye out for you.' He gave Billy an odd wink. Was he being kind, or a little threatening? Billy couldn't tell.

With the suspicious man behind him, Billy's confidence began to creep back. He'd experienced the first test of standing on his own two feet and hadn't fallen over. He boarded the coach and sat four rows from the front, window seat to the left. Seat number thirteen was in front.

'Lucky for some,' he whispered to himself.

'Unlucky for others,' a girl added, from the seat behind him. 'Mind if I join you?'

'Only if you don't mind us looking like a Duracell battery,' he replied, pointing to her black hair and his bright ginger.

She lifted her battery powered arm and wiggled her fingers. 'Maybe we could make this last longer.'

Billy smiled at her, impressed; she was quick witted.

The girl studied him for a moment, perhaps trying to decide if he was old enough to even be there, before she sat down and held out her hand. 'It's nice to meet you. I'm Louise.'

'Billy,' he responded, paying no real attention to the metallic hand he was holding. 'Are you competing in the tournament?'

'Um … I don't think I'd be here otherwise.'

Billy facepalmed himself when he realised what a daft question it was. Louise couldn't help but laugh out loud, causing a little niggle of uncertainty to enter her mind. She thought back to what she'd told herself not that long ago. 'Whatever it takes. Whoever gets in my way!' But now, after meeting Billy, a stranger who'd so quickly disarmed her with his innocence. She wasn't quite so sure … Quite …

Over the course of their journey, Billy and Louise talked a lot. They discussed where they were from, how and when they received their Black Insignias, and what they'd done since. They also exchanged ideas on what challenges they thought the tournament might entail. Billy was very careful not to say too much; he didn't want to give any of his training secrets away after all. For a lot of the journey, they hadn't managed to say anything at all; they'd been too caught up in fits of laughter, largely owing to the cans of cherry Heliyumm that Louise had shared between them. Billy learned that Louise liked anything black, while Louise learned that Billy liked anything that wasn't black. The one thing that they did have in common however, was that neither of them had siblings and they both liked it that way.

***

'Look, look!' someone shouted from the rear of the coach.

A wave of gasps swept through the passengers as everyone stood up and crowded towards Billy's side of the coach. He wiped the steamy glass with his hand, forcing a chill from his fingers all the way to his chest. Viewed through the streaky palm swipe, Kielder Forest's Splitwood Stadium rose from the ground and disappeared into the low-lying cloud.

They'd arrived.

25

Billy stepped from the coach and into the grounds of Splitwood Stadium. His hand dropped to his side spilling some of his precious Heliyumm as he gawped open mouthed. He'd seen the stadium on TV numerous times, but it had never done justice to the sight that was filling his eyes. Floating floodlights sat below the cloud and spat their gravity defying blue thrust downwards. Hidden in the grey blanket above him, they cast intense beams of light that danced through the drifting cloud.

Feeling a little weak at the knees, he stumbled away from the coach and walked across the carpark. In front of him, the square bulky timbers of Splitwood Stadium soared magnificently into the cloud. The stands were completely empty, but despite their silence, he could still hear the crowds of tournaments past. To his right, and stretching away from the stands, the earthy banks of Kielder Water ran for miles. Across the water, lay a tall, splintery forest known as the Hunting Grounds. Its towering trees climbed defiantly up a steep hillside and far into the distance.

'It's incredible, don't you think?' said a new voice from beside him.

'You got that right,' Billy replied, without even looking. 'I've seen this on the broadcast a hundred times, but it never looked so, so—'

'Awesome?' The boy finished.

'Yeah. Awesome! I'm Billy,' he said, turning to face the boy.

'Reuben,' his new acquaintance replied, giving a flick of his razor straight, blonde hair. 'I hope you don't mind me saying, but aren't you a little bit—'

'Young for this?' Billy cut in.

Reuben smiled a little sheepishly. 'I guess you've heard that before.'

'Yep, but it's cool.' Turning away, he took a big gulp Heliyumm.

'I'm pretty sure it's the squeaky voice,' he said, in a high-pitched squeal.

Reuben burst into fits of laughter, made ever worse by Billy laughing along with him.

'I think we're going to get on, you and me,' Rueben said.

Billy liked that idea very much. Friends were good!

'BILLY!' someone shouted, from across the car park.

At first, he neither recognised the voice, nor knew where it was coming from.

'OVER HERE!' the voice called.

Billy's eyes darted in all directions. Then, catching his eye, he saw Mr Peddleton waving. He was standing with Sue and Tom. He turned to Rueben. 'I better go,' he said, pointing to his parents. 'See you later.'

'Yeah, see you later, Squeaky.'

Billy covered the distance between himself and his parents at a flat-out sprint. By the time he arrived, he was utterly puffed out.

'How was the trip?' Mr Peddleton asked.

'Too long …' Billy replied, his hands firmly planted on his knees and puffing for breath. 'But worth every second.'

'I thought it would be. Splitwood is my favourite' Mr Peddleton said, admiringly. 'Anyway, you best get checked in. You've got a big night tomorrow.'

'Night?' Billy asked, straightening up at the news.

'Yes. It's a new challenge for this year. They've changed the start time to 10pm. Nobody knew about it until today.'

'Oh … well … we'd better get on with it then,' Billy stated, his voice sounding much calmer than his nerves felt.

With Mr Crankworth leading the way, Billy headed for check-in. Bravery, it seemed, was rapidly becoming his most practiced skill. It was no bad thing when you considered what he'd have to face up to the following night!

If anything, it would be essential.

***

'What do you think of the Demountables now you're finally stood in one?' Tom asked.

Billy's eyes sparkled brightly. 'Even better than on TV. I love it! I can't believe they put them up and take them down for every event?'

'It's amazing isn't it. And better than leaving them all over the place, don't you think? It's like mini hotel room and workshop all rolled into one,' Tom enthused. 'Shall I show you around, like a tour?'

Despite Billy's desire to run around the Demountable in a flash, he knew how much his dad had been looking forward to his first event. In truth it was an easy answer.

'Where do I buy a ticket?' Billy asked, with genuine enthusiasm.

First off, they stopped in Billy's bedroom. Despite being in a pop-up home, the bed was twice the size of his own and floated on a set of magnet-stands. His spare clothes were hanging on one wall and his Kinetic Skinsuit on another. The next room they visited was the lounge. The first thing Billy noticed was the main wall: it wasn't really wall, at all. Instead, it was the biggest VR-Wall he'd ever seen.

'The screen changes size depending on what you watch,' Tom said. 'Great for movies, but a bit too big for the fireplace.'

'What fireplace?' asked Billy, seeing no such thing.

'Go and stand over there,' Tom said, pointing to the wall.

Despite not having a clue what his dad could be up to, Billy did as he'd been asked.

'VR-Wall, fireplace mode,' Tom commanded.

'Whoa! That's hot!' Billy said, jumping away in surprise. He looked behind to see a roaring fire. 'That is awesome! Maybe we could get one, one day.'

'Maybe one day,' Tom said, thinking one day probably meant never.

The next stop on their tour was the workshop.

'I suppose this is probably the most important room of all,' Tom said, gazing at Billy's beautiful Saddleton Mimic.

'It certainly is,' Harvey agreed, stepping out from behind Billy's suit. 'What do you think?'

'It's amazing. I can't believe the whole place is held together with magnets.' Billy turned to his dad. 'Can we look around a bit more?'

'You go ahead, Billy. I think I'll stop here. Just don't go messing with fireplaces, Okay.'

'I won't Dad, I promise.' Billy didn't have any plans to mess with any fireplaces but jumping up and down on a floating bed … now that was practically an obligation.

***

With his heart still thumping from trampolining, Billy found another two bedrooms. Each had its own VR-Wall and a bed sitting on magnet stands. In the dining room there was a dinner table with a delivery unit. He'd heard about them being used at posh restaurants. Instead of someone bringing your food to the table, when you chose from the menu it just popped up on the table in front of you; Billy couldn't wait to try it out. The final room he visited was the bathroom. The only thing of interest in there was a voice activated shower. He secretly set it to ice-cold, just on the off chance his mum forgot to say otherwise.

Returning to the workshop, he found his dad sat in front of a Holo-Tab. Sue was pacing the floor, apparently finding things a bit stressful.

Tom spotted him. 'Come on in, Billy-boy. We've got the details of the first challenge.'

However fast he could move, it wasn't Billy who stood beside Tom first. It was Sue.

'What is it? What's he got to do?' Her voice was not entirely steady, and the sense of worry was apparent for all to hear.

Billy joined his mum and put an arm over her shoulder. She jumped with a nervous little twitch but took his hand in hers and offered a difficult smile.

'Right then,' Tom began. 'It looks like there are two sets of Hourglass Focus hidden in the grounds. Some are hidden in the forest, and some are hidden in an underground mine. You need to collect one by linking it with your Profiler. It says you can choose which type you try to find.'

'Well, that's easy,' Billy said. 'I'll look for one in the forest.'

'It's not quite that simple,' Tom replied. 'Underground Focuses are worth more Time Credits. And don't forget you can lose Credits too. It's to discourage things like bad sportsmanship,' he continued, utterly unaware that both Louise and Dean were already planning to cheat. 'It says that more details will be revealed at the dinner, later.'

'Speaking of which,' Sue said, 'I've left your outfit in your room, and some Space-Time magazines on your bed if you wanted to have a read. Maybe see if you can pick up any last-minute hints.'

With nothing more to learn from the Holo-Tab and the thought of re-reading his favourite magazines again, Billy disappeared into his temporary bedroom.

26

Via the magic of Port travel, Dean Tuffnell had arrived at Splitwood Stadium a mere five minutes after he'd left Weeweeler and his smart Alec dad behind. He'd been caught off guard by the overly nice way Weeweeler's dad had acted and didn't get the one up like he'd planned. It was made worse by the fact that his own dad had abandoned him. His excuse was that he'd needed to use the bathroom. But in truth, they both knew better.

After finding his feet in his own Demountable, Dean had enjoyed a bit of preparation. His little mission to locate Weeweeler's food and drink in the stadium food-store hadn't been as difficult as expected. Nobody saw him creeping through the timber lodge where they'd host the welcoming dinner, and in an incredible turn of luck, Billy's food was in the second freezer he'd checked; on the day of the main event, he'd be having lasagne. As for his pre-event snack, there might be a little extra ingredient too! As far as Dean was concerned, there could be no better way to prepare for the tournament other than to enjoy a nice, tasty snack.

***

Walking toward his Demountable after his very successful mission, Dean stumbled across a small teenaged girl with short black hair. She was standing at the edge of the forest and peering into the gloom like a child looking down the stairs into a dark basement

'Hi,' he said from behind, making her jump.

She spun around and took a small step back 'Oh, hi,'.

Dean was a little amused by her reaction, but he didn't show it. 'Sorry, I didn't mean to make you jump,' he said, submissively, knowing that for now at least, making friends was better than making enemies.

'It's okay, I just didn't hear you,' the girl replied more confidently.

'I guess you must be competing?'

'Yeah. My dad said it'd be a good idea to have a look around before the event tomorrow night.'

'Ah yes, the night challenge,' Dean said in a sarcastic spooky voice. 'Should be fun.'

'There may be a monster or two though. That's what I heard.'

'Hunters maybe, not monsters!' Dean scoffed. 'Unless they hid my mum in there.'

When the girl realised that he'd replied without any hint of humour, she took a small chance. 'Or my dad,' she whispered.

'Oh, it's the same for you, is it?'

She looked at the floor shamefully. 'You could say that.'

'Well … we'd better hope it is the Hunters you've heard about. It'd be better than finding our own parent monsters in there.'

Louise smiled. She liked the way he referred to their parents as monsters. It was quite accurate.

'I'm Dean by the way.'

The girl stepped forward and offered her robotic hand. 'I'm Louise.'

Like Billy did earlier, Dean shook her hand barely noticing it was robotic; at least they shared something in common. It was almost a pity. If either of them had paid it more attention, it might not become the thing that would bring them together in such a dangerous way.

Dean and Louise began to walk together and formed quite the tournament partnership. Dean, a boy with a mis-informed score to settle. And Louise, a girl so afraid of letting her father down that she'd likely do whatever it took to impress him.

Unsurprisingly, Dean didn't mention Billy at all; he wouldn't dare encourage any suspicion onto himself should anything accidentally mess with his tournament. But if he had mentioned Billy, Louise wouldn't have admitted that she knew him either. Her newest friend was someone with his own parent monster, and she liked that they shared this in common. But he certainly wasn't the bright and innocent boy she'd liked enough to share her Heliyumm with. Dean was a much darker character all together.

27

Darkness had fallen by the time Billy pushed his dad along the path toward Kielder Lodge. Leading the way, gentle glowing lamps hung from the trees, casting soft flickering light as if glow-bugs lived inside them. Tom listened to the gravel crunching beneath his wheels, but he could have sworn that Billy's feet were almost silent; the boy really was a Whisperer.

Following the pathway, they rounded a final tree bringing the ancient timber lodge into view. Giant Spruce logs curved gently skyward, creating steep pointed arches. The incredible building was topped by a heavy moss roof that hung over it like a green woolly blanket. Approaching the entrance, the mixed sounds of conversation and music drifted towards them.

'Good evening, Sir. May I take your name?' a man asked as they approached the door.

'I'm Billy … Um, I mean, Billy Wheeler.'

'Ah, very good, Mr Wheeler.' The man checked a holographic list that floated in front of him. 'You're on table twenty-two, right at the back. Should be easy to get to,' he said, looking at Tom's wheelchair and smiling.

'Oh, great. Another table at the back where we can't see anything!' The words had burst out of Billy before he could control his instant frustration. His dad was dumped at the back, yet again!

'Oh, um, I see. Um … we do have a very large VR-Wall,' the man suggested, genuinely trying to be kind.

'That'll be fine. Thank you,' Tom said politely, rather embarrassed by Billy's outburst.

The man blushed a little and pointed to a table in the back corner of the room. 'It's just over there. I do hope you enjoy your evening.'

'Off we go then,' Billy said sarcastically, brimming with protective frustration.

Tom wheeled himself in the direction of the table swiftly followed by Harvey and Sue. Billy gave the usher a defiant look before he too followed them away. When he reached the table, Sue collared him.

'It doesn't do any good to get annoyed or be rude,' she said. 'People make assumptions when they're trying to be helpful. It's just the way it is sometimes!'

Billy stood there defiantly. 'Well, it's not fair!'

'Oh, try not to let it bother you,' Tom said. 'Just enjoy the evening. Ooh, look, Space Rocks!' he continued, spotting his favourite chewy sweets on the table. He put two in his mouth at once. 'I love these things.'

Despite his dad's enthusiasm, Billy still grumbled. Then, making him feel even worse, he spotted Dean sitting right at the front. He was flanked by Louise on one side and Reuben on the other.

Oh, that just great, he thought. *The only two people I know are sat right by him!*

For the next twenty minutes, Billy sat with his parents and nursed a Cookies and Cream Heliyumm. His mood had taken an unexpected nosedive, and despite having his favourite drink, he was struggling to climb back out of it.

'Aren't you a little bit young to be doing this?' a familiar voice asked.

As quickly as it had left him, the sharp wit humour returned to Billy. With a mouthful of Heliyumm disappearing into his stomach, he turned around to greet his visitor. 'I think it's squeaky the voice,' he replied.

Reuben put his hand in the air ready for a high-five. Billy placed a stinger of a slap to meet it.

'I thought I'd come and sit with you if that's okay?'

Billy looked to his parents for approval who nodded without hesitation. He'd needed a friend to lift his spirits, and this young man had done the perfect job.

'I think I prefer it back here,' Reuben whispered. 'I'd rather be out of the way instead of sitting right up there.' He pointed to his table right in front of the VR-Wall. 'I didn't like the idea of getting called up in front of all these people.' He smiled sheepishly at Billy. 'I'm not very good at that kind of thing.'

Billy felt utterly surprised. It had never occurred to him that while he was annoyed about being at the back, maybe some people didn't enjoy being at the front, either. Before he could reply, the giant VR-Wall burst into life projecting a huge hourglass into the room. Instead of being filled with sand it was brimming with bright sparkling stars that tumbled from top to bottom.

'Ladies, Gentlemen, and of course, our competitors. It is my pleasure to welcome you to the Space-Time Tournament dinner. I'd like to take this opportunity say how wonderful it is to have you all here. It is always so exciting to see the new young faces that give such limitless value to Space-Time Industries.'

'Do you recognise that voice?' Billy asked, scanning the lodge and hoping to find the owner.

'Nope, never heard it before,' Reuben replied.

'I swear I know that voice, but I can't remember where from.'

'Be quiet, Billy,' Sue whispered. 'You need to listen.'

'To kick off the evening I am pleased to announce that our new initiative, Time for Charity, has been a tremendous success. The withdrawal of advanced travel funding for our competitors has resulted in a significant sum being donated to some wonderful causes. While I imagine that some of you were looking forward to your first Port experience, I can only ask that you forgive our decision when I say that the funding is making an incredible difference to those less fortunate than ourselves. So, as the Space-Time Tournament enters its twenty-second year, it strengthens my belief that this will be our best year yet! The only thing left to do right now, is to ask that you eat well, relax, and enjoy each other's company. Oh, there is the small matter of the tournament rules, of course. I'm sure you've all read the guide that came with your Black Insignia, but we're putting it on the VR-Wall in case any of you need a reminder.'

Billy looked at Rueben, eyes wide. 'I didn't read mine. Dad called it mumbo jumbo.'

'Guess you'd better start reading then, Squeaky.'

'Oh, this is stupid!' Billy complained. 'I'm sitting right at the back, and I need to watch the VR-Wall all night.'

Reuben gave an apologetic shrug and got up. 'Why don't you come and sit at my table? You'll be able to see better from there. I need to go and talk to someone, but I'll be back in a minute.'

Billy pointed at Dean. 'I don't want any grief. You could say we don't get on very well?'

'Oh … Well, if you change your mind just come over.'

With a defiant I'll manage, expression, Billy fixed his eyes on the wall. 'Thanks, but I think I'll do it from here.'

Reuben had only been sat for five minutes when he felt a gentle tap on his shoulder. Billy was standing there, looking slightly sheepish.

'Is it still okay to sit with you? My eyes were beginning to water from squinting.'

'More like you were crying,' came the sarcastic words from just behind him.

Billy's heart sank. He'd been stood there for less than a minute and Dean had already taken the time to come and hassle him. He left his back turned and began to walk away.

'Oi!' came a loud shout, into his right ear.

Billy snapped around thinking Dean had finally lost it and was about to thump him, but instead of finding an angry face, he found his nemesis cupping his ear and looking at a half-chewed Space Rock on the floor.

'Who did that?' he asked, looking around to see where it came from. Billy expected there to be an awkward stand-off in the middle of the hall, but then utterly straight-faced, Reuben stood up and offered a bowl of Space Rocks to Dean.

'Fancy another one?'

Still rubbing his ear, Dean glared at him angrily before turning away.

Reuben popped a sweet in his mouth. 'I love these things.'

A couple of tables away from Billy, Louise quietly popped another Space Rock in her mouth and pushed the bowl back across the table. Good deed done, she wouldn't feel so guilty if she betrayed him.

28

By the time their food arrived at the table, Billy had managed to memorise several rules as they scrolled across the screen. He already knew about the first one as he'd been wearing it since he'd received his Black Insignia: 'Profilers cannot be removed until after the tournament.' The purpose of the second rule was a little less obvious and had prompted Billy and Reuben to ask Mr Peddleton about it: 'Only one Gadget can be used during any event'. The explanation reminded Billy of when he and Katie escaped from Dean across Whitelake river. When they'd arrived at the riverbank it looked like they were stuck. The result? Billy had done the best he could with what he had – the apparent ability to defy gravity – and they'd escaped. So, in the tournament, armed with only one Gadget and their ingenuity, it would demonstrate who could make the best of a difficult situation.

Sitting at her own table near the front, Louise watched the rules scroll across the screen. Even though her dad made her read the guide several times, he still insisted that she read them again. It was all rather boring until a rule scrolled across the screen that made her face flush hot and pink: 'Competitors must not make modifications to their suits.' As if by some horrible coincidence, she felt tap on her shoulder and jumped out of her seat in fear; had she been found out already?

Dean offered an apologetic smile. 'Sorry, I didn't mean to make you jump again!'

'What did you do that for?' she asked, anger flourishing in her voice.

He took a step back, shying away from the darkness that filled her eyes. 'Hey, I said sorry!'

'Oh, Dean. No, I'm sorry. You made me jump, that's all.'

'Are you sure? You looked pretty annoyed.'

'Yes, of course, I think I'm just a bit on edge because of tomorrow.'

She certainly wasn't going to tell him that she was utterly paranoid about being caught with a Disruptor in her arm.

'Who's this?' Duncan Kelley asked, returning to the table.

'Oh, Dad, this is Dean. We met earlier today when I was having a look around.'

'I see … Well, Dean, you'll have to excuse us. Louise has more preparation to do.'

She looked at him apologetically. 'Parent-monster,' she mouthed.

'Oh, okay. I guess I'll see you tomorrow then.'

'Goodbye Dean,' Duncan said, flatly.

When Dean looked back a few minutes later, Louise was staring down at the table with her dad jabbering in her ear. *Yep, we both have parent-monsters*, he thought. Seemingly unwelcome wherever he went, he decided to sit at his own table and read some rules rather than face further rejection. In quick succession, three scrolled across the screen: 'Time Credits earned during the tournament will decide your starting position for the final challenge: An Hourglass Focus may be linked by more than one competitor.'

Yeah, yeah, I know that! he thought, bored already.

'Memory Traces operate at all times. Upon request, Traces must be submitted for inspection.'

This final rule took Dean by surprise, and for a moment, panic coursed through his veins; he'd forgotten all about the Memory Trace when he'd been on his little mission earlier. If the wrong person got to see it, he'd be kicked out of the tournament for sure.

'Dad,' he whispered, 'I think we've got a problem.'

'Oh, what's that then?'

'I did something earlier today. Something I shouldn't have.'

Kurt's expression didn't change. 'I know you did.'

'You know?' Dean asked, confused.

'Yeah. It's a good job I know you, too! Do you like your new hat?'

'What's that got to do with anything?'

'Take the hat off and look at it, boy.'

Dean took off his hat and looked it over. At first, he saw nothing of interest, nothing to hint to what his dad was getting at. But then he found it. Stitched into the side was a tiny power switch.; the hat was a Trace Blocker. If anyone tried to watch his Trace, it would simply show static.

'Thanks Dad,' he said, not daring to ask how he'd purchased such dubious an item.

Kurt gave him an unforgiving look. 'Don't be so dumb next time!'

Despite being together, they didn't speak for the rest of the night.

Anderson Toms sat with his engineer and observed the interesting variety of characters that surrounded him. Having watched a slightly grumpy and too-young-to-be-in-the tournament, boy at the back of the room. A worryingly jumpy girl being chastised by her dad at the front, and a very angry looking father calling his son dumb at the table next to him, he felt confident about his chances. Being told off wasn't something he'd ever experienced. For as long as he could remember, he'd never been in trouble. But that was because his dad was never home, and his mum spent her entire life at the gym or having dinner with friends. He didn't mind it that much; having anything you want when you want from parents who'd let you have it, was fun. Although when it really came to it, he'd swap the gifts they gave for their time and company in a heartbeat.

The tournament entry had been their most recent 'we'll make it up to you' gift. Not because he'd asked for it, but because he'd been talking about it and said how nice it would be to visit some of the locations on a family holiday. Needless to say, Anderson was visiting every location, just without the company of his parents. His only motivation to compete at all was to try and impress them so much that they noticed him a little bit more.

Almost all the contestants ended up re-reading the rules several times. Hiro Akita became fixated with, 'If a competitor has to ask for rescue, they will not earn any Time Credits for that event.'

Thinking about his time with Louise Kelley earlier in the day and comparing their parent-monsters, the rule that stuck in Dean's mind was, 'If a competitor is caught by a Hunter, they will not earn Time Credits for that event.'

Alisha May spent most of the evening chatting with friends on her Holo-Phone. She barely read the rules at all. The one time that she had looked up, it read, 'The competitor with the fewest Time Credits at the end of each event will leave the tournament.' From that point on she couldn't stop making jokes about how embarrassing it would be for the first contestant to leave the Tournament. It wouldn't be her – that much she was certain of!

***

Late evening had arrived when the VR-Wall finally went dark. The deep and powerful voice that had opened the dinner returned once again.

'Ladies, Gentlemen and competitors, I hope you've enjoyed your evening and each other's company. If I may offer some final advice, enjoy your rest and prepare. When faced with a challenge, do not be shy. When faced with fear, find your bravery. But most important of all, when faced with a decision, choose wisely. For tomorrow night, the search for a new tournament champion begins.'

Those two words rang loud and clear in Billy's ears yet again … Choose wisely .

29

The sun disappeared behind the horizon giving way to a hazy golden light. Soon after dusk, darkness enveloped Kielder Forest. There was an all-together different feeling to the place from when Louise and Dean had been looking around; heading out at night was considerably less appealing. Guiding the way, the floating floodlights cast their ghostly glow onto the spectators beneath. The stands had steadily filled as darkness fell, and un-known to those around him, the president of Space-Time Industries sat proudly within the crowd. Even though they would see very little without looking at the large VR-Walls, the stadium buzzed with a sense of excitement and expectation.

***

'You can do this,' Louise told herself, looking out into the gloom from her bedroom window. 'You won't get caught.'

'Five minutes Louise. Are you ready?'

'Yes Dad!' she replied, far too sharply. 'I'll be out in a minute.' She was trying to remain calm, but the pressure he'd been putting on her made it all but impossible. The thought of cheating with the Disruptor was becoming difficult to bear.

Elsewhere, and in his own Demountable, Dean was hoping that yesterday's mission would become a success.

'Remember what I told you yesterday,' Kurt said. 'No silly mistakes. Just beat Wheeler!'

'I'll be fine,' Dean replied. 'And Weeweeler won't be a problem either. I took care of it.' If it wasn't for his dad, Dean would have been caught and nothing would be fine, but he wasn't worried. If he needed to cheat again, he would. Anything to beat that Weeweeler!

In several other Demountables, contestants nervously awaited the start of their event. Alisha May and Reuben Alt, for example, both paced the floor, not feeling ready for what lay ahead. With the constant distraction of her phone and friends, Alisha hadn't managed any preparation at all. It was probably the reason she'd have the kind of night that was heading her way.

***

As the 10pm deadline approached, the first competitor to arrive at the arena was all alone. Their suit was entirely black, but for one significant feature that you simply couldn't miss: the aged bones of a human skeleton. From whichever direction you looked, the holographic bones would appear. In the greyness of the foggy night, it was like watching a living skeleton walk the earth.

Through the eyes of the skull, Dean Tuffnell viewed the world. He stepped through the control gate and looked back toward the Demountables. *No sign of Weeweeler*, he thought. *Looks like mission accomplished.*

Another two contestants arrived at the control gate and linked their Profilers. Despite walking together, they both remained silent in thought. Alisha May was thinking that her crystal white design was a terrible idea; while the dark forest absorbed any hint of light, her bright suit did not! Everyone would see exactly what she was doing – Hunters and all.

Dexter Jones was grateful that his suit was not white; the small person who walked beside him stood out like a storm cloud in a clear sky. Instead, he'd arrived in a suit sporting deep green armour. Shaped with scales and spurs, it had the appearance of an ancient, long-lost dragon.

Several young contestants hoping to prove their worth arrived and passed through the tournament control gate. Dexter's suit had wowed with his menacing dragon, and Dean's living skeleton made his fellow contestants shiver. Despite being for the wrong reason, even Alisha May's suit caught the eye of those around her. There was however, one notable exception. One suit that the Space-Time president had worryingly noted was missing. That one belonged to Billy Wheeler.

Past the control gate and inside the starting arena, Dean waited patiently. If Billy didn't make the start he'd be out of the tournament before it even began. Satisfied it was all going to plan, he turned his attention to the talent reveal.

'Spectators, please welcome your contestants,' the commentator bellowed through his voice-volumizer.

'Dean Tuffnell … Mighty.'

Dean puffed his chest out at the resulting applause. He'd hoped beyond anything else that being a Whisperer would not be his talent and he wasn't disappointed. He was utterly convinced that outstanding strength would win him the tournament.

'Alisha May… Nimble,' the commentator confirmed. This time the resulting cheer was notably louder and definitely contained the voices of several young females. Alisha's cheerleader friends were clearly delighted she was a Nimble – dexterity being her skill.

As each contestant was announced, their primary talent and skills were revealed. Dexter was confirmed as a Heed – he could hear beyond the silence of a whisper. Anderson was delighted to be a Visual – confirming the ability to see without light and spot the smallest of details. Louise Kelley was also announced as a Heed. It was unsurprising, given how often she'd listen to her dad go on at her about achievement.

'Ladies and gentlemen, all our contestants have now … oh!' The commentator stopped talking when a tournament marshal whispered in his ear. 'Oh dear, it looks like we have one missing. Now, where did I put him?' he said with a chuckle.

The crowd laughed. So did Dean.

30

'Stop … Just STOP!'

The chaos of noise and confusion filling the Demountable ceased into shocked silence. Both Tom and Billy had never heard the gentle voice of Sue Wheeler be so, not gentle. She stood there with her hands on her hips like a disapproving matron and glared at them. A shadow crept away from her feet and up the wall behind her. It wasn't cast by a light in the room, but by the face of Billy himself.

'How could you eat Glow Candy just before a night-time event?' asked Tom, for the umpteenth time.

'I haven't eaten anything other than my dinner,' Billy said, defiantly.

'You're not going to solve anything by blaming anyone,' Sue said. 'We all know he wouldn't have eaten Glow Candy on purpose.'

Sue was merely stating the obvious, but when panic sets in, the obvious can often get missed. As for Billy, his skin was glowing like a green neon sign; it was Glow Candy alright!

Interrupting the brief moment of silence, the front door of the Demountable swung open, banging hard against the wall.

'OK, I've got it,' Harvey said, breathing heavily. He held out both hands and offered a sloppy, gritty pile of mud that he'd scraped from the peaty earth outside. 'It's the best I could come up with.'

Billy looked at Mr Peddleton. 'What are we going to do with that?'

'Put it on your face,' Sue said, already taking the mud from Harvey's hands. 'Take your helmet off, quickly.'

Billy was about to protest, horrified by the thought of putting that filth on his face, but Mr Peddleton was one step ahead.

'Unless you want the Hunters to see your face lit up like a torch?'

Billy's mouth snapped shut in frustration. He wasn't to blame for this, but he was certainly paying the price.

'Just think of it as black sun-cream,' Sue suggested, rubbing the gritty dirt all over his face.

Billy thought sun-cream could never smell so bad.

Unrelenting, the seconds flashed past while Sue's hands did their work, but with every smear, the greenish light that cast her shadow up the wall faded until it was gone.

'Now go, Billy. Right now!'

***

Back in the starting arena, Dean watched the clock flick past 9:58pm. The seconds were ticking by too slowly ... thirty-one, thirty-two, thirty-three ...

In the stand, the Space-Time president stared at the control gate filled with sheer frustration. For him, the seconds were ticking by too fast... forty-five, forty-six, forty-seven ...

Dean's eyes remained locked on the control gate. It was deserted, just the way he liked it. A ripple of chatter drifted across the stadium. Some of the people were pointing. He scoured the stands, searching for the cause of their interest but it was just some stupid flag fluttering in the breeze. Disinterested, he returned his attention to the control gate and promptly received the fright of his life. Billy was standing just centimetres away, glaring at him in silence. He hadn't heard him approaching at all! Not even the slightest sound.

'He's finally here,' the commentator announced. 'Billy Wheeler ... Whisperer!'

In acknowledgement of his late arrival, the cheers and applause echoed around the stadium. They were not the loudest of the night, but they were the only ones led by a relieved Space-Time President.

Despite the applause being for him, Billy didn't register his introduction; the last ten minutes had consumed what little free thought he had left. What he did manage, was to offer Dean a very generous smile before turning his back and waiting for the event to start. While he would never know for sure, there was one possible explanation for how he could have eaten Glow Candy, and it was standing right behind him. He walked away and looked at the shimmering blue wires of the Electrobeam barrier. It crackled and fizzed, daring anyone feel their sting should they jump the start.

Within his skeleton suit and staring at Billy's back, Dean's thoughts turned dark. *Don't smile at me Weeweeler. You might have gotten this far, but you won't win the tournament. I'll make sure of it!*

A second wave of chatter began to spread through the crowd as a man wearing a Space-Time Industries jacket walked into the arena.

'Oh, my goodness,' Billy said, feeing utterly starstruck. 'You're Willy Schrader.'

'The one and only, young man. But you can just call me Schrader,' he added, winking.

Dean snickered at Billy's faux pas. The man known as Schrader never used his first name for reasons that should have been obvious. Although seemingly not that bothered, Schrader returned to his voice-volumizer and began to do what he did best.

'Welcome ... welcome all ... to the Space-Time Tournament,' he sang. He drew long, tension building breaths, stretching the words out before each dramatic pause. 'In a matter of moments ... our brave young contestants will begin their journey to win a scholarship with Space-Time Industries ... In this first challenge, contestants will undertake a perilous search for an Hourglass Focus ... Racing against the clock, contestants who collect a Focus in the quickest time will earn Time Credits. The faster they are, the more Credits they'll collect ... Contestants, I remind you ... the more challenging the Focus is to find ... the more credits you'll be awarded. So, I wish you all good luck ... for it is time ... to begin!'

First in line, Alisha May and Anderson Toms took their place against the Electrobeam barrier. One would return, the other would not.

'Three ... two ... one ... GO!'

31

The Electrobeam barrier evaporated, triggering Alisha May to react instantly. Racing Anderson off the line, she ran at a flat-out sprint toward the Hunting Grounds before quickly disappearing into the shadowy forest.

Anderson could have gone with her, but he already knew that you couldn't be faster than someone if you only ever followed them. So, with a different plan in mind, he headed towards Kielder Water. The other competitors looked on as the fog wrapped around Anderson like a heavy grey blanket and swallowed him whole. With both contestants disappearing into the night, the countdown began again.

'Three … Two … One … Go!'

One by one, each contestant took their turn at the Electrobeam barrier before disappearing into the darkness. Waiting patiently for his own turn to arrive, Billy watched Dean and Ruben sprint away. The speed at which Reuben left Dean behind was astounding. He was a Swift, and boy could he move! On the downside and completely the opposite to a Whisperer, you could hear him a mile away. Quickly falling behind, Dean's skeleton suit cut its own spooky lines through the darkness, before he too, was gone.

Finally, it was time for Billy to take his turn. He stood against the Electrobeam barrier and waited for the countdown to begin. He was delightfully unaware that beside him and inside a suit that looked like a Black Widow spider, stood Louise Kelley.

Louise herself was acutely aware of who was standing next to her. He was the funny and innocent boy she'd met only yesterday. She hadn't intended for it to be this way, but his unusually innocent character had gotten under her skin. Could she use her Disruptor on him if she had to? She wasn't so sure.

The countdown began and snapped her out of the thought. The subject of Billy would have to wait for another time.

'Three … Two … One … Go!'

Billy leapt off the line and ran like fury toward the water's edge, although he'd barely gone anywhere when the first problem arrived. Given all the time he'd waited to get going, he still hadn't decided which path to take. His eyes darted frantically between them, unable to decide. Should he follow the water's edge for a while in the hope of finding the abandoned mine: scary, dark, and claustrophobic? Or maybe one of the other paths that led into Kielder Forest: a vast area where an Hourglass Focus could be just about anywhere.

He stood for a moment in silent indecision when he became aware of the subtle sounds around him. Listening to the other competitors run through the forest he could hear branches snapping and dry leaves crackling under their clumsy feet. He knew that being surrounded by so much noise would do him no good as a Whisperer; he needed to be alone. But then the thought of actually being on his own was daunting. Slightly uncertain, he started for the path that followed the water's edge. To his left, the swirling greyness of fog offered little but the sounds that had pushed him away. With one final snap of wood, it was decided. The abandoned mine it would be.

The darkness completely swallowed Billy as Louise watched him disappear. She'd paused on the bank of Kielder Water long enough to lose sight of him and was pleased with the outcome; no Billy meant no decision about the Disruptor. Should she stumble across anyone else however – even Dean – they were fair game. With that one thought fixed in her mind, she ran into the darkness herself.

***

Billy half ran and half walked along the water's edge for several minutes before taking a sharp left and ducking into the trees. Fifty meters further along, the trail it split in several directions like splayed out fingers, each pointing to destinations unknown. His eyes jumped from trail to trail not having the slightest clue where each would lead. Hoping he wouldn't get lost and acting on pure impulse, he chose the narrowest one and ran aimlessly into the dark. Sprinting between the trees, small branches tapped and scratched at suit as if the trees were trying to grab hold of him. The fog was making it hard to see and different tracks kept appearing all over the place. The first niggle of fear began to poke at his skin; he was slowly losing his way.

A hundred meters later, Billy stumbled into a small clearing. Around its edge, yet more trails led into the darkness. Panic began to grab at his ankles, threatening to drag him away and be lost forever. But then appearing from within the gloom, he spotted his saviour. Skewed and twisted by years of ancient weather, a blocky wooden doorway emerged from the fog. It was almost impossible to believe and completely by chance, but he'd found the mine!

He stood there for a moment and filled his lungs with precious cool air while trying to calm his racing heart. In the silence of the moment, he could hear a quiet beeping sound coming from the mine's entrance. *It's an Hourglass Focus!* he thought, *I can't believe it, I've found one already* – little did he know that it was hundreds of meters away, echoing along the tunnels like a lost mouse trapped in a maze.

Filled with fresh excitement he started to move, but he'd only taken three steps into the clearing when a tingling sensation scurried across his skin, forcing an involuntary shiver to rattle down his spine. He tried to take another step, but the Mimic suit refused. Harvey was right, Billy had felt like something was wrong and the suit had reacted, rooting him to the spot. That's when he realised something was nearby. Something lurking just out of sight. His calming heart began to race once again. Was he being watched? He stared into the darkness desperately wishing he was a Visual, because then he'd be able to see what it was, before whatever it was, saw him.

32

Hiding in the shadow of the mine's entrance, Anderson could see Billy very well. He'd reached the doorway just as Billy stepped into the clearing and froze solid. He already knew what Billy had sensed, because he'd seen what was out there, watching and waiting. Thankfully, he'd seen its subtle movement before it could see him. In his attempt to sneak around it, panic had almost consumed him; a snapping branch nearby had made its ears perk threateningly. Thankfully, it didn't search for the cause. Confident that Billy had his own problem to solve, Anderson turned away and walked into the blackness of the mine.

For anybody else, the tunnels would have to be navigated by torch, or with the use of a night vision Gadget. Without them, you simply couldn't make sense of the maze-like tunnels. Anderson, however, was different. As a Visual, he didn't need any such device. The visor in his suit enhanced his sight, enabling him to see even beyond complete darkness. Instead of the endless tunnels scaring him, they became a simple but rewarding challenge. Full of confidence, he strode toward his goal: the hidden Hourglass Focus.

***

Far away from Billy and in his own patch of Kielder Grounds, Dean Tuffnell ploughed deep into the forest, making all manner of noise and mischief just like he thought a Mighty should. When he finally stopped and fell silent, he quickly realised that nobody else had followed. In fact, he felt quite alone. *Fine by me,* he thought.

He pondered for a moment to catch his breath when a flash of inspiration struck him. Flying into action, he began to climb the nearest tree. It was neither nimble nor quiet, but instead, utterly chaotic. Branches snapped and fell while the trees creaked and groaned under his heavy-handed dash. He was tearing up into the canopy making great heavy strides as only a Mighty could, when he heard the angry shout of a female voice from within the darkness.

'Be quiet you idiot! BE QUIET!'

Far below, he spotted the flash of a light beam reflecting from a diamond white Kinetic suit.

'You gave me away,' the girl shouted. 'I nearly had a Focus, and now it's chasing me!'

Dean watched from his vantage point as the girl ran through the trees and scrub that he'd destroyed only moments ago. She was desperately trying to escape something, but he quickly decided that she wouldn't be successful. From his makeshift lookout he watched a pair of headlamps dart left and right, scanning the low-lying scrub, hunting their target. At first, he didn't know what the lights belonged to, but then he thought back to his VR-Wall and of scaring his friends with the virtual Leopard attack and smiled. He had a pretty good idea of what the real-life counterpart might be. *Thank you, Alisha*, he thought with glee. *While it's chasing you, I'll be getting your Focus.* Just like that, he forgot about Alisha's perilous chase. All he cared for was the flickering blue light and rhythmic beep of her Hourglass Focus.

***

Back in Billy's patch of the forest, an identical set of headlamps sat motionless and dark. The ears behind them, however, were listening intently. It was lucky for Billy that he was a whisperer; tournament Hunters were taught to behave like their real-life counterpart, and this one had been programmed to listen, prowl, and wait. Its reward ... an unsuspecting competitor.

Billy stood still for several agonising seconds waiting for the suit to let him move, but it wouldn't. He was rooted to the spot like the ancient trees that surrounded him. Every time he tried to take a step the suit refused to listen. *Why won't you move?* he thought, his entire body tense with frustration.

Behind him, a crackle of leaves invaded the silence. Beads of sweat to burst from his skin. Was it coming for him? The thing that was out there. He half gave up and sighed, expecting it to be over, but instead, nothing came and the suit relaxed. Relieved that it hadn't found him, he took another step forward and immediately felt that strange tingle returning to his skin. *I've got to get going,* he complained. *I can't just stand here.*

He was about to take another tentative step when abruptly and breaking the silence, a loud shout came from within the forest. Somebody was yelling and they sounded angry. A bright flash of light swept across his eyes as the nearby Hunter sprang into life. It was so intense that it left him with half-moon crescents blurring his vision. The sound of scurrying feet reached his ears, quickly followed by a storm of twigs being kicked at his visor.

'That was close!' he whispered, watching the headlamps disappear into the forest. A minute or so later and observed by nobody, Billy slipped silently into the abandoned mine.

33

For ten minutes Billy stumbled aimlessly into the dark. Wide tunnel after narrow tunnel, flat tunnel after dangerously steep tunnel, he was simply getting nowhere. Dean's Glow Candy and the ensuing panic continued to fog his mind, and in his haste to get into the mine and avoid whatever it was outside, he'd totally forgotten about his Gadget. Although he wasn't normally afraid of the dark, the blackness that surrounded him was colder and heavier than anything he could remember. It was all but impossible to remain calm in the chilly maze. Despite the cold, Billy continued to sweat.

After another three tunnels, Billy was no closer to finding the Hourglass Focus. Inside his suit he was sticky with sweat and frustrated by his discomfort. Unable to take it anymore, he stopped and removed his helmet. The chilly damp air was a wonderful remedy to his hot and prickly face. He rested for a moment and listened. He was straining his ears, trying to understand where the beeping was coming from, when a new noise put him on high alert – footsteps! Was it a repeat of his encounter outside – four legs bad, two legs good? He couldn't tell.

With fearful urgency he ran, but in the complete and utter blackness he tripped over a rock and came to a shuddering halt on the ground. Face down to the floor and on his elbows, a faint glow of light reached the ground. Washed away by his sweat, tiny rivers of glowing green skin began to shine through the mud on his face.

'What am I doing?' he said out loud, clambering back to his feet.

'Making a bit of a mess of things,' a voice answered from within the dark.

Billy jumped in shock at his invisible visitor, forcing his suit to freeze once again.

'Sorry. I didn't mean to make you jump. I forgot you probably can't see me. I can see you though. Especially with those green streaks on your face.'

Billy's eyes swept left to right expecting to see at least something, but there was only darkness. 'I ate Glow Candy,' he said, through gritted teeth. 'Is that Anderson?'

'That's a good guess considering you can't see anything!'

'Well, if you can see me then you must be the Visual,' Billy explained, 'You're the only one. I think?'

'Very good!' Anderson replied, admiringly. 'You got lucky outside, with that wolf. It didn't hear you, so I guess that makes you the Whisperer, right?'

'A wolf?' asked Billy, receiving a fresh dose of surprise.

'Well, not a real wolf. A mechanical one. A Hunter.'

'Are there any in here?' Billy asked, now feeling more nervous than he had done all evening.

'I've been hearing quite a few noises,' Anderson said, allowing Billy's imagination to play in his favour. 'I suppose it's possible.'

'You think there are!'

'Well, I didn't say that. But we should probably be careful. Anyway, I've got to go.' Before there could be any more questions, Anderson took off, leaving Billy behind with that slightly teasing suggestion: There might be more of them.

Listening to Anderson's footsteps fade away, Billy closed his eyes and took a deep breath. Slowly, his suit released its frozen grip. He put his helmet on and started along the tunnel once more. There wasn't any point in trying to follow Anderson. In the darkness it would be futile. Despite the faint glow from his face, with his helmet back on, he could barely see anything at all. Frankly, he felt hopeless! He thought about Anderson's comment, about what might be lurking in the dark, forcing a chill spread across his sweaty skin. *I should have worn thermals*, he thought, absurdly. But it was that one flippant thought that unlocked a memory. The returning idea was like a face palm from the BFG; he'd remembered his Gadget.

He touched his hand to the side of his helmet and activated the Thermal Visor-Cam. Instantly, the tunnel ahead of him popped wonderfully into life. It was far from perfect, but there was certainly enough detail to guide the way.

Finally, able to move with some confidence, Billy picked up his pace. He stumbled across several junctions that lead who knows where, climbed old wooden ladders that creaked and complained under his weight and scraped through several craggy gaps between different passages. It could have been fun, but whenever there was a creak in the ceiling or a tumble of rock, he'd jump, and his suit would lock solid.

Gradually, he began to understand that it was responding to his muscles as if it *were* his muscles. If only he could work out how to stop it happening – it was so frustrating. Soon enough though, he'd be grateful for this unique connection; it would just about save his life.

'Yes! Finally!' he said, through gritted teeth. Ahead of him, Billy could see the soft glow of a blue flashing light. It pulsed rhythmically like a welcoming neon sign and was just about bright enough to bring the walls into momentary life. Making a final dash for his prize he emerged into a small cave and flicked his Profiler against the Hourglass Focus. He didn't have a clue how long it had taken, but at least he'd found it. Already in escape mode he turned around and looked to the tunnel that brought him here. *Just double back,* he told himself, already planning his escape. *Can't be that hard can it!*

***

Outside the mine and at least fifty meters above him, Louise Kelley wasted no time in looking for her prize. The soft beeping of the overground Focus was much quieter than the one Billy hunted – almost silent in fact – but as a Heed, she could still hear it. She'd been creeping through the forest and looking over her shoulder every few seconds, when she too had heard the same shouting that Billy had heard. She was too far away to know that Dean was watching from up in the treetops, but she knew someone was running in her direction; she could hear multiple sets of feet – some slapping the ground, others clawing at the earth.

Someone's being chased, she thought. She ducked behind a tree with barely a moment to spare before Alisha's white studded suit thundered past. Louise watched her manage another five steps before the chasing wolf leapt into the air and seized her ankle.

'No, no, NO!' Alisha screamed, as her suit shut down.

Satisfied its task was complete, the mechanical wolf backed away and gave a chilling howl before it slinked away in search of its next victim.

'Why me?' Alisha whispered to herself. 'If it wasn't for that Dean, I would've had it.'

Louise stepped out from behind the tree and crouched down beside the stricken girl. 'I know you're not going to get that Focus, but if you tell me where it was then I'll make sure he doesn't either.'

She had no real intention of stopping Dean. Not only had they formed a sort of friendship, but she remembered her dad's words. 'If you're going to be an achiever, do whatever it takes.'

'Will you?' Alisha asked. 'You'll really stop him getting it?'

'I will. You'll have more luck next time. Just tell me where the Focus was, and I'll do the rest.'

'It's down there on the left,' Alisha said, pointing to where she'd run from. 'There's a massive tree trunk in a clearing. It's in the top.'

'I'll break it so he can't get it,' Louise told her, standing up to leave. 'Now, ask for rescue.'

Alisha watched Louise disappear before giving her command. 'Help. I need rescue.'

A hundred meters further into the forest, the tree trunk Louise was searching for emerged from the fog. Looking like an out of place lighthouse, the faint blue light of an Hourglass Focus flashed on top of it. She could have easily missed it if Alisha hadn't pointed her in the right direction, but that didn't matter anymore – it was hers. She sneaked across the clearing and clambered up a couple of dead branches before linking her Profiler.

'Stupid girl thought I was really going to break it', she whispered. She held her breath and listened to the silence around her. Certain nobody else was on their way, she dropped from the trunk and started for home.

She'd only made it to the edge of the clearing when a new noise brought her an abrupt halt; it turned out she wasn't alone after all.

34

Dean had long since dismissed any thought of Alisha; leaving the memory of her behind was easier than leaving her to the wolf. And despite not being able to find her Focus, his annoyance had been short lived – he had a new competitor to watch.

Sitting on a branch high in the trees, he waited like a vulture waiting to steal the hunter's catch. Below him and oblivious to his presence, Hiro Akita was fighting with the remains of a fallen tree.

'Keep on trying,' Dean muttered, finding the sight rather comical. Despite trying everything he could think of, Hiro simply lacked the strength to move the rotten trunk; it was like watching a child trying to wrestle a bear. Eventually, he had no choice but to give up and look elsewhere for a Focus.

Seizing the opportunity, Dean leapt down, impacting the ground like a dislodged boulder. Lacking almost any skill, he used brute force to tear the rotten trunk apart and throw it aside. To anybody watching he would have looked like a thoughtless caveman in a fit of rage. Not that he would have cared of course. He had his prize.

With his Focus collected, Dean turned tail and began to storm back through the forest. He didn't need to bother following pathways or traversing the treetops like before, but instead, tore through the undergrowth like a jungle explorer in a new land. It was foolish to make so much noise, but fate was on his side. Because of his actions one competitor had already fallen foul of a Hunter, and another would follow.

Although Dean wasn't heading back to the starting arena like he thought. He was on a collision course with the mine's entrance where Billy would soon emerge. The other thing he didn't know, was that following behind was a suit that looked like a Black Widow spider.

***

Back below ground, Billy was hopelessly lost. Ahead of him, yet another tunnel stretched away into darkness. Thanks to Anderson, a horrible fear of being found by a Hunter continued to pester his mind. He was certain that something was following, he'd heard it in the distance. He began to pick up his pace, desperate to get out of the dark when a noise from right behind him triggered panic to flourish. It was only a loose stone that he'd just disturbed, but Billy didn't know that.

With fear taking over he rushed aimlessly along the tunnel and stepped forward … onto nothing. Billy's body flew into panic like falling in a dream before being jolted awake. Reacting to his flinching muscles the Kinetic suit froze once again. Unable to stop himself, he closed his eyes and fell. The seconds that followed dragged endlessly. His eyes were tight shut, protecting him from the truth, but when he mustered the bravery to open them, it was worse than he'd thought. Like a fallen tree bridging a raging river, he found himself precariously balanced across a hidden mineshaft.

Do not relax. Do not relax! he repeated in his mind, desperately hoping his suit was listening. The panic filled thought looped in his head, forcing his heart to pound faster than he'd ever known. It was hard to think of anything else, but still the next thought managed to invade his mind. *If I call for rescue, I'm out.* Billy gave up – he knew the frustrating truth – it was over. 'Help, I need resc—'

'Hold on, Billy, I'm coming.' Anderson Toms scrambled down the narrow tunnel and grabbed hold of his arms. 'I've got you.'

'Anderson? What are you doing?'

'I'm saving you of course.'

'But—'

'Oh, don't worry about it. I got lost trying to find the way out. Lucky for you I guess!'

'Accidental air biscuit,' Billy said, shakily. 'It stinks of fart in this suit. I couldn't help it!'

Anderson fell back and dragged Billy with him before he burst into fits of laughter. 'Air biscuit?' he asked. 'Let's go before you gas us out.'

Billy's suit relaxed with their easy laughter. 'No complaints here,' he said. 'Thanks for saving me. I thought I was out.'

Anderson smiled. 'No worries. Come on. Let's go!'

With a lucky turn or two, Anderson and Billy emerged from the mine just a few minutes later. They were still chuckling about Billy's fart, when they came face to face with an unwelcome enemy.

'Well-well, what do we have here?' Dean said, sarcastically. 'The Whisperer and the Visual playing together in the mine. I hope you've been having fun, because I already got my Focus.'

'Oh really?' Anderson replied, defiantly. 'And?'

'And,' Dean said, stepping forward and shoving them both over. 'I hope you have fun with the wolf.' He turned away and gave a piercing whistle into the forest before running off, laughing.

Anderson and Billy looked at each other in disbelief and shared a knowing look of imminent trouble. Barely any distance away from within the shadow of the trees, a mechanical howl invaded their ears. Terrified into action, Anderson jumped up and chased after Dean, leaving a cloud of dust and Billy behind.

***

Back at the starting gate and first to arrive, Reuben Alt stood watching the shoreline of Kielder Water. He along with everybody else had heard the wolf's howl, and a sense of tension filled the cool air. As if on cue, Dean Tuffnell's skeleton suit burst through the fog that hugged the forest. Ghostly wisps reached out behind him as if trying to prevent his escape. Following his appearance on the large screens, a cheer of voices rose into the air.

He was only the second person to return.

***

Scrambling through the shadows and running as fast as possible, Billy was increasingly aware of the chasing feet getting closer – four legs bad, two legs good. *I hope it doesn't hurt!* he thought. He tried to steal a glance of his pursuer as if it might help him escape – it didn't. As fast as lighting strikes, a crackle of electricity invaded Billy's ears before his suit shuddered erratically and blinked out of life. He was mid-tumble on his way to the ground when he saw a flash of red sweep across his visor and the outline of a Kinetic suit disappearing into the fog.

Sprawled in a frozen star jump he lay still and waited for the howl of a triumphant Hunter, but it didn't come. Instead, his suit sprang back into life. He started to get to his feet, but then the unwelcome sound of scampering feet came at him once again.

It must have missed me and now it's trying again! he thought, miserably. He scrambled hurriedly, trying to get up, when for the third time of the night he shrieked with shock. Touching his leg, was the motionless body of a mechanical wolf. Whatever had happened Billy had also stunned his pursuer into an unwelcome sleep.

'What happened to you?' Billy asked, as if expecting an answer. Although the lack of a reply quickly didn't matter when a contestant ran past him.

'Snooze you lose, baby,' Hiro shouted.

On the brink of elimination, Billy jumped up and gave chase. If he finished last, all the Time Credits would be gone.

***

Another cheer erupted from the spectators when Anderson Toms emerged from the fog, rapidly followed by Louise Kelley. Within the crowd the Space-Time president waited anxiously; the top four positions were gone and only the first five contestants would score Credits. Billy could barely afford to be third, let alone fifth or worse.

'And so, we wait,' Schrader boomed over the speakers, doing an admirable job of building the tension. 'Who will be next? Who will be the final contestant to score valuable Time Credits and move on to the next event?'

The loudest cheer of the night spread through the crowd as the lonely figure of a contestant finally emerged from the fog.

'Here they are ladies and gentlemen … The final contestant to score valuable Time Credits before the next round is … Hiro Akita!'

35

Tom and Sue watched Billy emerge from the fog, already knowing it was too late. If Tom had been capable of standing – if someone hadn't taken that away from him, that is – he would have needed to sit down.

High up in the stands, the Space-Time president also sat in miserable silence. He'd only had one wish: to fix a very big mistake, but he'd already done everything he could to make that possible. The only hope now, was that Billy would do better at the Grand Canyon. If he didn't, then perhaps for ever more he'd have to live with the secret he'd been keeping all these years.

Dean Tuffnell stood in the starting arena and grinned with satisfaction. All it had taken was a quick whistle and one of those useless wolves had stopped Billy scoring any credits. *It's just pathetic*, he thought, watching Billy run from the fog and toward the starting arena. *He hasn't scored any Credits and he still doesn't know when to give up!*

Louise Kelley watched Billy with a mixture of confusion and admiration. Despite not scoring any Credits he was still determined to finish. Although how he'd appeared from the forest after Hiro, left her utterly stumped.

***

It was creeping up to midnight when Billy poked his head around the door of his Demountable. Tom was sipping a coffee and reading the results for the umpteenth time. Rather predictably, Sue was pacing the floor with hands firmly on her hips.

'Well, that was a bit … shocking,' Billy remarked, trying to put a brave face on things. 'Although I bet the wolf thought it was a stunning performance.'

'That was you being chased by the wolf?' asked Sue, in surprise.

'How did it not catch you?' Tom asked. 'No-one escapes a Hunter!'

'Well, I was running away from it when there was this massive—'

'Billy Wheeler! I repeat, Billy Wheeler!' It was Schrader, his voice booming throughout Splitwood Stadium. 'Please return to the starting arena. That's Billy Wheeler to the staring arena!'

Tom spat coffee over his Holo-Tab in surprise. 'Billy! Hiro's been caught cheating. He put a Hunter charm on Alisha while she was in the starting arena. He's been demoted to last place, and you've been promoted to fifth. Get down there, quickly!'

In the rush to get Billy back to the starting arena, both Tom and Sue completely forgot to ask about the Hunter and how he'd managed to escape it.

Luckily for Billy, Katie wouldn't forget so easily.

***

Before Billy's first event had even begun, Katie had started to watch from the comfort of her bedroom, but from the moment she'd sat down it was obvious how difficult it would be to follow. She'd watched him arrive at the starting arena late – goodness knows what he'd been doing – and then complained to the screen when he ran into the shadows and out of sight. Once in the forest, it had been a challenge to keep up with him at all. Hampered by the fog, the images from the drone mounted cameras were next to useless. Most of the time, you could see the contestants, but you couldn't tell who, was who. And some things – like Alisha May getting bitten by the wolf, for example – went completely unseen.

Half an hour into the event, Katie was getting bored; it was all rather dull, not being able to see anything. Hoping to see more, she switched camera to Forest Drone 5. Hovering high above the ground, the camera focused on the entrance to the mine

'There's nothing there,' she complained to the empty room. 'I want to find Billy!' She leaned forward intending to change to the next camera, when two contestants emerged from the wooden doorway. 'Why are you two together?' she asked, now fully talking to herself.

The two of them were larking about, looking more like they were having fun rather than competing against each other, but then a third person appeared from the shadows and the two of them froze solid like naughty children who'd been caught stealing cake. Despite the fog, the skeleton suit of their new visitor stood out clearly.

Katie looked on as Dean lurched forward and shoved them both over. 'You can't do that!' she shouted at the screen, angrily. 'Oh, you just wait till I see you next!'

Like someone scared of being told off, Dean ran from the mine's entrance and disappeared from the screen, quickly followed by one of the contestants.

Katie watched, both concerned and confused; the other wasn't moving. 'Get up then,' she demanded of the unknown figure. 'Don't you know you're in a competition?' She moved closer to the screen, eager to see who it was, but quickly jumped back in surprise when the lights of a Hunter swept through the nearby trees. 'Get up you idiot. Get up!'

As if responding to her demand, the contestant leapt up and sprinted into the forest. The camera drone swept down from its lofty position and gave chase, but by the time it caught up, the wolf was already snapping at the contestant's heels. With terrifying speed, it closed in on its hapless victim and sent them both sprawling across the floor.

'Please don't be Billy,' Katie begged, desperately hoping she wasn't watching her best friend. She waited for a moment, expecting the wolf to get up and run off, but it didn't. It just laid there next to the contestant. Her surprise at seeing it's lifeless body quickly transformed into a sense of dismay when another competitor appeared from behind a nearby tree before disappearing into the fog.

***

Now, as Katie watched the contestants preparing for the Credits presentation, her frustration boiled over. Despite him being fine, it had been Billy who was stunned. He had been the one sprawled on the floor, and she hadn't been able do anything about it. Although now that she'd watched the video several times over, maybe there was something she could do. Focusing her mind on what she'd seen in the forest, she became ever more convinced that she'd spotted something; an immeasurably brief flash had jumped from Billy to the wolf. That spark – which only she had noticed – had originated from behind the tree where someone was hiding. Whoever that was, they'd not only flattened Billy, but the wolf too. Certain of her suspicions, Katie promised herself that she'd find out who that person was and whether they'd wanted to help Billy or hurt him.

***

The clock struck midnight as Anderson Toms watched Billy scan himself back into the starting arena. 'Why didn't you get up?' he asked, thinking of when he'd left Billy at the mine.

'My stupid suit froze again!'

'Well, 'I'm pleased you didn't get caught by the Hunter. How did you get away?'

'Floated another air biscuit. Wolf repellent fart,' Billy replied sincerely. 'Call yourself a Visual? You didn't see that coming did you!'

Anderson laughed easily. He liked this new friend very much.

'Thanks again … for saving me in the mine.'

'Ah, no problemo mi amigo,' Anderson replied, in his best Spanish accent. He turned and looked at Dean. 'With your amigo over there, we might need to stick together.'

Billy glared at Dean through narrow, accusing eyes. 'I think you might be right.'

36

'Here we go. It's the Time Credits presentation,' Schrader sang, beginning his exuberant speech. 'Please welcome the competitors of The Space-Time Tournament, Kielder Grounds Challenge. First to score and top of the pile, Reuben Alt, followed by Dean Tuffnell, Anderson Toms, Louise Kelley, and in a surprise result our final contestant, Billy Wheeler!'

The spectators erupted into applause, but none more so than the Space-Time President; redemption it seemed, was still possible.

'So, let's confirm the final scores. To Reuben Alt, for returning in the fastest time, we award ten Credits, and for collecting a low difficulty Insignia, a further five Credits. To Dean Tuffnell, for the second fastest time, its nine Credits. And for collecting a medium difficulty Insignia, ten Credits. To Anderson Toms, with the third fastest time, eight Credits. And for his high difficulty Insignia, a further twelve Credits. In addition, we award two Credits for excellent sportsmanship when helping a fellow competitor. To Louise Kelley, who returned in the fourth fastest time, seven Credits. And for collecting a medium difficulty Insignia, ten Credits. And finally, to Billy Wheeler. For returning with the fifth fastest time, we award six Credits. And for a high difficulty Insignia, twelve Credits. However, for being rescued by a fellow contestant, we deduct two Credits.'

A summary of the contestant's names and their Time Credits then scrolled across Splitwood stadium's scoreboard.

Anderson Toms …22… Dean Tuffnell …19… Louise Kelley …17… Billy Wheeler …16… Reuben Alt …15… Dexter Jones …0… Alisha May …0… Hiro Akita …0…

Dean almost fell over with shock when he read the scoreboard: he was only in second position. Worse than that, Weeweeler was fourth.

If that stupid wolf had done its job, he wouldn't have finished at all! he thought.

The crowd clapped and cheered as the results were announced. This was especially true for Sue and Tom, who'd watched it all from their Demountable. But Kurt Tuffnell, who was utterly alone in his own portable house, did not clap even once. It had not gone to plan.

The top five contestants stood below the tournament podium waiting for the presentation to begin. Like the stadium surrounding it, large and blocky timbers that looked older than the forest itself climbed defiantly into the sky.

Louise Kelley waited below the podium feeling more than a little regret over her actions. Her one chance to use the Disruptor had not been selfish as planned, but completely selfless; saving Billy had almost certainly cost her a higher step on the podium. All she could do now was hope that paying it forward really did work. If her parent-monster ever found out about her misjudgement, she'd be in more trouble than she dared think about.

Dean Tuffnell lurked uncomfortably close to Billy and repeatedly shot him dark looks. He'd become ever more frustrated by Weeweeler and his incessant good luck. What made it worse was the fact that Anderson had helped him. Was that boy just as stupid?

You can have all the help you want Weeweeler, Dean thought, *but you still won't win if I've got anything to do with it.*

'And so, to the podium presentation,' Schrader sang. 'Please show your support for our top five finishers.'

Anderson ran up the steps and punched his hands into the air. He was closely followed by Reuben and the other podium contestants, each celebrating their achievement in their own personal way. Even Dean – who remained fed up and annoyed inside his suit – managed a blasé wave. Billy was last to take his place, and despite it being the bottom step, he wasn't the least bit downhearted. He'd only ever dreamed of taking part in the Space-Time Tournament – he was the not-very-well-off boy from Pilton, after all – but here he was at the end of his first event.

Schrader joined Anderson on the top step and presented him with the Kielder Grounds Insignia. Like an army General presenting an honourable medal, he pinned the platinum howling wolf on his suit. 'Ladies and Gentlemen, I present to you our Kielder Grounds winner, Anderson Toms!'

In celebration, drone-mounted laser fireworks flooded the sky with a mesmerising show of light and sound. High above the stadium and its occupants, a pulsating message shimmered like a stencil carved into the night sky: 'Congratulations to Anderson Toms! Kielder Grounds winner.'

Unable to contain his excitement anymore, Billy left the podium and ran to his Demountable at a flat-out sprint. He arrived to find his parents and Mr Peddleton ready and waiting with Light Poppers, Whistling Streamers, and his favourite sweets: a full box of Pop-Rockets.

They would celebrate his first podium in style with an indoor firework display of their own. Although Billy's highlight wouldn't be the fireworks, it would be the side-splitting laughter after watching Mr Peddleton try to catch Pop-Rockets in his mouth and getting one stuck up his nose.

Later that night, a satisfied Billy would fall asleep with his face still shining with the effects GlowCandy, but not caring one bit.

37

Billy stepped off the train thinking that the effects of Glow Candy had worn off completely. But Katie – who'd waited patiently at the Travel Station like the loyal friend she was – could still see a definite glow about him; the kind you have when you're so happy to see someone that it shines from your face like the night's brightest star.

'Where was your sign, Billy-Boy?' she asked, hands firmly placed on her hips.

'Sorry K, I couldn't think of a design, and then I started to glow, and then I had to put mud on my face, and then I got lost in the mine and—'

A warm smile crept across her face, silencing him.

'Still the same old Billy-Boy,' she said, affectionately. 'Well, I know what design you can use next time.' She leaned forward and whispered in his ear.

Billy stood back and howled with laughter. Everybody within ten meters stopped and stared. 'Katie Jack, you are amazing,' he stated, with the same explosive volume.

Katie's cheeks began to take on a fresh glow of their own and she promptly returned to her disapproving hands-on-hips stance.

'Sorry,' Billy said sheepishly, even though he wasn't. 'I'll get Mr Peddleton working on it as soon as we get home.' He smiled at her without the slightest hint of regret. As far as he was concerned, she truly was amazing.

'I saw something you might be interested in,' Katie said, when Tom and Sue joined them. She took her backpack off and pulled out a shiny, printed-less-than-an-hour-ago copy, of Space-Time magazine. On the front cover was a large glossy photo of Anderson Toms standing on the podium. He was flanked by the other contestants along with Billy.

The headline asked a simple question: 'Terrific Tournament Winner?'

Billy looked at the cover and beamed from ear to ear. If getting on the podium wasn't already enough, seeing himself on the front cover of Space-Time magazine was simply ridiculous.

'Well, I guess Anderson was pretty good,' Tom said, looking at the headline and the picture.

'I don't think you understand, Mr Wheeler. It's not talking about Anderson. It's talking about Billy.'

Tom checked the picture again and realised that Katie was right. Anderson was in the middle of the cover, but he wasn't the person in focus. That honour belonged to Billy.

She handed Tom the magazine. 'It makes for an interesting read.'

Tom opened first page but then closed it immediately, seemingly having second thoughts. He handed it to Billy with a smile. 'Perhaps you should read it first.'

Billy took the magazine and stared at the cover. He felt utterly stunned. 'I think I'll read it a bit later if that's okay?'

'Of course. I could do with a rest anyway. I'll have a look after.'

Sue had spotted the change in Tom before he knew it himself. Terrible fatigue frequently crept up on him since his accident and gave little warning of an imminent attack. When it did, there was little to be done but go home and rest.

'Come on then you lot. Let's get home.'

***

Katie and Billy arrived at Worthy Park not long after Tom had gone to bed. Sue had given them strict instructions to be back by six if they wanted a treat of home-cut chips and egg; Katie had no intention of being late!

They were only halfway across the park when Katie couldn't stand it any longer. 'Come on Billy-Boy, I want you to read it,' she said, pleadingly.

He'd been jabbering on so much about his encounter with the wolf and his suit failure that he hadn't even looked at the magazine. 'As soon as we sit down, we can—' he stopped in his tracks and grabbed her arm. 'Can you see that? he whispered.

'See what?' Katie replied, now whispering herself.

'Over there in the trees.' He pointed into the woods.

Katie could barely make out what Billy was pointing at, but when she got her eyes focussed on it, she could see what looked like an old brick shack. It was nestled deep within the trees and heavily disguised by an abundance of fluffy moss and creeping Ivy.

'Let's check it out,' Billy said. 'If it's alright we'll use it. I've always wanted a hideout.'

Without waiting for her to agree and before she could say anything about it, he ran into the trees and disappeared. By the time she caught up, he was already inside.

'You won't believe what I've found,' he said, poking his head through a hole that used to be a window. 'Check it out. It's awesome!'

When Katie stepped through the crooked doorway, she promptly gawped at what Billy was holding in his hand. The pages were tattered and worn, but she could easily read the words. He was holding a Glastonbury Festival programme.

'Two thousand and seventeen?' she said, in disbelief. 'That's more than 80 years old! How has it lasted this long?'

It was then that Billy stood aside to reveal an open metal box. Inside, there were at least another ten programmes.

'What's Glastonbury Festival?' she asked.

'This is Worthy Park, K. You must have heard about the festival that used to be here?'

'No,' she replied, hand-on-hips firmly in place.

'It was a huge music festival,' he said. 'It was really famous because of the dancing cows.'

Katie raised her eyebrows. 'Dancing cows? What, like to music?'

'Yeah … I heard they were … udderly brilliant.'

'Oh Billy, you idiot,' she complained, resisting the urge to poke him in the ribs. She squatted down to study the box. 'It must be a time capsule.' She brushed a thick layer of dirt from the lid and found that she could just about see a stuttering line of text stamped across it. A simple name from who-knows-when. 'The Vault,' she whispered.

'That's what we should call it,' Billy said excitedly, thinking of their shack. 'It needs fixing up, but this could be our space. We could come to the park without being bothered by Dean and his idiot mates.'

Katie looked around the dilapidated building. There were holes in the walls full of weed and holes in the roof where ivy fingers sneakily crept inside. There were even holes in the ground – probably dug up by rabbits or some other secretive creature. Although surprisingly, it had a safe kind of feeling to it. One that made her feel quite at home.

'The Vault,' she whispered under her breath, as if mulling the idea over. She spun around and beamed at him before pointing at the Space-Time magazine he'd dropped into the time capsule. 'Let's do it! But before we start, you've got to read that!'

'Billy beamed at her. 'It's a deal!'

For the first time of many, they sat down in the Vault together and began to read.

"In a scintillating start to this year's tournament, Kielder Grounds kicked off the competition in reassuring fashion. Emerging from the shadows as our tournament leader, Anderson Toms displayed both skill and compassion to steal an early march on his competitors. But do not allow the headline to lead you astray, for it is not only Anderson that has gathered my attention, but a certain Billy Wheeler.

Despite his relatively tender years, Billy's display of bravery and unwavering commitment earned him a podium position, when by all rights, he should have been sharing dinner with the wolves. How he achieved such a result from the brink of catastrophe must surely mark him as the one to watch. In fact, I would go so far as to say—"

Billy stopped reading the article and stared blankly at Katie. 'Whoever wrote this knows about the wolf,' he said, obviously surprised by the revelation.

'I think maybe everybody knows about the wolf,' Katie said, flatly. *But I think maybe it's only me that's investigating what really happened,* she thought. She glanced at her watch. 'We'd better get going. Your mum said six.'

'You're always so sensible,' Billy teased.

'But chips and egg at yours are the best,' she replied, dreamily. 'Let's come back tomorrow. We can start doing this place up.'

They didn't know it yet, but Katie and Billy had found what would become their new sanctuary. One to which they would add posters and rugs and rickety home-made chairs, along with all manner of exceptional objects. Soon it would be theirs, their own Vault. More than that, it would be the place where Dean and Billy would see each other for the final time in their lives.

38

Sue and Billy arrived at Peddleton's bike shop bright and early. Despite wanting to help Billy choose the Gadget for his next event, Tom had stayed at home, still suffering from his latest bout of fatigue. Sue had done her best to reassure him that Harvey knew what he was doing, and that so far, Billy had done a fine job himself. On that account, Tom agreed completely, but before they'd left, he'd still offered one piece of advice: Choose wisely. Billy found himself struggling to decide if it was just a coincidence that he kept on hearing that phrase.

'Hi Mr Peddleton,' he said, opening the door to Peddleton's.

'Billy!' came a reply more animatedly than intended.

'Morning Harvey. How are you today?' Sue asked.

'Oh, you know. Busy looking at Gadgets for Billy, mostly.'

'What a coincidence. That's why we've come to visit.'

'That's great!' Harvey replied, far too enthusiastically – or was it nervously? 'I was going to suggest that Billy and I take it from here. I think he probably knows what he wants, and I can take him through all the options. It'd do him good to be in charge. I can give you a call when we're ready to choose, if you like?'

Sue eyed Harvey a little uncertainly – he wasn't normally so … animated. 'Well … I don't really have any plan—'

'You should go and do something nice like a bit of window shopping,' Harvey cut in. 'Or maybe have a coffee. Don't you agree, Billy?' he said, nodding encouragingly.

At first, Billy wondered why Mr Peddleton was acting so strange. But then it struck him what he was trying to do.

'Oh, yeah, go for it, Mum,' he agreed, joining in. 'Mr Peddleton and I can choose, and then you and Dad can double-check things before we finalise it. You deserve a rest after the last few days.'

'I guess I could pop in and see Tilly for a quick chat,' she began.

'Excellent!' Harvey agreed, grasping the opportunity to get some privacy. 'We'll see you in about an hour then?'

Sue gave them both a suspicious stare as if she knew they were up to something, but then appeared to dismiss the notion without further questions. 'You're probably right. It'll do me good. Okay, I'll see you in about an hour.'

Harvey watched Sue cross the car park. 'We need to talk,' he said, still looking through the glass. 'Let's go out the back.'

When they arrived in the showroom, Billy could see his Kinetic suit spread out in several pieces on the work bench. It was not the awe-inspiring piece of technology that it once was but instead, looked like a rather pitiful jumble of parts.

'I've literally pulled it apart to find a fault, but there isn't one. If it had one, I would have found it. Whatever it was that shut you and the wolf down, I'm telling you now, it wasn't your suit!'

Billy thought back to the moment in Kielder Grounds when he'd heard the electric crackle and caught a glimpse of someone fading into the fog. 'Do you think it could have been someone else?'

'I don't know. The tournament stewards said it was either a fault with your suit or the Hunter, but I'm not so sure. Something just doesn't feel right. I didn't want to worry your mum, but I should probably talk to your dad.'

A hot prickle of fear ran across Billy's body. 'No, no, please don't say anything. Please don't. Not to either of them.'

'But Billy, if the shock came from something or someone else, then we need to find out who it was. It could be dangerous.'

'But Mum will try and stop me competing,' Billy explained. 'Maybe Dad wouldn't, but Mum would. Then I'll have no hope of winning.' He tried to compose himself, but before he could decide if it was wise to tell someone else about his big idea, it came flooding out. 'I need to win. If I win, I can change the past and fix Dad.'

Mr Peddleton didn't know what to say. He didn't think Billy could change the past whether he won the tournament or not, but there wasn't much point in telling him that right now, the boy seemed desperate. 'I need to think about it for a while,' he said. 'Maybe you should go and have a look at the Gadgets.'

Billy slouched off toward the Gadgets and pretended to look at them, but he couldn't think straight. Not when his tournament could end only just after it had started.

Ten minutes later, Mr Peddleton joined Billy at the Gadgets. In the end it was just too hard to believe that someone was willing to cheat. What could they possibly have hoped to achieve by stopping Billy and the wolf? 'Right, I won't say anything just yet, but I'll be keeping a close eye on things. The moment I think I need to I will talk to your parents. Okay!'

'Thank you Mr Peddleton. I'll be careful, I promise.'

'Okay, okay, it's fine. Come on, we need to look for a Gadget. If your mum comes back early, she'll wonder what we've been up to.'

The truth of it, was that neither Harvey or the tournament stewards would ever get to the truth about Billy's suit and the wolf, so it was a good job that Katie was performing her own investigation. If she kept going long enough, she'd eventually have the answer – although by then, it might be too late.

Billy and Mr Peddleton spent the next forty minutes discussing the positives and negatives of several Gadgets. Mr Peddleton thought that a grappling hook with hyper-wind would be fast at climbing cliffs. But Billy rightly pointed out that it wouldn't be much use in water. Then there was Billy's all-time favourite – Instinct Claws. They'd connect to his hands and feet like mechanical tiger paws and help him grip both the ground and the cliffs. The problem was that they'd be very difficult to master in the amount of time he had to practice. Mr Peddleton suggested that he should imagine the consequences if he started thinking about something else when he was halfway up a cliff.

Eventually, they settled on a Gadget that Mr Peddleton described as thinking outside the box. In this instance, Billy had to trust in his mentor's experience – even if he didn't think the Gadget would be useful. All that remained was get his parent's approval and Billy would be set for the Grand Canyon.

***

On the other side of the Atlantic and after visiting Worthies Bike Outlet for a second time, Louise Kelley was on the receiving end of her father's – parent-monster – temper.

'What did you think you were doing, girl? How are you ever going to win the tournament if you accidentally trigger the Disruptor?' He took the time to sarcastically quote 'accidentally' with his fingers.

'It *was* an accident, Dad' she pleaded pointlessly. 'Something in the shadows made me jump and I just flinched. I'll do better next time, I promise.'

'You'd better, Louise, or you'll end up being a nobody for the rest of your life like everyone else.'

Despite reading about Billy's escape from the wolf in Space-Time magazine, Duncan Kelley didn't think his daughter was anywhere near the incident. Thankfully, he'd not made any presumptuous link between the two events. Right now, he was too annoyed at having to Port to America to get the disruptor recharged! To top it off, Fletch had been difficult about meeting them. Saying that he didn't want to draw attention to himself if the girl was going to be foolish; he didn't want anybody to become suspicious and start knocking on his door.

When Louise finally went to bed for some much-needed peace and quiet, she promised herself that next time, she really would do whatever it took. She'd helped Billy escape the wolf and thankfully nobody seemed to have noticed. But look what that had got her: a whole bunch of grief from her dad. No, next time she'd use the Disruptor to her advantage. Even if that meant hurting whoever got in her way.

39

An early morning mist kept Katie and Billy company as they'd crept silently through Worthy Park and into their Vault. Finally finished, it had been quite the transformation from rundown brickwork box, into a satisfyingly cosy home. They had chairs to sit on – oddly comfortable given the wonky nature of Billy's first attempt at carpentry – and a green stripy rug that covered all but the very edges of the floor. Piles of earth had been moved to fill holes in the ground and the weeds and ivy were cut back. They'd even used a plastic sheet that Billy found in his dad's shed to fix the roof and make a new window. The place was pleasingly weatherproof and surprisingly homely.

Several posters had arrived from Katie's bedroom – after Billy had pleaded that 'nothing too girlie' was used – completing their hideaway perfectly. All in all, it was a ramshackle masterpiece. The best part in Billy's opinion, was the real Vault. With its treasure of ancient festival guides and the addition of his Space-Time magazines, it was simply perfect. When the day would come that he didn't return to The Vault – which given his big idea, seemed almost inevitable – they'd be left for somebody else.

Billy looked at Katie over the time capsule that sat between them forming a make-shift table. Sitting on top, were two empty cans of Heliyumm. Having joked around together with their squeaky voices, they'd both laughed so hard that Katie had nearly wet herself; she probably would have if she hadn't run outside! Now, with them back under control – although Billy couldn't help but smirk a little when he thought of her frantic escape – it was almost time to leave for his next event.

'Right then, Billy-boy, let's be serious for a moment. You definitely told Mr Peddleton about the design for your suit, yes?'

'I did,' he said, knowing what was coming next – another question. 'And I'll be able to recognise you whether it's light or dark, yes?'

'Yes K,' he said, drearily as if getting a lecture from his mum.

'Good, because I want to be able to watch you this time.' She left out the part that she'd be waiting to see who was nearby if there happened to be another strange electrical spark incident. 'And you're going to be super careful, yes?'

Billy mimicked her hands-on-hips pose whilst giving her his best, 'really?' expression.

'Great, well—' she trailed off into thought, looking at him in that way. Hadn't the days of working on the Vault together brought them a little closer? She thought it probably had, because this time she felt more worried about him, as if something worse might happen than the suspicious spark in Kielder Forest. 'Just go and win,' she finished.

'Keep a look out for the ginger,' he said, with his usual cheeky smile. This time she wouldn't be able to miss it!

***

A full hour after Billy and Katie had hugged their goodbye's – probably after holding on for that little bit too long – Billy, his parents and Mr Peddleton arrived at Bristol International Travel Station. Just like it was at the local station, an abundance of people rushed around beginning various journeys to who knows where. The difference this time: no Dean Tuffnell, no Kurt Tuffnell, and no repeat of their awkward meeting a week ago. Travelling by Ion-Jet, their journey time would be several hours longer than Port passengers would experience, but Billy didn't mind one bit. Knowing that Dean was miles away meant there would be no drama during their journey.

Halfway through the station, Billy saw one of the souped-up Port booths in action and stopped to watch. His local Travel Station only had a single Nano-port. If you wanted to go further afield you needed a Deca-port. He watched in awe when a man in a smart grey suit linked his Profiler to the Port Focus and walked into a large liquid bubble. A dancing smear of rainbow colours swirled around the sphere as it wrapped itself around the man's body. Then, just as quickly as you could blink, it popped! Both the bubble and the man were gone.

Billy watched as another bubble began to inflate, but then he caught a glimpse of someone's reflection shining back at him as if it was a mirror. He spun around expectantly. Had he really seen who he thought he had? Falling foul of his 'typical Billy' antics, he stumbled over the small boy that was standing right behind him.

'You're Billy Wheeler,' the small boy declared, tugging at his t-shirt. 'You're brilliant! Can I get a selfie? Can I, can I?'

Billy didn't have a chance to react before a chorus of voices began to fill the air. Thanks to Space-Time Magazine he was big news, and quickly found himself surrounded by adults and children alike. Standing on tiptoes, he peered over the crowd to catch a glimpse of who he'd seen, but the two people – a large man and a slim woman – were gone. *It couldn't have been,* he thought. *Why would they be here together?*

As if being pulled from a daydream by the tugging of his t-shirt, Billy once again became aware of the boy at his feet and the chattering crowd surrounding him. Instead of thinking about who he had or hadn't seen, his focus changed to his new-found fans.

40

Billy arrived at the Grand Canyon Travel Station less than two hours after leaving Bristol. Having never flown in a Trans-Atlantic Ion-Jet, he'd been struck by a severe case of verbal-diarrhoea. He'd talked excitedly about what he could see from his window seat almost as fast as the landmarks had passed.

Walking through the travel Station, Billy found another Deca-port. Just as before, he watched in awe as rainbow smeared bubbles inflated and popped, leaving behind a long-distance traveller who looked as if they'd simply stepped through a doorway.

'Why can't we Port, Dad?' he asked, despite knowing what the answer would be. It was perhaps wishful thinking on his behalf that if he asked often enough, his dad would give in and say they could. But as always, the truth came back as the only possible answer.

'You know why. We can't afford to. But imagine all the sights you'd miss if we Ported. I'm sure it's great and all, but flying, now that's cool!'

Billy looked at his dad with genuine admiration. Money could provide a lot of things, but loving parents that did everything in their power to show you the good in life – that was priceless. As if fate wanted to demonstrate how right he was, Dean Tuffnell popped into existence from the nearby Deca-port, quickly followed by his dad.

'Well-well,' Dean remarked. 'If it isn't Weeweeler acting all rich and travelling by Ion-Jet.'

'That's enough, boy,' Kurt said, angrily. The last time he'd nearly been this close to the Wheelers, he'd performed a disappearing act and escaped. But this time he was caught like a rabbit in the headlights with nowhere to go and he didn't like it one bit. It was fine to be angry and shout at Harvey or Tom, but something about Sue seemed to bother him more than anyone else. 'We're late,' he said. 'Move!' He shoved

Dean in the back and hastily made off without saying another word.

Billy watched Dean being forced along the corridor before getting a whack to the back of the head. He felt a fleeting sense of pity; he didn't like the idea of having a parent like that. But then it didn't take too much effort to recall how often he'd been the one on the receiving end of Dean's frequent unkindness. Do you get what you deserve? He wondered.

The short journey from the Travel Station to Overhang Arena began with good news; Billy's parents would travel on the same coach and sit with the other parents and engineers. Sue had already found a fellow worrier in Alisha May's mum – not surprising, given what happened with the wolf. But in stark contrast, and having forgotten about Billy's own wolf, Tom's only concern was how his son might win with their choice of Gadget. Despite several conversations with Harvey, he was still unconvinced it was the right choice.

Unlike his parents who both enjoyed company, Billy sat alone. Having gotten on so well last time he'd simply assumed Louise would sit next to him, but she hadn't. Instead, she sat much further up the coach with an empty seat beside her. As far as he could tell she hadn't spoken to anyone for the entire journey. Worrying that he'd done something wrong, he looked back at her once again.

From her seat at the back of the coach, Louise saw Billy looking back. He owned the distinct look of someone who wanted to come and ask if you were okay, when all you wanted was to be left alone. *Don't come back here Billy. I can't be your friend. If I'm going to win, I can't be friends with you.*

She was convinced that Billy wouldn't understand what life was like for her. A life where winning and achieving was everything to her dad and therefore her too. And she was certain that he wouldn't understand why she needed a Disruptor in her arm. If there was anything obvious about Billy, it's that he's as honest as the day is long.

Much to her relief, she was saved from any awkward conversation when the coach arrived at Overhang Arena ahead of schedule. Pulling into a large earthy bowl of a car park, it kicked up a series of giant dust clouds that completely obscured the view. It had barely come to a stop when Billy dashed down the aisle and excitedly jumped off.

Emerging from the dust cloud moments later, he yet again found himself utterly awestruck by the wonder of what he'd only ever seen on TV. The blue sky above him was impeccably clear without the slightest hint of a cloud. Below that, the landscape was barren and uninviting, stretching for mile upon mile into the distance. The only clue suggesting this place was anywhere but nowhere, was the tournament control gate that stood at the edge of the dustbowl. What lay beyond the gate – or more accurately, below it – was Overhang Arena.

Billy and his parents made their way to the control gate whilst listening to a man squawk through his voice-volumizer.

'All contestants for the Grand Canyon Challenge, please register your attendance here.'

The sharp and screechy sound cut through the air like a flying dart, attacking Billy's ears as it passed. Eager to get away from the harsh sound, Billy quickly queued at the gate and linked his Profiler without incident. For the second time in the same day, he'd not been questioned about his age. From now on the event would surely be plain sailing.

41

Billy's stomach grumbled unhappily as he descended the stone steps that started high above him in the canyon cliffs. It was way past lunch time, and he hadn't eaten for hours.

'Two hundred and three, two hundred and four, two hundred—'

'Are you going to count all the way down?'

Billy stopped and turned to see Reuben a few steps behind. 'I don't think I can count that high.'

Reuben smiled and descended the steps between them. The hazy orange light from the harbour caged lamps cast a warm glow cementing their friendly fist-pump.

'I'm glad to see you made it. I could do with some competition,' Reuben said, jokingly.

'If you need competition, let's see how quickly you can get down the steps. I've got proper gut-rumbles. Race you to the bottom?'

'Try and keep up, squeaky,' Reuben replied, bolting down the stairs ahead of him.

Once again, during the southward flight, Billy made no noise at all, whilst Reuben's feet slapped heavily on each step.

'Whoa, Whoa!' Reuben shouted, just twenty steps into their race.

Unable to stop, Billy clattered right into him, nearly sending them both over the low wall Reuben clung onto. Their joint gasps of relief mimicked each other like identical twins; they were still over fifty meters above the Colorado River.

'That was close!' Billy said, shakily.

'You're telling me!' Rueben replied, looking out from their perch. 'Hey, I know where we are. We're at the top of Overhang stands.'

Hanging from the cliff face like a collection of giant limpets clinging to a rock, they'd arrived in Overhang One. Directly opposite them,

Overhang Two flanked the river below. It was cast into deep ribbons of shadow by the passing mid-day sun. Pleasingly, Billy and Reuben were bathed in hot bright sunshine. Below them and completing the wonderful sight, the green Colorado river thrashed over the rocks throwing white misty clouds into the air.

'Reubs,' Billy said, with a mischievous smile on his face, 'check this out.' He cupped his hands around his mouth and bellowed with all his might. 'Shut up!'

Almost instantly, the echo replied as if someone on the other side of the canyon had shouted back at him … 'Shut up.'

Billy continued his performance. 'No! You shut up!'

Once again, the echo replied as if part of some comedy double act.

Billy began to shout yet again. 'No! I said—'

'Why don't you shut up, Weeweeler?' came a shout from far below.

'Who was that?' Reuben asked, looking down into the canyon.

'I've got a pretty good idea,' Billy answered, dejectedly.

'Oh. Your friend Dean, I presume?'

'Yep.' Billy turned away from the fence looking as if he'd seen his favourite Aerial Rugby team lose the Cup Final.

'What is it with you two? It was obvious he didn't like you when we came out of the mine at the last event.'

Billy walked off and continued down the steps with his shoulders slumped. 'There's only one thing I know for sure, and it's that I didn't do anything.'

'Maybe you should just ask him?' Reuben suggested.

From the bottom of the canyon, Dean Tuffnell looked up at the sound of Billy's echoing voice. What that boy was doing here, he had no idea. And how he'd managed to get out of the forest in Kielder Grounds when the wolf should have got him; that had bugged him for the entire week afterward. Now, seeing him here, fooling around, well, that got on his nerves even more. Shouting back to shut up was satisfying, but it wasn't enough – not yet.

'He doesn't even deserve to be here,' Dean said, leaving for his Demountable.

'Oh, he's okay,' said a low and strong voice from behind.

Dean turned around to see a tall athletic boy standing a few meters away. He had blonde hair shaved skin-short on both sides and was deeply tanned making his spiked mohawk stand out even more.

Thinking quickly, Dean seized the opportunity that stood before him. 'That's not what I hear he said about you!' It was a blatant lie of course, but Dexter Jones wouldn't know that, would he. 'I hear that he thinks you're the next person to be out of the tournament.' Dean double checked Dexter's shoes with a sly glance. 'In fact, I'm pretty sure he said that blonde boys like you are too stupid to tie their own shoelaces.'

Dexter looked down to see that he was wearing magnet-latch shoes. 'Is that so?' he replied. His eyes had darkened, suggesting that Dean had struck a nerve.

Seeing that his words were taking effect, Dean went in for the finish. 'The last thing I heard is that he's given himself a new nickname. Something like … oh, now what was it? Oh, yes … Dragon Slayer.' Dean knew very well that Dexter's suit was the ancient dragon that he'd seen at Kielder Grounds. He remembered it because he was jealous of how menacing it looked.

Dexter's demeanour had completely changed. When he was first looking up at Billy acting out his silly play, it was almost with fond amusement. Now when he looked up it was full of disliking and vengeful thought. *Dragon slayer, is it? We'll see about that!*

42

Billy left the relative cool of the canyon stairs and stepped into the searing heat of the sun. He looked back wishfully at the cool shadowy doorway and imagined the stone steps as they zig-zagged their way up to the dusty bowl. A bit of him wanted to retreat into their cool safety and not risk finding Dean's unkindness yet again. Stretching away from his feet, multiple wooden pathways snaked away in different directions. Some meandered to the Demountables, while others headed toward the river and the starting arena. Viewed from the top of the canyon, they looked like a giant bowl of wooden spaghetti.

Billy took a pathway that headed toward the Demountables. Climbing up and down like a big dipper rollercoaster it was far from the cool and easy walks in Worthy Park. Ahead of him, a long row of the pop-up houses nestled snugly against the cliff. Like most of the wooden pathways, they perched precariously on spindly wooden stilts.

Several ups and downs later and headed for his own pop-up home, Billy passed a Demountable who's door was open. Dexter Jones was standing in the doorway watching him. He'd read about Dexter in the Space-Time magazine. In his picture, he'd looked happy and relaxed. But now, as he stared back, he had a dark scowl on his face; Dean had done a good job!

I wonder what's bothering him, Billy thought, uncomfortably. Feeling Dexter's eyes on him, he looked at the ground and sped up a little.

***

'Hey, Billy. I think you're staying next to me.'

Billy looked up to see Anderson standing in the doorway of his own Demountable. His smile was a wonderful remedy both to Dean's shouting and Dexter's moody expression. 'Anderson!' he called, delighted to see a friendly face. 'How's life at the top?'

'Wouldn't you like to know. If I'm honest, it's awesome. I was interviewed by Space-Time magazine a few days ago. I've even had people stopping me to ask for a selfie. How crazy is that?'

'A selfie? That's brilliant.' Inside, Billy was beaming. Only a few hours ago, he'd been the one posing for a selfie with a fan.

'Can you come in for a bit?' Anderson asked. 'I've got something to show you.'

'Quick, grab the door handle!' Billy shouted, surprising Anderson into doing that. 'Hold on. I'll be back in a minute.' He smirked and ran off toward the next Demountable, leaving his friend to hold on. Anderson looked to the sky and tutted. He'd been pranked.

Billy arrived at his own Demountable and found Mr Peddleton adding a finishing touch to the design on his suit.

'Like it?' he asked, stepping back to reveal the new look.

'That ... is ... brilliant!' Billy said, enthusiastically. 'K will definitely know who I am now!'

'After tomorrow, Billy, I think everyone will know who you are.'

'Excellent!' he replied, with a satisfied smile. 'Listen, I'm going to visit Anderson. Can you tell Mum and Dad I'll be back later?'

'Sure, no problem. But don't be late. The details of your next task are here. The message unlocks at six tonight.'

'Really? Uh, okay. I'll be back soon then.' With that, Billy was gone.

43

Much to his delight, when Billy returned to Anderson, he found him sat on the ground and still holding the door handle.

'Billy, you're back!' he said, faking exhaustion as if he'd been there for hours. 'Can I let go now? Please say I can. Please.'

'Alright, Dramatic Doris. You can let go now.'

'Dramatic Doris?' Anderson repeated feigning disbelief. 'I don't think I want to show you what I was going to now!'

Billy did his best sad-face and turned away shoulders slouched.

'I was joking. Come on. You gotta see it.' Arriving in the kitchen, he pointed to the table in the middle of the room. 'What do you think?'

'No way! You got the new The Space-Time board game!'

Anderson sat at the table, delighted at Billy's amazement. Laid out in front of him, the three locations of the tournament were created by large hologram arenas with interactive displays. Kielder Grounds, the Grand Canyon and Mount Everest were all replicated in stunning detail. All eight of the tournament competitors were also present – each a perfect robotic replica of their real-life counterparts. The tiny robot characters responded to voice commands. They could walk, jump, duck and of course, fall over. The game was simple: get from one end of the arena to the other by completing tasks, avoiding obstacles, or being caught by a Hunter. The player whose character reached the end first, would win.

'What do you think about this one?' Anderson asked, throwing Billy's own character to him.

Billy caught the tiny robot figure and immediately dropped it. 'Ow!' he cried. 'It gave me a shock!'

'Ha! That'll learn ya,' Anderson stated, laughing. 'I fixed it so you'd get a shock. That's for leaving me hanging.'

'Oh, very funny,' Billy replied. He did think it was quite funny, but it hurt bad enough that it made his eyes water. Did Anderson know it would be that bad? Unfortunately, the next time he'd remember his buzzing fingers, it wouldn't be in a good way. 'Can we play it?' he asked, still shaking his hand. 'I'll never be able afford one myself.'

'Oh, I don't have long, but I guess we can have a quick go. I tell you what. Let's have a look at the Grand Canyon. You can go first.'

'Really? Are you sure?'

'Yeah, It's cool.' He stood up and puffed his chest out. 'Let the tournament begin.'

Responding to Anderson's command, the gameboard sprang into life. Holographic images appeared right in front of them, recreating the Grand Canyon arena in stunning detail. The Colorado river began to flow from one end of the board to the other, thrashing and foaming as it flowed between the rocky canyon cliffs.

'I can hear the river,' Billy said, stating the obvious. 'It's so realistic!' He placed his robot character on the starting platform where it stood proudly to attention. 'Come on then robot. Let's see what you've got!' Right on cue, a deep, powerful voice filled his ears.

'I'm sometimes a pet, but don't ask me why. Some think I am slimy, but really, I'm dry. Sometimes I'm big and sometimes I'm small, I live in this canyon, do you think I can crawl? You'll hear me, not see me so don't come too close. With my weapon all ready, I'll dish out a dose. What am I?'

Billy repeated the riddle in his mind, trying to solve the puzzle. Then, as if trying to swat a fly, he slapped himself on the head. 'Oh, why did that take so long? It's obvious! It's a—'

'Billy? Billy?' It was Mr Peddleton. He was somewhere outside.

'Ah man, I gotta go. Can I come back later?'

'Um, I'm not sure. I need to get ready for tomorrow. My engineer says I should try using my Gadget before the start.'

'Oh yeah, I should probably do the same. OK, well, I'll see you tomorrow then.' He started for door when Anderson called out.

'Billy, before you go. What was your answer going to be? You know, for the riddle.'

Billy was on the brink of giving an answer, but then had a sudden flash of clarity. If the game version of the event was a riddle, then maybe the real challenge would be a riddle too. If that turned out to be true, he'd be giving a competitor the answer, friend or otherwise. 'Sorry, I better not. What if it's … you know, the challenge tomorrow!'

Before Anderson could say anything else, Billy ran from the door.

***

At 6pm the riddles of the Grand Canyon were revealed. Billy retreated to his bedroom and took his Space-Time Magazines for inspiration. He studied the riddle one bit at a time like an archaeologist slowly revealing clues of the past: 'I'm remarkably strong but I cannot stand for long. I'm often a question of which one came first and looked after properly I'm likely to burst. Inside me might soar, up high in the air, look up for the twigs and find me up there. What am I?'

'Mum, Dad, I've got it,' he declared triumphantly, running into the lounge. 'I've got the answer to the riddle; it's an egg.'

'Just an egg?' asked Tom, sounding a little underwhelmed.

'Well, no, not just an egg,' he replied, somewhat deflated. He began to recite the riddle in his mind. He was obviously missing something. At least that's how it felt. *Inside will soar … twigs … look up …* He stepped outside and looked up along the cliff. A defiant slither of sunlight reached into the canyon, clinging to the tip of a tall rocky spire. It glowed, a wonderful, golden brown beneath the pink bellies of the sunset clouds. He gazed in awe at the gentle golden colours. He'd never seen anything like it in Pilton. That's when it hit him.

'It's gold!' he said, returning to his parents. 'I've got to find a Golden Eagle's egg.' He looked for approval, but nobody said a word. Tom simply smiled, and Billy had his answer.

By contrast, Dexter Jones was infuriatingly baffled. He'd spent over an hour trying to solve his first riddle and failed. It should have been simple, he knew that, but it felt like a large wooden door in his mind had been slammed shut. And thanks to his encounter with Dean and the perfectly crafted lie, he believed the person who'd locked the door and hidden the key was Billy.

Later that night, and still unable to solve his riddle, Dexter would take a late-night walk through Overhang Arena. Little over an hour later he'd return and go to bed clinging to the hope that a good night's sleep would reveal the answer. Although the one thing he had managed to work out – care of his little walk – was how he'd deal with Billy.

44

After spending the entire day with his head buried in Space-Time magazines, Billy emerged from his Demountable and stepped into the cool air of late afternoon. He'd slept incredibly well the previous night, owing much of that to the single clue he'd taken to bed. As it happened, it was the same clue that had kept Dexter Jones awake half the night and woke him early with its frustrating absence. Although in time, Dexter would solve his riddle – with little nudge from Dean – and find himself in the right place when it mattered most.

Looking along the canyon Billy could see that Overhang stands were full of spectators. Above them, the early evening sky was the deepest blue he'd ever seen. He walked towards the starting arena captivated by Schrader's echoing voice. Intermittently, he could hear the crowd cheer as contestant's arrivals were announced. He found himself thinking it wouldn't be too long before his own name would echo across the canyon floor; it made his skin tingle with excitement. He passed Dexter's Demountable and felt a hint of déjà vu. Dexter was leaning against the doorframe again, but instead of the dark scowl he'd been wearing yesterday, he gave a generous smile and waved. Billy offered a friendly wave back, clueless to the fate that Dexter had in mind for him.

'And so,' Schrader declared, watching a dark blue suit with its red lightning bolt arrive in the starting arena. 'I encourage you to welcome our current tournament leader, Anderson Toms!'

The crowd dutifully played their role, creating such a noise that the echoes bouncing around the canyon vibrated the very stands they sat in.

'This is getting exciting,' Schrader continued, when he spotted Billy. 'We have another contestant arriving in the arena. Please show your appreciation for our latest arrival and Space-Time Magazine's newly acclaimed tournament favourite … Billy Wheeeeeelerrrr.'

Billy stepped into the arena and onto the circular stone platform. Despite having read his Space-Time magazine in the Vault, he hadn't really believed what it had said: tournament favourite. But now that Schrader was quoting it to goodness knows how many people, it really felt possible.

'So, Billy, what do you think about that? It's quite a bold claim wouldn't you agree?'

Billy didn't know what he was supposed to say. He hadn't planned on speaking to one person, let alone to such a large audience – frankly, he was terrified. But then an idea popped out of his mind like a jack in the box and saved him. He hadn't planned to reveal Katie's design in this way, but the timing and atmosphere felt perfect!

'I … I think ginger rules!' he declared, activating a switch on his suit and walking toward the other contestants, swaggering like an unruly rock star.

Both Schrader and crowd cheered with approval. Glowing in bright orange on the back of Billy's suit was Katie's design: The Ginger Ninja.

'You heard it here first,' Schrader said, admiring Billy's witty reply. 'Now, let the fun begin!'

When Billy spotted Anderson, he'd expected to see him smiling, but instead he looked a little glum. 'Are you okay? he asked.

'Not really. I'm stuck on the riddle. I solved the bit about white water, but I can't figure out what I'm looking for when I get there.'

Billy turned to face him. 'White water? I didn't get a riddle about white water.'

'My engineer said they're random. Sometimes they're the same, sometimes not.'

'I guess it stops us cheating.'

Anderson put on a posh voice. 'One does not cheat, Sir! One improvises.' He gave Billy an odd suggestive wink. Unfortunately for both of them, Billy would remember that wink too – cheating was cheating, wasn't it?

Standing just behind them, Dean and Dexter were shoulder to shoulder. 'What was your riddle?' Dean whispered.

'I'm remarkably strong but I just can't stand for long. I'm often a question of which one came first and looked after properly I'm likely to burst. Inside me might soar, up high in the air, look up for the twigs and find me up there. What am I?'

'And you solved it, right?' Dean asked, frowning.

Dexter shook his head like a confused nodding dog.

How did you get this far if you couldn't even work that out? Dean asked himself. *Maybe Billy was right, and you really can't tie your own shoelaces*, he thought, forgetting that Billy hadn't even said such a thing. A fresh wave of contempt for Dexter swept over him, but he still wanted Billy out of the tournament and Dexter was his weapon. He leaned in and whispered so quietly that he could barely hear himself speak, but as a Heed, Dexter heard just fine. 'It's a Golden Eagle's egg.'

Dexter's eyes opened wide with embarrassed surprise and his tanned skin still managed to flush bright pink. He'd been made to look a fool by Billy yet again.

'Welcome to the second round of the Space-Time Tournament,' Schrader sang. 'The riddles of the Grand Canyon! It's a full twenty-four hours since the riddles were released, so I hope our contestants have solved them by now. Before we get going, I should remind you of the rules. You must solve three riddles. If you can solve all three, the Grand Canyon Insignia will await you. Contestants, unlike your first event at Kielder Grounds, you will all begin at the same time. Once again, Time Credits will be awarded for how quickly you find and solve each riddle. The first challenger to collect the hidden Insignia, will win bonus Credits!' Schrader left the stone platform, allowing the Electrobeam barrier to crackle into life. 'Ladies and gentlemen, without further delay, three ... two ... one ... go!'

45

The Electrobeam barrier evaporated, but instead of running off, the contestants just stood still as if waiting to see where the others would go before making their own move.

Seizing the moment, Dean knelt on down like someone tying their shoelaces and then sprang high into the air. It was an audacious move that was met with cheers of approval and admiration; his strength was apparent for all to see. He landed on a rocky outcrop at several meters away. *This is going to be too easy,* he thought smugly – he was wrong!

As if woken by Dean's eye-catching start, the remaining contestants sprang into life and leapt from the platform. Anderson headed for the white waters of the Colorado River: having solved his own riddle, he believed the foaming rapids created a formidable overcoat to the clue hidden beneath. Dexter Jones however, remained motionless, slowly digesting the answer that Dean had given him. It seemed obvious what a Golden Eagle egg might look like, but the canyon walls towered countless meters above him. He couldn't see any nests all that way up! In desperation to get going, he simply left the platform and ran down the first path he came to.

When Billy left the platform, he was grateful for how quickly he'd solved his riddle; it had given him plenty of time to think about where an eagle egg might be hidden, including how he might get there. Unlike at Kielder Grounds, he'd planned exactly which way he was going. The closest trail to the platform stretched away from him before twisting out of sight into a mini canyon of its own. It was into this shadowy pathway that Billy disappeared, closely watched by someone who was already having second thoughts.

Running along the dusty trail, Billy found himself flanked by a stone rock face that grew higher and higher above him. The sun was low in the sky and shone brightly, but in the depths of his mini canyon he was smothered in heavy shadow. Before long, he arrived at a fork in the trail. To the left, the path snaked out of sight. To the right, the shadows faded into sunlight. He didn't know which way to go, but he needed to choose a path. Somewhere far behind he heard the faint sound of Schrader's voice reporting to the audience. He was too far away to hear anything clearly, but for a moment – before dismissing it as a canyon echo – he thought he heard the word, Hunter. Ignoring his ears and returning his attention to finding the egg, Billy chose the path that led to the cliffs on his right. The other path would have been safer, but he didn't know that. Yet!

Striding along the path, it wasn't long before Billy ran into another obstacle. His mini canyon narrowed abruptly and finished at an impossibly tight gap with a bright slither of sunlight cutting through it. He could have tried to get through, but he already knew he wouldn't fit; it was simply too tight. His only option was to go up and over.

He turned to the rock face beside him and crouched into a low tuck, before springing up with all his strength. Miraculously, both his hands hooked solidly onto the stony ledge. He pulled himself up and scraped his suit on the rock, causing little waterfalls of dust to drift gently to the ground. Looking down, and trying not to scratch his precious suit, he was oblivious to the fact that thirty meters away and swooping down from the sky towards his fingers, the Hunter that he'd dismissed, approached.

***

Far away from Billy, Alisha May was tracking Dean. She hadn't forgotten how he'd ruined her first event and she wanted revenge. It hadn't been difficult to follow him, what with all the noise he'd made as his feet pounded the stone. And once she'd spotted him, she hadn't lost sight. More than once he'd stopped and looked back, as if suspecting he was being followed, but being a Nimble, Alisha had simply danced out of sight. She'd hidden beside him in a thicket of bushes, and above him on the smallest of ledges. Neither had posed a problem.

So now, here they were, less than two meters apart after Dean finally came to a stop. His riddle had been the same as Billy's from the

Space-Time board game; he was looking for a snake. Alisha stood above him on the narrow ledge and watched as he edged towards a spiny cactus. He was moving more carefully than she'd thought possible, and at first, she didn't understand what he was doing holding a massive boulder over his head like he was. But then elation came when she spotted flashes of sunlight reflecting from the body of a mechanical rattle snake.

Delight filled her entire body; he'd been searching for the same thing she was. She didn't like to think of herself as a cheat, but hadn't he been the one to leave her to the wolf without any care for her feelings? She certainly hadn't deserved that! The thought of cheating was bad, but when the snake rattled beneath her, it was the wolf biting her ankle that filled her mind. Without hesitation, she straightened up and got ready to jump. Feet first, teeth gritted.

Dean stared at the mechanical rattle snake, concentrating like somebody who was trying to thread a needle. Everything around him faded into the background, but the snake remained in sharp focus. The once loud rush of the river softened into a distant background hush, as if he were wearing earmuffs. *Just a little closer and you're done for,* he thought, ready to smash the rock on its head.

When the snake spotted Dean moving the muffled quiet was ruined by the harsh rattle of its tail. But it wasn't the rattling chatter that astonished Dean, it was the raging shriek that came from above. Before he could react, a bright white flash attacked his eyes, followed by a heavy thump to his chest. He was knocked onto his back where the heavy rock pulled at his arms, stretching him out as if he were on some medieval rack. By the time he'd gotten over the shock and managed to sit up, whatever had hit him was gone. Most infuriating of all, so was the snake.

On the other side of a narrow boulder and not more than three meters away, Alisha May huddled down with the limp, stolen snake in her hands. Across its belly, the next riddle was revealed.

46

The top of Billy's head edged closer and closer to the ledge that his fingers hung onto. In the time he'd taken to pull himself up, the metallic feathered Hunter had gained another ten meters. His fingers stood out like black spider legs against the reddish stone, inviting the Hunter to stalk them like prey. It dived abruptly, stretched out its talons and screeched. It had arrived.

Billy was consumed with fear as a vice-like grip took hold of his legs and dragged him down from the ledge. His fingers gave up their grip and he fell to the floor in a sprawling heap. Looking skyward he was stunned to see the mechanical eagle swoop across his mini canyon and out of sight.

'Urgh, get off. You're squashing me.'

Billy took his second shock of the moment and leapt off the floor. 'DEXTER?' he asked, surprised to see the ancient dragon suit in front of him. 'What are you doing here?'

Dexter stood up and brushed himself off. 'Is that all the thanks I get for saving you?' he asked, incredulously. 'That was a Hunter!

'You're pulling my leg!' Billy joked, a little nervously

'Ha-ha, very funny,' Dexter replied sarcastically, finding Billy's joke funnier than he wanted to.

'Seriously though,' Billy continued, 'thanks for saving me.'

'Let's just say you owe me one,' Dexter told him. 'Listen, I wouldn't climb up there if I were you. With that Hunter around, you'd be better off taking the other path about fifty meters back. Take a left at the fork and then turn right. I think it takes you towards the cliffs. If that's where you're going, that is?' he added, backtracking a little.

'Thanks. That's two I owe you.'

'You can pay me back later,' he said, fully believing that Billy would be out of the tournament by the end of the day. 'Anyway, I've got to go. We are competing after all. See-ya.'

Having ducked out of sight a short way back, Dexter hid within the shadow of a nearby crevice and waited for Billy. Sure enough, he only had to wait a few moments before Billy's silent feet ran past. Once he was out of sight, Dexter returned to the rocky wall where Billy's fingers had left dusty claw marks down the rock. Satisfied with his work, he scrambled over the top, but not before looking back with a dark smile. *Call yourself the Dragon Slayer? We'll see about that.* He could have let the eagle have Billy, but why risk it? It might have dropped him or missed him altogether. No, it was far more satisfying to be the reason Billy would fail and send him to the pit that he'd found on last night's walk.

***

Dexter reached the bottom of the canyon cliff after an easy dash across the scrubby canyon floor. Choosing to follow Billy had been an inspired idea. Not only did he send him in the wrong direction, but Billy had shown him the route to what he himself was looking for: A Golden Eagle's egg. He stood at the foot of the cliff and looked up. Directly above him and perhaps thirty meters away, he could just make out a brownish mess of branches that could well have passed for a dead bush. When he'd stopped moving and listened – one thing that being a Heed made him particularly good at – he could hear a conversation of squeaks that surely only an eagle would make. From that moment on, there was no doubt in his mind. It held the clue was looking for.

With his decision made he activated his Gadget, triggering a miniature winch and grappling hook to appear from the chest-plate of his suit. He craned his neck and quickly spotted his target. A couple of meters above the eagle's nest, a craggy rock jutted upwards like a finger pointing at the sky. He smiled as a plan took shape in his mind. This was going to be easy!

Using a crosshair on his visor, he aimed his grappling hook and fired. A high-pitched pulse like a bat's sonar filled his ears as the tiny hook cut through the air. It skittered momentarily, scrabbling at the rock before sticking firm within a tiny crack. When the cable began to wind in and pull at his suit, Dexter realised just how close he'd come to disaster; disturbed by the noise, a Hunter took flight from the nest, engulfing him in the shadow of its enormous wingspan. He could only hope it wouldn't return while he was up there.

Placing one foot in front of the other he began to walk up the cliff face as if doing a reverse abseil. With each forward step the cable pulled at his chest, twanging loudly like an out of tune guitar string.

'I know what you just did to Billy, Dexter. That wasn't very nice, was it!'

Dexter jumped at the sound of the stranger's voice. He tried to turn and look, but while the cable continued to pull him upward, he couldn't twist enough to see who it was.

'What do you think I should do about it?' the voice asked.

The voice belonged to a girl, and she was whispering so quietly that only a Heed would hear her. Dexter's body began to fill with fear like a bottle under a running tap; if he didn't do something soon it would overflow. He tried to unwind the cable, but his abrupt movement jammed it solid. He was halfway up the cliff and utterly helpless.

Eight eyes stared at Dexter from beneath the grassy scrub. Eight eyes of the Black Widow spider that her Kinetic suit mimicked. The only giveaway amid the shadow, was the bright red hourglass across her chest.

'I'm sorry, Dexter,' she whispered. 'I have to do this. I need to win more than you.'

He was on the brink of panic and bashing the winch on his chest when a powerful shock coursed through his suit. Frozen and unable to move, he found himself wondering how lightning could possibly strike from such a clear blue sky. But then none of it mattered. The winch broke, and he fell.

Later that night, Dexter's Memory Trace would show that a suspected failure of the winding mechanism had caused his fall. Despite his uncertainty about it being the real cause, the bang he'd taken to the head meant that he'd never remember exactly what happened. Either way, after a better night's sleep than the one before, he'd wake up the following morning, out of the Space-Time Tournament.

47

Louise stopped sprinting and stooped over with her hands pressing hard on her knees. If she hadn't, she probably would have passed out. When she'd collected the egg from high above Dexter's sleeping body a sudden need to run and hide had overwhelmed her; she'd never intended for him to fall so far, but she needed that egg.

Mercifully, as her breathing returned to normal her world stopped spinning. It had felt like she'd been riding an awful theme-park Waltzer, but now able to think more clearly, she could concentrate on the golden egg in her hand. Despite the shade she stood in, the tiny hourglasses engraved on it sparkled like a shimmering sea at sunset.

'Come on then,' she said, whispering to the egg. 'What do you have to say?' She flicked her Profiler over it and watched in awe as the top cracked open, spilling fragments of golden shell on the floor. A glowing hologram then lit up and floated in front of her eyes.

Her third and final riddle was revealed.

The truth of the matter, however, was that when Louise read it, she was almost the last person to do so. Dexter Jones wouldn't be reading riddles anytime soon of course. And then there was Billy, sent in the wrong direction without a whiff of a riddle and on a collision course with the pit.

***

For the second time in two events, Katie had decided to watch the tournament on her own. Although on this occasion she'd chosen to watch it in the Vault: somehow it made her feel that little bit closer to Billy. Whilst she'd been waiting for the event to start, she'd covered an entire wall of the Vault with screenshots and pieces of paper, all containing theories on who the person she'd named The Shocker, might be. It had been a welcome break from investigating when Billy had revealed his Ginger Ninja design. She'd laughed hard enough that a dog walker had stopped and stared accusingly into the woods. It was all she could do to bite the sleeve of her hoodie and muffle her hysterics.

Now back in investigation mode and in a far more serious mood, she watched as pair of Space-Time medics put Dexter Jones onto a stretcher. Like it or not, she'd found that tournament officials were very clear about the dangers that existed – after all, time travel and space exploration were hardly safe occupations. But the thing she'd found most difficult to accept was that officials would not interfere. For better or worse, contestants would be left to their own devices during the events. Officials would be watching, and they'd have access to Memory Traces for all the contestants, but they would only interfere if they suspected cheating. In the case of Dexter Jones, a camera drone had been watching when he fell and officials knew that Louise was nearby, but that was all; Fletcher's disruptor really was very clever!

Re-watching the footage of him lying on the ground yet again, Katie spotted something that at first, she hadn't seen. It wasn't the almost imperceptible white spark that her now experienced eye had seen before he fell. Neither was it the bloom of stone dust that filled the air as if someone had kicked a sandcastle at the beach. No, when Dexter lay motionless on the ground, it was a flash of red dancing across his visor that got her heart beating.

With the camera drone looking at Dexter, nobody had seen Louise using her chosen Gadget; an Ion Backthruster. She'd activated it and scurried up the cliff face looking like a real Black Widow spider. But now that Katie had seen the red flash on Dexter's visor, she began to connect two parts of a puzzle: the spark, and the red flash.

'Does the Shocker wear red?' she asked the empty room.

She began switching through the different cameras, searching for a contestant wearing a red suit, when she came to an image that stopped her in her tracks. It wasn't a red suited contestant that she'd found – it was Billy.

48

Billy scrambled across a steep gravel slope that ran between the river and the canyon cliffs. To his right and a small way behind, threatening white water cascaded over a mass of highly polished rocks. Looking at them, he could only hope that Anderson had been able to find his own riddle safely. Especially now that most of the canyon was cast in heavy shade like it had been smothered by a grey woollen blanket.

Billy continued to traverse the slope forcing loose shingle to tumble away like sand running through an hourglass. It had become so difficult to move that he had to use both his hands and feet to make any progress. His apprehension had begun to grow from the moment he'd found himself edging not across, but down the slope – if he turned back, he'd end up in the rapids. Despite his growing concern, he found himself chuckling at the thought that he must look more like a clumsy Orangutan than the newly named Ginger Ninja. *Where have you sent me, Dexter?*

In answer to his question, it was now that Billy saw his destination; the slope had rapidly become a one-way ticket to his demise. To his dismay, on a stony outcrop that flanked the river was what looked like a writhing metallic Medusa's head. What it was of course, was the Hunter's snake-pit!

A shiver scurried across his body as if tiny snakes were in his suit. He looked along the slope and considered whether the rapids offered another route, but they were more severe than the ones he'd seen Anderson heading towards. *I wish you were here, Anderson. You'd help me!* He closed his eyes and tried to think of a plan when out of the blue and thinking of Anderson, he found himself transported back in time.

***

The Space-Time board game filled the table in front of him. On it, a holographic image of the Grand Canyon flickered brightly. Mr Peddleton was calling from outside and he was walking towards the door when Anderson stopped him.

'Billy, before you go. What was your answer going to be? You know, about the riddle.'

'Sorry, I better not. What if it's … you know, the challenge tomorrow!

***

Billy snapped back to reality with Andersons's voice echoing inside his head. *It was a snake!* he thought. *I had to find a snake in the board game.*

Having no other choice, he made his mind up; if a snake held the riddle, he had to catch one. Katie, Billy's parents, and the hundreds of people in Overhang stands fell into stunned silence. With the drone looking on, he turned to face down the gravelly slope and looked directly at the writhing chaos of Hunter snakes.

'What are you doing?' Katie shouted at the screen. 'Turn around! Leave!'

Captivated, the spectators watched in anticipation as he drew one hand back to his hip and pushed the other out in front making a target through the loop of his finger and thumb. A collective gasp then raced through the canyon. To overwhelming disbelief, Billy leapt into the air and hovered momentarily – seeming to defy gravity yet again – before surfing down the gravel slope toward the snakes. The distance between them closed at an alarming rate from thirty meters to twenty meters, to ten.

Katie closed her eyes. The Ginger Ninja crouched … and jumped.

Billy clutched his fingers into a tight fist. *If I don't get this right, I'm toast,* he thought, exhilarated. Floating down the slope he bore down on the snake-pit, eyes narrow as if staring at a bright light. In a fragment of time quicker than a blink, he punched his hand out and activated his Gadget: An Airshield 2.0. The powerful shield of air blasted from his fist and struck the snake-pit dead centre, sending snakes in all directions like he'd punched his hand into a bowl of metal spaghetti. When the dust settled around him, he stood on the rocky outcrop and looked at the stunned circle of snakes – not one of them moved. He crouched down and picked one up, holding it aloft like a trophy. In the distance he heard a cheer drift across the canyon. The entire population of Overhang Arena could breathe once again.

Despite his thundering heart, Billy managed to hold the snake steady; calmness and purpose were returning. He stared at the limp body, pleading for something to happen, when, filling his world with wonderful relief, words began to glow across its belly. Like a newsfeed, they scrolled along the body in quick succession before repeating once again: 'If three riddles you find, I'll show you the way. Don't run off and look, my advice is to stay. I may be the first, but plenty you found, so close is another now don't make a sound.'

Billy stared at the words as if he were reading foreign language. How was he supposed to find another riddle if he didn't go anywhere? Although right now, what felt more important was escaping the trap he'd been sent to. He looked along the river and spotted a pencil-thin ledge. It was certainly tempting, but it was far too narrow. Falling into the river and swimming was one thing, but tackling the rapids? That would be foolish.

Looking for another way to escape, Billy's eyes followed the canyon slope and settled on the trench that he'd carved into the gravel. That's when his heart began to race once again. Scattered up the slope, multiple snakes lay motionless, each with a new riddle scrolling brightly across its belly. Although it wasn't the riddles that had got Billy's attention, it was the metal pipe that had been hidden under the gravel that excited him. It might have been the snake's way into the tournament arena, but more than that, it was his way out of Dexter's trap.

49

Louise Kelley waited beneath a cactus that she'd taken refuge below a whole thirty minutes ago. In fact, having found and solved her final riddle, she'd sat down and waited. Elsewhere in the canyon, Anderson also sat quietly and waited. It was the same for Alisha too. Surprisingly, for the entire time Billy had struggled along the gravel slope and stomped into the snake-pit, everybody else had just sat and waited.

Well … nearly everybody.

The third and final riddle of the challenge was the same for all contestants; no matter when they found it or where they were, it read the same: 'From where you began, watch me set. Not before then or impatience you'll regret. The last of my warmth at this spot you will feel. And when I'm gone, in my place, your prize will be real.'

***

Dean sat and waited all by himself. The sun was setting, and he could just about feel the last of its warmth creeping through his visor. His fist was clenched tightly, partly because he held the prize in his hand, and partly in annoyance at the crowd, who hadn't cheered when he grabbed the Snake Insignia. Annoyingly, what happened was the complete opposite. The crowd had clapped and cheered as Schrader announced his arrival. And upon seeing him they'd reacted with wonderful approval – something that he rarely received. But when he'd picked up the Insignia, they'd stopped. Even Schrader went quiet. It suddenly felt like they didn't want him to be the winner.

But I have won, he thought defiantly. *It was just as the final riddle had said it would be. It was at the start. And the sun is setting.*

Dean was right about the location: he'd found it in the centre of the stone platform where they'd all began the challenge. But he'd made a terrible mistake. One that would bother him for days: in his rush to be first he hadn't read the riddle properly.

Schrader spotted Louise come into view and immediately sprang back into life.

'Ladies and Gentlemen … our other contestants are beginning to return. The sun is setting, and the final moment will soon be upon us … Let's hear it for our fantastic competitors.'

Louise raced towards the starting platform full of excited expectation. She'd timed her run perfectly and was first back; she was going to win! Finally, her dad was going to be pleased, proud even. But then she saw Dean on the platform, and it all came crashing down. Beaten, she slowed to the dejected walk of disheartened defeat.

Dean greeted Louise with a generous smile and revelled in seeing the expression on her face. When Alisha arrived, swiftly followed by Anderson and Reuben, his satisfaction grew: There was no sign of Billy or Dexter.

I got rid of them both, he said to himself proudly. But then his pleasure was shattered when Schrader spoke once again.

'Here he comes, ladies and gentlemen. Our last competitor is here.'

Everybody's attention turned to the mini canyon that led away from the platform. Billy was hiking up the final climb.

'You're making a habit of turning up late, Mr Wheeler,' Schrader remarked, triggering laughter within the crowd. Dean didn't laugh with them, but instead, stepped to the edge of the platform and held out his hand. Everybody watched, expecting him to help Billy up. But what he really wanted to do was show off the Snake Insignia.

'I don't need any help thank you,' Billy said, watching the final slither of reflected sunlight disappeared from Dean's visor.

Dean ignored his words and grabbed Billy's arm, dragging him onto the platform. A shocked gasp spread through the crowd, but then they broke into cheers and applause. Somehow, instead of sprawling across the floor, Billy had managed to grab onto a stone pillar behind Dean. Pulling himself up, his chin came level with the top where his eyes fell upon the most wonderful sight. Sitting right there under his fingertips, was the true Snake Insignia.

'We have a WINNER!' Schrader bellowed. 'Congratulations to our youngest ever victor … the Ginger Ninja!'

'WHAT?' Dean shrieked, spinning round to look at Billy. 'That wasn't there a minute ago!' he shouted, pointing at the stone pillar under Billy's hand.

'That's because the sun hadn't set,' Anderson replied, now realising the mistake they'd all made; Dean hadn't found the real Insignia at all like they'd thought – he'd arrived too early and grabbed the false one. They'd all been so busy watching Billy arrive late that they'd missed the last slither of sunlight disappearing from the platform, leaving a stone pillar and the true Insignia in its place.

Realising his foolish mistake, Dean thundered past Billy, outraged and embarrassed. He had no intention of standing on the podium to be humiliated by Weeweeler or anybody else.

'Ladies and gentlemen. Before we begin the podium presentation, we should recognise the achievements of both Dexter Jones and Rueben Alt. They have both proven themselves to be fantastic competitors, but only the best can survive. Ruben was snared by a Hunter, while Dexter suffered a suit malfunction. As a result, both were unable to score enough Credits to qualify for the next event. And so, please welcome our top five finishers to the podium.'

Without warning, the platform that Billy was standing on began to rumble and groan under his feet. A heavy grinding sound filled his ears as five stone steps climbed skyward around him. Rising from the edge of the platform like a rugged half-built amphitheatre, each block stacked higher and higher, building the pyramid-like podium.

'For a remarkable win and taking the top step, please cheer for our Grand Canyon winner: Billy Wheeler. And, following in order of Time Credits awarded, please congratulate Dean Tuffnell; Louise Kelley; Anderson Toms and last but not least, Alisha May.'

Climbing the stone steps, Billy tried to remain calm. It wasn't easy; his entire body felt like a shaken-up bottle of Heliyumm. He was so full of excited energy that his legs trembled. Despite the number of people watching from the limpet-like stands, when he looked for his parents, he found them easily. Tom was waving a Ginger Ninja flag with all the energy he could muster, while Sue stood beside him waving her arms like a windsock flapping in a hurricane. To anybody else it might have been embarrassing, but Billy felt nothing but pride.

'And so, to the Time Credits. To Billy Wheeler, for collecting the true Insignia, we award five Credits. And for solving three riddles in the slowest time, a further sixteen Credits. To Dean Tuffnell, for solving three riddles in the fastest time, twenty Credits. But, for collecting the false Insignia, we deduct two Credits.'

If Dean had been on the podium, he'd probably have screamed in frustration. Instead, he was hiding from his dad in their Demountable, too ashamed to even show his face.

'To Louise Kelley, for solving three riddles in the second fastest time, nineteen Credits. To Anderson Toms, for solving three riddles in the third fastest time, we award eighteen Credits. And finally, to Alisha May, for solving three riddles in the fourth fastest time, we award seventeen Credits.'

The screens across Overhang arena displayed the competitor's Credits and tournament positions, while Schrader took the Snake Insignia and pressed it to Billy's chest like a medal of honour. Billy looked down at it sitting proudly on his suit, rapidly becoming glassy eyed.

'Congratulations Billy, I'm sure your parents must be very proud.' Schrader prompted him to reply by holding the voice-volumizer under his chin.

Billy looked at his parents through watery eyes, but before he spoke, found his attention drawn to the face of a man standing beside his dad. *Wait a minute. Isn't that …* He wiped at his face trying to clear his blurry vision, but as if sensing Billy's intention, the man dropped his head and disappeared beneath his hat. Seconds later, the black raincoated figure disappeared altogether. Billy scratched at his head. *Why would he be with Dad?*

'So, Billy. Do you have anything to say?' Schrader asked.

Distracted, Billy's suspicions fell to the back of his mind, there were more immediate things to concentrate on. He looked at Schrader and smiled cheekily. 'I told you ginger rules!'

50

Billy woke up to the real world when he arrived at home and found Katie waiting at the front door. She'd been so eager to show him what she'd been working on in the Vault that she'd arrived at the house an hour early. When Billy saw her through the window, he could hardly get out of the car fast enough.

'Hi K,' he said, casually. Trying to play down his happiness at seeing her. He put his hand out as if he intended to shake hers.

'What's that for?' she asked, snorting out a laugh. 'Come here, Billy-boy.' Before he could react, she hugged him tightly and whispered in his ear. 'Welcome back, winner.'

If his parents hadn't been watching, Billy felt like he could have stayed there all day.

'Can you come to the Vault?' She asked. 'There's something I want to show you.'

'Sorry K, I can't. Dad's not well again.'

'Oh, that's okay. How about tomorrow?'

'Yeah, tomorrow's cool.'

She leaned around him, 'I hope you feel better soon Mr Wheeler.'

Tom smiled wearily. 'Thanks Katie.'

'See you tomorrow,' Billy said, watching her walk down the drive. It couldn't come soon enough.

***

Katie and Billy wondered through Worthy Park while the morning mist still hung in the air. Billy's dad was suffering from a bout of fatigue and was resting in bed, but after a good nudge from his mum, Billy had felt a little better about going out.

'What do you think?' he asked, long after handing over the Insignia.

'It's beautiful,' she replied, after a considerable delay.

'Are you okay?' Billy asked, realising she'd been silent for most of their walk.

'Of course I am!' She looked at him apologetically. 'Sorry, Billy-boy, it really is stunning. It's just, well, I'm worried about you.'

'You don't to worry about me, K. I'm the Ginger Ninja.' He ran into the woods that edged the park and re-appeared leaping through the air. 'Ninja slow, Ninja fast, turn your back I'll kick your—'

'Self into in a puddle of mud?' Katie finished, spotting the slop he was going to land in.

'Grass!' Billy said wishfully, landing backside first in the dirt.

Katie burst into laughter and performed her hands-on-hips stance. 'Told you!' she said, looking smug.

'Eat dirt, squirt,' Billy replied, throwing a handful of sloppy mud in her direction.

Katie ducked to the side, easily dodging the muddy missile before running off. 'See you in the Vault, Billy-boy.'

Dripping wet and covered in mud, Billy appeared in the doorway of the Vault. 'My backside is absolutely soak—' he stopped mid-sentence, stumped for words. The sight of the wall that Katie had covered in photos was startling. 'What is that?' he asked, taking a step back.

Katie pointed to the blue threadbare cushion on Billy's chair. 'Sit down and I'll tell you,' she ordered, having already covered it with a plastic bag.

Same old sensible K, he thought, affectionately.

'Right then, Billy-boy,' she said, pointing to a photo labelled: Incident one. 'This is a blown-up capture of when your suit froze in the Kielder Forest. Can you see that?' she asked, pointing to a tiny faint white line. 'That's a spark. It appeared just before your suit stopped working.'

'You can see a spark?' asked Billy, surprised. 'Mr Peddleton said maybe something hit me and the wolf. But I didn't know you could actually see it!'

'That's not all,' Katie declared, impressively. 'I found another one at the Grand Canyon event. It's the same!' She pointed to a second photo where Dexter Jones was halfway up the cliff face, frozen in time.

Billy had to get up and stand right against the photo before the faintest white line became apparent. 'No way!' he said, turning to face her. 'You must have spent ages looking through these.'

'You don't want to know,' she mumbled, looking sheepishly at the ground. 'Anyway, this is what I wanted to show you.'

Billy followed her to a third photo. It was an image of a sleeping Dexter. Circled in the middle with a thick black marker, an innocent looking red mark on his visor took centre stage. The word Shocker was written beside it along with a big accusing question mark.

'I bet whoever shocked you and the wolf, shocked Dexter too. And I bet whoever it was, has a red mark on their suit.'

Billy's body shuddered at her words. He looked closely at the photo, hoping to find fault with her theory, but there was no room for doubt; there was a red reflection alright. He thought back to the Kielder Forest when his suit had shut down – he'd seen someone run into the fog. Had he seen something red too? He wasn't entirely sure, but when he thought about the Grand Canyon event his memory was much clearer. He wiggled his fingers, remembering how badly they'd hurt after he'd been shocked by the robot character! His mind flew into overdrive. He didn't want to believe the answer he'd come up with, but he had no choice. With the red lightning bolt on his suit and the shock from the robot … It was unavoidable!

'Billy, are you okay?'

'No, I'm not!' he replied with a sigh.

'What's the matter?'

'I only know two people with any red on their suit. Louise Kelley and—' Billy fell silent, hardly able to get the name out.

'And?' Katie asked. 'Who else?'

'It can't be,' Billy groaned. 'It can't.'

'Who, Billy? Tell me.'

He looked at her with sadness in his eyes. 'My friend Anderson.'

51

Three days after leaving the Grand Canyon, a nervous Louise Kelley sat beside her dad in Worthies Bike Outlet and waited patiently for Fletch to return. They'd all been talking happily enough while he'd recharged the Disruptor, but when he'd spotted someone enter the store on the CCTV, he fell into a stunned silence. The look of sheer panic on his face was almost scary, and before they knew it, he'd shot upstairs ordering them not to follow at any cost.

She studied the screen to see who had spooked Fletch, but they hid beneath a black raincoat and a wide brimmed hat. 'I wonder who it is,' she said, anxiously.

'There's no need for you to worry about that. You just concentrate on being ready for the race.' Duncan pointed to the large folder of on her lap, labelled, Mount Everest. He'd given it to her because 'achievers come prepared.' 'Fletch sold us the finest suit and Magbike that money can buy,' he continued. 'But you still need to be at your best. You did well at the Grand Canyon by the way. That Dexter Jones should have been more careful.'

'We're not going to get caught, are we?' Louise asked, anxiously.

'No dear, don't be silly. If anyone suspected anything they'd be here by now.'

Louise looked back to the CCTV screen just in time to see the man in the black raincoat leaving the store. *Maybe they are*, she thought.

'When Fletch comes back we'll take the suit and get going, okay? Will that make you feel any better?'

'Yes,' she agreed, thinking about the man in the raincoat. 'It would.'

Fletch appeared in the doorway. Small beads of sweat stood out on his forehead, and he looked decidedly flustered. Wasting no time, he went directly to Louise's Disruptor and disconnected it from the charger. 'Right then. I think this is the last time we'll see each other, Duncan. You won't need to come back again.'

'But what about the Mag—'

'I've done all I can to help you,' Fletch barked. 'I'll refund you for the Magbike.'

'But—'

'Now, I must ask you to leave.'

With any hint of friendliness gone, Louise and her dad were shoved out the back door of Worthies Bike Outlet. The Magbike Louise had chosen would not be hers after all and it looked like an emergency visit Peddleton's might be necessary: unless Mr Rimmel at Carbon Copy Magbikes could help, that was. One thing was for certain though. Louise Kelley and her dad would never visit Worthies again.

***

Elsewhere in the world and sitting in his bedroom, Dean Tuffnell was having an equally hard time of it.

'I don't know what you think you were trying to do,' Kurt said, yet again. 'It was such a stupid mistake. Didn't you even read the riddle? I go to all the effort of getting you there, and you just mess it up.'

'I already said I'm sorry, Dad. I messed up. But I don't care about winning the tournament anymore. All I care about is beating Wheeler. Besides, we're even on Credits, so I only need to finish in front of him and I'll probably win the tournament anyway.'

'You should care about winning it, Dean! They took it from me. Now you have to take it back.'

'If mum was here, she wouldn't be giving me such a hard time,' Dean replied, resentfully.

'But that's exactly it, Dean. She's not here … because of them!'

It was the first time that Kurt had ever openly blamed the Wheelers for the fact that his wife had left him. Although Dean had known for a long time that his dad held them responsible; it was why he gave Billy such a hard time.

'Fine. I'll beat him and win the tournament … Okay!'

Dean turned his back and waited for his dad to leave. After a silent moment, that's exactly what he did, oblivious to the tears that ran down Dean's cheeks.

**

The day before the Mount Everest event, Anderson and his engineer walked through the door of Carbon Copy bike shop. In contrast to Peddleton's, it wasn't the gentle note of a bell ring that welcomed them but a brash electronic buzz.

Anderson arrived at the counter and was about to ring the service bell when he spotted Mr Rimmel's grey wiry hair hiding behind the counter. 'Mr Rimmel?' he asked.

'Oh, thank goodness?' the man replied, popping up from behind the counter. 'I thought that awful customer had come back to make more demands.'

'It's just me,' Anderson replied with a smile. 'We've come to collect my bike. Is it ready?'

'Yes, it is. Just about. You wouldn't believe the morning I've had.' He gave a disapproving shake of his head. 'A quite awful man came in creating all sorts of trouble. Complaining about being let down by some guy who was supplying his daughter's bike and so having to buy one. Can you believe that he tried to buy yours? He wouldn't stop demanding to take it, no matter how many times I told him it was already allocated. When I asked who his supplier was his daughter started having a strange coughing fit. She carried on so long that he got all angry with her and left.'

'I think I know who you mean,' Anderson said. 'He sounds like the one that was giving his daughter a hard time at the tournament dinner. With parents like mine I can't say I know what it's like,' he said bluntly, feeling a pang of sadness. He was right. His parents never gave him a hard time. He wouldn't have minded if they did; it would be better than what he got now: no attention at all.

'I thought they'd have been here,' Mr Rimmel said.

Anderson raised his eyebrows and shrugged. 'I didn't.'

'Right, um, well, follow me and we'll get your bike.'

With James Rimmel leading the way, Anderson disappeared through an identical Holographic display to the one at Peddleton's bike shop and headed for the showroom. He didn't know it yet, but he was just about to say hello to the Magbike that would win him a place in the Space Exploration Programme.

52

The words invaded his ears before he could see who was shouting them. He didn't like the sound of whoever it was, regardless.

'What's going on?' Katie whispered, as she stepped through the door with Billy.

'I don't know,' he mouthed in silence.

They'd caught the bus to Peddleton's so he could show Katie his Magbike before he left for Everest, but something more significant was already happening. The two of them crept into the shop and sneaked along a narrow aisle between some shelving. Whoever owned the raised voice was being loud enough that Mr Peddleton's doorbell hadn't disturbed them.

'Please calm down, Mr—'

'I am calm!' the man butted in.

Billy didn't have a clue who the voice belonged to, but the owner was clearly frustrated and desperate. Suddenly feeling protective, Billy wanted to see who it was, but before he looked, somebody else spoke.

'Dad, please calm down. He said he might be able to help.'

In utter surprise, Billy jumped up. His head popped over the shelf like a meerkat on high alert.

'Louise? What are you doing here?' He began to make his way toward them. Katie went after him, tugging nervously on his sleeve.

'Oh, Billy?' Louise said, full of surprise and clear embarrassment.

'What's going on?' asked Billy.

Duncan gave him a distrustful glare, forgetting that he'd watched this very boy win the last event. 'Who's this?'

Billy shrank back from his stare. He looked as every bit as mean as he sounded.

'This is Billy Wheeler. He's in the tournament.'

'Really?' Duncan replied. 'Wheeler, eh? Now, why does that name ring a bell? Ah yes, I remember … Tom Wheeler. Your dad I presume? Nasty accident that … Quite shocking.'

Before Billy could reply, Mr Peddleton spotted an opportunity to take control while Duncan's rant had been disturbed.

'Mr Kelley, I'm sure I can help you with a Magbike, but I need a little time. Why don't you come through and we'll see what we can do? Billy, perhaps you can keep Mr Kelley's daughter company while we sort things out.'

Duncan exhaled loudly. 'Very well, Mr Peddleton. Although you'd better not be wasting my time. I need results. Louise, wait here. And don't babble!'

'Right then, Mr Kelley. Please follow me.'

When Duncan and Mr Peddleton stepped through the holographic display – taking the horrible atmosphere with them – Billy returned to his question.

'What's going on, Louise? Why is your dad freaking out?'

'Oh, it's nothing. He always gets cranky after Porting.'

'Have you only just got back from America?' Billy asked.

Louise looked down to the floor and fidgeted uncomfortably. 'No. We've been back for a while. We've just been travelling around a lot.'

Listening to Louise, Katie's instincts began to poke at her stomach. Something about the way she was fidgeting made her look uneasy. But why?

'Anyway, who's this?' Louise asked more confidently and managing a forced smile.

'This is Katie,' Billy told her, proudly.

Louise offered another uneasy smile. 'Hi, it's nice to meet you.'

Why do you look so nervous? Katie wanted to ask. 'It's nice to meet you too,' came instead. 'It must be awful trying to sort out a Magbike this close to the final?'

Louise nervously scratched at the back of her head. 'It's doing my head in. Our supplier let us down at the last minute, so we've got to find a new one.'

'No way! That's terrible? Who was it? We should probably tell the other competitors in case they have the same problem.

Louise was feeling an increasing amount of pressure: What were they doing here? Did they know something? Were they spying? Slightly panicked, she used the first excuse that came into her head. 'I don't think anyone else used them. Dad obviously forgot to do any research. Otherwise, we wouldn't have used them either.'

Billy found that very hard to believe. If he'd had any impression of Louise's dad, it was that he was all about being prepared. He'd seen it being put into practice during the tournament dinner. Although why she might lie about something like that, he didn't know. What he did know, was that things had begun to feel rather awkward. Louise didn't look comfortable at all.

Katie noticed it too. There was something about the conversation that was making Louise uneasy. She took a step closer. 'Well, I'm sure you'll get it sorted,' she said, reassuringly. 'You know ... I really do think we should contact—'

'Louise ... LOUISE?' Duncan shouted, from behind the spare parts display. 'Come here. We need to scan your Profiler.'

'Okay Dad, I'm coming.' She turned to Billy. 'I'd better go.'

The chance to ask more questions disappeared with Louise as she turned her back and dashed through the display.

I don't like your friend, Louise thought. *And I'm not sure I like you anymore, either. Not after you were sneaking around trying to catch me out. Whatever you were up to, you both need to mind your own business!*

Louise's paranoia about being caught cheating had rapidly turned into a defiant belief that people were trying to catch her out. Firstly, the man at Carbon Copy had wanted to know who her bike supplier was, and then the old man with her dad now, he'd wanted to know who had let them down too. To make it worse, after those two nosey old men, there was Billy, the one person she'd thought was so innocent when they first met. Even he was trying to trip her up.

Billy was the final straw. It was like a door had been opened in her mind that could never be closed again. If she was going to risk it all, then she'd get rid of anyone who got in her way. Friend, enemy, whatever, it didn't matter; she needed to achieve.

Back in Mr Peddleton's shop, Katie couldn't help but think that something was wrong. Louise's behaviour just didn't feel right. But what was it? Worry, fear, guilt, maybe? What if she was the Shocker? What if Anderson was the Shocker and Louise was just anxious about the final event? She couldn't go around accusing people; she'd make enemies for Billy and make herself look like a foolish little girl. But then there was what Duncan Kelley had said. He'd remembered Tom's accident and how it had been shocking. Was that what happened? Was Tom struck by the Shocker too?

I've got to tell someone, she thought. *Someone needs to know. But if I don't have proof, they'll think I'm just making it up to help Billy.* She looked at her best friend. Could she risk ruining his tournament by making false accusations? No, but the one thing she could do was talk to his dad.

In the run-up to the Mount Everest event, Katie would make three wrong decisions. Not telling someone at Space-Time Industries about the Shocker straight away: that was number one.

'Let's come back tomorrow, Billy. You can show me the Magbike then. It's probably best not to get in Louise's dad's way. Besides, I've just remembered I'm staying at Sophie's tonight. She wants me to help setup her new LifeEcho account.'

'Um, that's a no-can-do, K. I'm leaving tomorrow.'

'Oh, Billy. I'm sorry. But I really don't want to be here with Louise's dad acting the way he is. And I really do need to go and see Sophie, too. I'll make it up to you somehow, I promise.'

Billy tilted his head in that way. 'Don't worry about it, K. It's cool. But I'm going to wait and talk to Mr Peddleton and then go to the park. See you tomorrow before we go?'

'Yeah, of course. See you tomorrow.'

What Katie didn't want to explain was that several pieces of a puzzle were coming together, and they were all linked by suit failures: Billy's suit had shut down after receiving a shock, and then Dexter had his accident after he'd been shocked too – they had to be linked. But there was also a third accident, the one that belonged to Billy's Dad. His suit had failed in the same way.

Katie knew it wasn't possible that the Shocker was the same person, because Tom's accident had happened years ago. That only left her with one option: someone else was behind it all and they were helping the Shocker yet again. But who? That's what she needed to know, and fast. The last thing they needed was a repeat of Tom's accident. The problem was that nobody had stopped Tom's accident from happening back then, and nobody in Space-Time Industries appeared to know what was happening now.

Unfortunately for Katie, when the lights went out at the start of the final event, she wouldn't be able to do anything about it either.

53

'Hi Mrs Wheeler,' Katie said, puffing heavily, having run from the bus, all the way to Billy's front door.

'Katie,' Sue said, peering down the driveway. 'Isn't Billy with you?'

'No, he said he was going to the park. I think he's on the AirTube.' She kicked her feet at the ground looking a little sheepish. 'Actually, I came over because I wanted to talk to Mr Wheeler, if that's okay?'

Sue's expression changed from welcoming to questioning, but she seemed to accept Katie's silence when an explanation didn't arrive.

'He's in the lounge. Go right ahead.'

Katie shot through the door like a timid rabbit getting out of sight.

'Hi Katie,' Tom said, warmly. 'You didn't fancy another flight on the Air-Tube with Billy then?'

'No way! It makes me feel sick,' she replied, holding her stomach.

'I can well imagine,' Tom agreed, wishing he had the chance to find out for himself. 'So, what can I do for you?'

Katie had already decided that she wouldn't tell him everything – sometimes adults took over when all you needed was someone to listen – but she needed to know something very specific that maybe only he would know.

'I'm a bit worried about Billy. I think someone's cheating in the tournament.'

'Oh … what makes you think that?' asked Tom, intrigued. 'And how exactly do you think that I can help?'

'Well, Mr Wheeler—'

'Katie, after all this time, don't you think you should call me Tom?'

'Oh, right, yes.' Katie felt her cheeks begin to flush. 'Well, I was wondering if you … you know … your accident, whether you knew anything about it that you didn't ever tell Billy?'

'My … my accident?' Tom stammered, surprised by her question.

'Yeah,' she whispered, timidly. 'You see, the thing is, I was watching Billy in the forest when his suit locked up, and I watched a replay of Dexter's accident when his Gadget failed. It … it made me think about your accident.'

Tom was struggling to understand how his accident could have anything to do with a couple of suit glitches. Especially when it happened so long ago. 'I'm a bit confused, Katie. What could my accident have to do with anything that's happening now?'

'Well, I think there might be a link between them. I watched an old video of your accident, but the snow was too thick to see anything properly. I thought maybe you might have a Trace'

'A Memory Trace?'

'Um, yes.'

Katie's cheeks were burning with guilty embarrassment. She had no right to be bothering Tom and asking him questions about his accident. Billy had told her several times that he still got frustrated about it and she could sense it now.

'So, you think if I have a Trace, that you might see something in it which shows someone is cheating in the tournament now? I'm sorry Katie but you're barking up the wrong tree.' Tom's voice had changed – some of the gentle nature had disappeared. 'Space-Time industries investigated my accident. They said it was caused by a fault, just like they reported about Dexter's.' Tom knew in his heart that he'd never truly believed this, but there had never been proof to say otherwise.

'I know, but maybe—'

'I'm sorry Katie, but you've got things wrong. Nobody could get away with cheating these days and my accident certainly can't mean anything now.'

'I'm sorry Mr Wheeler. I didn't mean to upset you, I just … I'd better go.' Her cheeks felt like they were on fire. 'Is it still okay if I come and see Billy in the morning?'

Tom's smile didn't quite reach his eyes. 'Yes, of course Katie. That's fine. He'd love to see you.'

Katie stood up and left the house as quickly as her legs could carry her. Rushing through the garden gate she wondered if she could ever come back, but then Billy was her best friend. It didn't matter how embarrassed she felt, she had to see him off, no matter what.

***

Well on her way home, the blissfully cool breeze chilled Katie's cheeks like a cold wet flannel on sunburn. Despite Tom's insistence that she was wrong, she couldn't ignore the fact that she'd seen the same white spark before two suit failures. Someone had to be cheating. It was dishonest and wrong, not to mention the fact they risked hurting someone. The idea of a link between Tom, Billy and Dexter refused to go away. She'd been hoping that Tom would help, but it seemed he didn't have the Memory Trace she needed after all. Alone with her thoughts and her earphones playing music, she racked her brains. *Evidence,* she thought. *I need evidence.*

Startling her out of the puzzled thoughts, a firm hand grabbed hold of her shoulder. She whipped around, momentarily sure that Dean had finally caught up with her. But when she came face to face with her assailant, she found the worried eyes of Mrs Wheeler.

'Crikey Mrs Wheeler. You scared the life out of me!'

'Sorry Katie, I didn't mean to scare you, but I heard you talking to Tom. Do you know something about his accident?' She didn't have a clue how a teenager born several years later could possibly know anything about it, but if there was any hope what-so-ever of proving that Kurt Tuffnell was responsible, she'd take anything she could.

'I think I might know something,' Katie said, tentatively.

'Then take this,' Sue said, handing Katie Tom's Memory Trace. 'If it can help you, then use it. When Tom had his accident, they said it was a fault with the suit. But if you can prove otherwise, I need to know!'

'I'll do my best,' Katie whispered, still full of embarrassment. 'I really should go. I'll see you in the morning.'

'Yes, of course. You'll be wanting to see Billy.'

Katie smiled before running off, oblivious to the fact that she would not be returning.

54

Katie arrived at the Vault holding a photo of Tom that she'd printed straight from the Space-Time archives. He was dressed in a smart blue suit and was posing with his fellow contestants at the tournament dinner – no need for a wheelchair just yet. Thinking about him as she looked at the photo, it struck her what a terrible injustice it would be if his injury hadn't been an accident after all, but instead, that someone had done that to him on purpose. All of a sudden, the promise she'd made to Sue felt more important than ever.

Feeling like a crime detective, she pinned it up and studied the puzzle of pictures and random scribbles that filled the wall. There had to be a clue somewhere. It seemed impossible, but the idea that one person was responsible for it all refused to go away. Whoever had caused Tom's accident all those years ago might well be helping the Shocker now. Desperate to know more she grabbed her Holo-Tab and connected Tom's Memory Trace. Seeing it through his eyes, the Everest event flickered into life. It was time to find the truth.

***

Viewed through Tom's visor, Katie found herself staring at the red lights of the starting grid. Beneath him, the Magbike breathed – a powerful machine ready to launch. Before she could blink, the lights had changed, and Tom was tearing away from the start. His bike thrust through the bone chilling air, smothering the competitors behind him in a heavy blanket of white powder. As he raced toward the first climb his snow-track Gadget ripped at the icy surface, propelling him into a nail-biting battle with Kurt. Although she was only watching on her Holo-Tab, her skin prickled every time Kurt appeared.

When the edge of the first chasm neared, Katie watched Kurt veer into view from within the whirling snow. He had that knowing smile spread across his face. At first, it was all she could think about. Time and time again, she replayed the Trace, always transfixed by his unpleasant, cold smile. But then something at the edge of the screen caught her eye. It was so brief that at first, she thought her eyes were playing tricks on her. But the more she watched, the more it stood out. With her detective mind in full flow, she maxed the brightness on her Holo-Tab and pressed play once more.

At first it didn't make sense; she'd been expecting to see Kurt at the same time, but he was nowhere to be seen. But still, there it was, like a horrible little scratch on the pristine glass: a tiny white spark flashing across Tom's mirror. To Katie, the flash had lost all significance, it was where it came from that mattered. Frame by frame she played the Trace in reverse and followed the spark until it reached its owner.

She covered her mouth in shock! No longer hidden in darkness, she saw a face behind a visor. One with a mean and threatening scowl. It wasn't Kurt's face, but the face that belonged to Tom's attacker. She frantically paused the video and ripped Tom's tournament dinner photo from the wall. Her hands trembled as she placed it side by side with the Holo-Tab. Seeing it so clearly, sadness swept over her as if someone had erased all her happy memories in one go. It hadn't been an accident at all; somebody had stolen Tom's dreams by putting him in a wheelchair, and all these years later, she'd found the thief.

***

Alone in her bedroom, Katie churned through page after page of photos from the Space-Time archive. There were hundreds of images to look at, and every one of them had the name of the competitor above it. There were plenty of Tom, and lots of Kurt too, but whenever she saw the face from Tom's Memory Trace, his name didn't appear. What struck her as even more significant, was that the archive for 2081 simply had a blank space for whoever had finished the tournament in second place. Kurt Tuffnell had won, and Tom Wheeler was credited with third, but in second… nothing. It was like the man's identity had been erased all together. For Katie, it was evidence enough. She didn't need to be a genius to put it all together. The scowling face in Tom's mirror. The missing name on his photos. The blank space in the tournament results. They had to be to the same person.

In a spontaneous moment, she typed 'Space-Time Tournament 2081' into Google and pressed search. *Surely it can't be that simple*, she thought. But to her utter surprise, it was. In absolute shock and disbelief, she dropped her Holo-Tab, smashing the screen on the floor. Staring back at her through the spider web of cracks was a name that stunned her as if she'd just been attacked by the Shocker herself. 'It can't be,' she whispered pointlessly.

Anger and frustration began to boil in her like lava. If the name on the Holo-Tab belonged to the face in Tom's mirror, an awful injustice had been committed. She tapped on the screen and waited patiently for a new page to load. When it did, six words appeared that changed Katie's day irreversibly. They simply read: Head of Sales: Worthies Bike Outlet.

It was as this point that Katie made her second wrong decision – two down, one to go! She grabbed her backpack and dashed downstairs. Spying a piece of paper on the kitchen side she scribbled a note to her parents: she wasn't really staying at a friend's house overnight, but that's what she wrote. Then, before she could convince herself otherwise, she left for the International Travel Station. She was going to confront the thief!

55

At 8:55am, Sue Wheeler was sleeping peacefully when she woke to a cold rush of air engulfing her entire body.

'Quilt snatch!' Billy declared, snorting with laughter.

'Oh Billy, you little—'

'Now-now, Sue,' Tom said. 'I think they call that Karma.'

'You two are a pair of scoundrels,' she complained falsely.

Billy started for the door. 'Come on then! Breakfast is ready. We're leaving at eleven.' Without waiting for a reply, he disappeared from their bedroom and into the kitchen.

Sue could hear all manner of clatter and commotion when he started to serve up their breakfast, but she couldn't think about food, or even helping Tom out of bed. What played on her mind was the talk she'd had with Katie yesterday and whether there might be some chance of her finding the truth about Tom's accident.

***

It was 11:08am and long after he was ready to leave when Billy walked into the kitchen looking utterly miserable. Time had all but run out for Katie to see them off.

'I don't understand. She told me she'd be here,' he said, miserably. 'She's not answering her phone or anything.'

'Did you try calling her at home?' Sue asked, a niggle of concern beginning to grow.

'Yeah. There's no answer! Can we wait a bit longer?'

Tom wheeled himself into the kitchen, catching the end of their conversation. 'That's a no-can-do, Billy. If we don't leave now, we'll miss our flight. You know Katie, she'd have been here if she could.'

'But Dad,' Billy pleaded.

'Sorry Billy, you'll just have to call her when we get there.'

Billy groaned miserably before slouching off into the hallway. He was going to miss out on the hug he'd been hoping to repeat.

At 12:30pm Billy boarded an Ion-Jet at Bristol International Travel Station, headed for Kathmandu. Despite her promise to see him off and despite Billy making them wait five minutes longer than they could afford to, Katie was nowhere to be seen.

***

Billy stood in front of a Nano-port at Kathmandu Travel Station and gawped at it like a child staring at a pile of Christmas presents; he was moments away from experiencing his first ever Port. Having heard you can't breathe during Port jumps, he found himself hoping that he could hold his breath long enough to get through it. For now, at least, Katie's absence had slipped his mind.

Tom fidgeted impatiently. 'Come on then Billy. Hurry up or they'll fix the bus, and we'll have to take that.' Tom had never Ported either and given his permanent wheelchair status, he was eager to feel the freedom of weightlessness. 'Unless you want me to go first?' he half joked.

Not feeling entirely ready, Billy pressed his Profiler against the Focus before taking a deep breath and pressing his lips together. He stepped into the rainbow smeared bubble allowing it to take hold of him, pulling him into itself like a vacuum cleaner. Despite his feet never leaving the ground, he felt utterly weightless. A gentle squeeze then overwhelmed his entire body as if he were swimming deep under water before the hustle and bustle of the station shrank to a muffled hum. Outside, the blurry image of his parents disappeared. Everything turned as black as space, before instantly brightened to reveal completely new surroundings. To finish his journey, the bubble gave a heavy squeeze on his body before it popped, leaving him standing there in the Port.

His muffled hearing cleared to reveal the gentle whisper of mountain winds. He walked forwards feeling a mixture of elation and disbelief. His pale skin tingled with the bitter cold that welcomed him while the Himalayan mountains towered ominously above him – he'd arrived at Everest Base Camp. He stood and watched as the Port produce another bubble, before it popped to reveal his dad sitting in its place. Worry and concern instantly gripped at his lungs, stealing his breath. 'Dad are you okay?' he asked, dashing to the Port.

Tom's eyes glistened with tears. 'That was incredible,' he said, through a broken voice. 'I haven't felt that kind of freedom for as long as I can remember.'

'Maybe one day it can be forever,' Billy whispered.

'What was that?' Tom asked.

'Oh, nothing Dad.' The last time Billy and his dad had spoken about him getting any silly ideas – his Big Idea – he'd been saved from lying by Katie knocking at the front door. He hadn't told them about it then, and he wasn't about to tell anybody now. 'Can we check-in and go to our Demountable,' he said, changing the subject. 'I'm freezing out here.'

***

Anderson stood on the balcony of his own Demountable and gazed at the stunning landscape through his brand-new Sight Amplifier – yet another "sorry we can't be with you" gift from his parents. Spotting Khumbu Icefall, he shivered with fearful nerves: he knew that beneath the slow-moving sea of ice, lay a labyrinth of deep bluish chasms. They were the most dangerous part of the Everest event, and he dreaded the thought of navigating through them.

Resisting a second shudder he'd begun to look elsewhere when Billy popped up in the viewfinder. He was wearing a bright orange inflatable jacket and was pushing his dad's wheelchair toward the Demountables. Anderson's mood lifted at the sight of his friend, but it would soon drop out of sight like a discarded stone sinking beneath the ocean; Billy's strongest memory of Anderson was his conversation with Katie – the one putting him firmly in the frame as being the Shocker. Billy didn't really think Anderson could do such a thing, but after their next meeting, he'd struggle to believe anything else.

56

Sitting in his bedroom in Pilton, the bitter cold of the Himalayas felt more like a million miles away than just a simple Port journey. And it might as well have been, seeing as he wasn't planning on going.

The last argument Dean had endured with his dad refused to leave him alone. He'd laid awake half the night thinking about what had gone wrong with his family and spent most it staring into the dark. He was tired of the arguments, and tired of feeling worthless.

Maybe it's my fault, he said to himself, thinking of how his dad had always treated him. *Maybe if I'd been better then he wouldn't be so angry all the time. Maybe even Mum would still be here.* Fresh tears began to surface, but he quickly rubbed them away when his dad walked in.

'Why aren't you ready? We're leaving in five minutes!'

Dean looked down at the floor. 'I don't feel very well. I don't want to go anymore.'

'What do you mean, you don't want to go anymore? You have to!'

'Why, Dad? Why do I have to go?' Fresh tears were threatening to come back, and this time he wouldn't be able to stop them. He turned away knowing that in his dad's eyes, crying would only show weakness.

'You know why! They took away my tournament and everything else that mattered to me. So, you need to take it back. You'll be fine once we get moving. Now hurry up.' The moment the words had left his mouth, Kurt felt a black cloud of guilt settle over him. Did nothing else matter? Not even his own son? He hesitated for a moment on the brink of an apology, before walking out. He couldn't take it back. 'Five minutes,' he barked, from the hallway.

Try as he might to ignore it, the cloud of guilt that settled over Kurt would refuse to leave for the rest of that day. But when the time would come that it was too heavy to bear, Dean wouldn't be there to listen.

***

Back at Mount Everest, Louise was walking to her Demountable when she spotted Alisha leaving hers. Barely able to believe her luck, she seized the opportunity and offered her best fake smile.

'Hi Alisha.'

'Oh, hi Louise.'

'Listen. We've got to stick together, you and me.'

'We do?' Alisha asked, caught by surprise.

'Yeah. We're outnumbered by know-it-all boys who just don't care about us.' Louise offered a sympathetic voice. 'You remember what they did to you in Kielder Grounds, don't you?'

'How could I forget,' Alisha replied. 'At least Hiro got disqualified for putting a Hunter charm on me. But Dean, he got me trapped by the wolf and got away with it. You're right. We should stick together. Maybe we can do something to wind him up.'

Louise subconsciously rubbed her robotic arm. This time, there wasn't a Disruptor hidden inside, but a trigger. 'I already had an idea,' she said. 'I thought it might be fun to send them a message in the middle of the event.'

'A message?' asked Alisha, looking somewhat uneasy. 'What kind of message?'

Louise pulled a miniature silver cylinder from her backpack that had Holo-Laser Displays stamped on the side. 'It's a hologram laser display. You can programme them with messages like happy birthday and stuff. It hovers in the air like a giant sign. I thought it might be fun to put our own message up.'

'That's brilliant. What are we going to say?' Alisha asked, her eyes lighting up.

'I thought maybe you might like to choose,' Louise replied. 'Maybe something that would put off what they're doing or where they're going. There is just one thing though. I need you to go and set it up in the snow dunes above Khumbu Icefall. It's the best place for everyone to see it. I would do it, but I'd get spotted because my suit is black. but being white, yours would be completely hidden. We don't want anyone to know what we're up to. It'll ruin the fun.'

Alisha frowned a little. 'Uh … I guess I can,'

'Excellent,' Louise continued, before Alisha could change her mind. 'It'll be so funny. Let's go to the practice arena so we can plan what to say. Then afterwards, you can put the laser in the snow dunes. We'll need to be quick though, the final event starts in a couple of hours.'

Alisha and Louise left for the practice arena walking arm in arm like two best friends going to a party. One of them believing she would be planting a cheeky message, the other knowing the alarming truth.

57

Having scanned himself into the practice arena, Billy stood beside his bike and looked at the enormous crater of snow and ice. He'd never ridden a Magbike before, and his usual self-confidence seemed to have locked itself away. It felt all the worse, given that he'd left his parents at the Demountable and only had Mr Peddleton for company.

'It's bigger than I thought it would be,' he said with a trembling voice.

'Oh, it always looks worse than it is,' Mr Peddleton, said offering encouragement.' You'll be fine once you're on the bike.'

'But what if I can't—'

WHAP! Billy's visor turned completely white.

'Ha-ha … I got you!'

Billy wiped a hand across his visor to see Anderson preparing another snowball.

'I didn't think I'd hit you from all the way over here. Come on, snowball fight!'

Billy bent down and prepared his own snowball before launching it at Anderson. It hit him square in the chest.

'I don't think you really have time for a that, Billy.'

Billy looked at Mr Peddleton and then at the snowball in his hand. Reluctantly, he dropped it. 'I better not,' he said, turning to face Anderson. 'I need to practice.'

'We don't need to practice,' Anderson replied, wiping the remnants of Billy's snowball from his chest to reveal the red slash that cut across it. 'We'll be fine.'

'But I've never ridden a Magbike before.'

'Oh, don't worry about it! Practice is for Noobs.'

'How can you not want to practice?' Billy argued. 'It's the final!'

Unable to resist its draw, Billy's eyes settled on the bright red slash that cut across Anderson's suit. Out of nowhere, Katie's words came flooding back: 'I bet whoever shocked you and the wolf, shocked Dexter too. And I bet whoever it was, has a red mark on their suit.'

He thought of the jolt that sent him sprawling across the floor in Kielder Forest; his eyes *had* seen a fuzzy blur of red before it disappeared into the fog. It had to be Anderson's red lightning bolt, didn't it? As if to further re-enforce his suspicion, he remembered the way Anderson had modified the robotic character in his Space-Time bard game; it gave him a shock when he'd picked it up. It really hurt! *Maybe you want to have a snowball fight because you don't need to practice. Maybe you really are the Shocker Katie told me about.* 'I don't want to,' he said, before he could think more rationally.

'Why not?' Anderson asked in surprise. 'I thought you'd be the first one to join in.'

'I just don't want to. I need to practice.'

'But I wanted to have a snowball fight.'

Billy turned his back and walked toward his bike … WHAP! Another snowball disintegrated on the back of his head.

'Come on, Billy. Don't be a Noob.'

'I said no. I'm not interested.' Then, under his breath, 'I don't like cheats.'

Somewhat annoyed and totally out of character, Anderson smashed a snowball into the ground. 'Fine! Sorry for bothering you!'

Billy felt a pang of guilt, but he couldn't help himself. Look at the way Anderson was acting, just messing about and not even wanting to practice. Surely you needed to practice! Unless you knew something that others didn't. Billy had thought only people like Dean would cheat, but it looked like others did too.

'Um, maybe you should get on the bike,' Mr Peddleton suggested, feeling rather awkward. 'Just get yourself moving and take it steady. Do a couple of laps so you can feel what it's like. Then maybe try riding some of the banked curves.'

Trying to put Anderson out of his mind, Billy focused on the arena. He didn't mind the idea of the banked curves: they looked quite smooth and forgiving. It was the ramps over the chasms that bothered him; the normally soft looking dunes of snow had given way to grey fingers of rock that looked ready to poke a hole right through you.

Taking a deep breath, he stood by the bike and gripped the handlebars. The moment his hands touched them the bike took a deep breath as if it had come to life. When he twisted the throttle, vents on the side of the bike opened and closed like fish gills breathing Ion energy. With each twist, the handlebars pulled at his hands, challenging his grip. It felt like he was playing tug-of-war with a team of rugby players.

'You need to step over the bike and sit down,' Mr Peddleton told him. 'The magnetic bond needs to activate otherwise you won't be able to hold on.'

A freshly nervous Billy did as he was told and stepped over the bike. Instantaneously, his legs and feet were sucked onto the bodywork by the magnetic bond. 'I'm tipping over. I'm going to fall!' he yelled in panic.

'I thought you were brave,' Mr Peddleton teased, knowing that no such thing would happen.

Instead of falling over Billy sat there with his feet off the ground, completely balanced. Inside his mind, a key was turning, unlocking his confidence once again.

'This is awesome! It's like I'm hovering.'

Before Mr Peddleton could tell him what to do next, Billy twisted the grip, forcing the Magbike to lurch forwards with a ferocious burst of Ion energy. It blew Mr Peddleton clean off his feet and sent him bum first into a pile of snow. Billy's voice came drifting back in sporadic bursts as he Kangaroo jumped across the snow. 'Whoa … sorry … Mr Peddleton … I'll … be back.'

For all his effort, Billy couldn't control the bike. Every time he tried to twist the throttle it lurched wildly back and forth like a bucking bronco. Clouds of snow blew into the air filling most of the arena with an icy fog.

'Look at that idiot,' Dean said to his dad, watching Billy from across the practice arena. 'I'm glad I came now. This is going to be easy.'

He jumped on his bike and gripped the bars. When the same familiar breath signalled that his bike was ready, he opened the throttle to max and shot off like a bullet from a gun. He sped across the crater of icy snow, deliberately aiming at Billy before throwing his bike into a slide, ploughing an enormous wave of snow directly into Billy's path.

'Let's see you deal with that, Weeweeler!'

Mr Peddleton watched Billy disappear into the snow, expecting to see him crawl from the cloud on his hands and knees. But instead, saw him burst from it doing a ridiculous wheelie.

'I've got it Mr Peddleton. This is brilliant!'

Billy raced around the practice arena picking up speed with every lap. Despite his confidence growing, he still avoided the menacing jumps. Every time he approached, his nerve gave way, forcing him to swoop sheepishly around the side.

'I was right, Weeweeler. You don't have what it takes,' Dean yelled, annoyed that Billy hadn't fallen off already. 'You're a wuss.'

Billy's mind was thrown back to school where Dean had taunted him relentlessly in front of the other kids. Like a shaken bottle of Heliyumm, determination bubbled ferociously inside of him. He didn't have to put up with being bullied anymore. On the very next lap he powered his bike out of the curve at full throttle and launched himself at the ramp. Dean watched from the seat of his bike, stunned into silent awe as Billy appeared to defy gravity and floated over the chasm with ease.

Maybe this isn't going to be so easy after all, he thought, begrudgingly.

Thanks to what Louise was planning, little did he know just how difficult things would become.

***

On the opposite side of the world, Katie was sitting in the bus stop opposite Worthies Bike Outlet. After spending the night at the Travel Station – having used some of her sizeable allowance to Port to America – she'd arrived at Worthies full of angry determination. But when she'd called her parents to say she'd be staying at her friends for another night, her phone had died, and her nerve had died with it. She was a million miles from the infinitely sensible Katie Jack that Billy adored so much.

It was over an hour since she'd sat down, and she hadn't moved an inch – bravery was a hard thing to find when you were all alone. Deep in thought, she was deciding if she should go ahead and confront the Shocker when a news article popped up on the screen beside her. The headline flashed brightly, easily grabbing her attention: 'Space-Time USA competitor involved in mysterious suit failure; suffers injury.'

It scrolled across the screen several times before an unseen newsreader began to describe the incident.

This was the point when Katie made her third and final wrong decision. By the time the newsreader had finished her story, Katie was storming towards Worthies Bike Outlet, fists clenched like she was ready to fight.

'Hello, how can I help you?' the pleasant looking man asked.

The man she'd seen scowling in Tom's mirror was much younger than the one who'd just offered his help, but still, there was no doubt: it was him.

'I know who you are, and I know what you've been doing!' she said, angrily.

'I'm sorry? I don't understand,' the man replied, looking quite calm.

Katie's blood began to boil at his blatant lie. 'I know who you are, and I know what you did to Tom Wheeler.'

The welcoming expression that had greeted her disappeared faster than a click of fingers and was replaced with a scowl that made her shiver with fear.

'Is that so?' he sneered. 'Then you'd better come with me.'

Frightened, Katie tried to retreat, but he was too fast. He grabbed at her arm and snatched her sleeve; she wouldn't be leaving anytime soon, and she knew it.

58

Billy stood with his hands on his hips – subconsciously copying the missing Katie – and stared at the Magbike that Harvey was cleaning. Just like his Kinetic suit, it was covered with interlocking fish-like scales forming a dense chainmail skin.

'It looks even more aerodynamic than Miss Cravity,' he joked.

'Billy, you shouldn't say things like that about your teacher!'

'Sorry Mum, you're right. There isn't anything more aerodynamic than Miss Cravity.' Billy burst into fits of laughter at his own joke.

Despite being serious, Sue couldn't help but break into a smile herself. 'Oh Billy, you are terrible.'

'What's so funny?' Tom asked, wheeling himself into the garage.

'Your son's been telling jokes about his teacher. Saying that she's aerodynamic. But we shouldn't be making jokes about her, should we!'

'You're absolutely right, Sue. Being slim enough to blow away in a stiff breeze is no joking matter.'

Billy bellowed fresh fits of laughter at his dad's comical reply.

'Tom! Seriously!' Sue scolded.

'Misbehaving again are we, Tom?'

Everyone in the room froze as if a bucket of ice-water had been thrown over them. Billy immediately recognised the voice but couldn't believe his ears: it didn't make sense. He slowly turned around and found a large, suit filling man standing in the doorway. He was wearing a full-length black raincoat with his face hidden beneath a wide brimmed hat.

'Hello Billy. I thought I'd come and wish you good luck for the final. It's been quite the rollercoaster, watching you compete – almost as good as watching your father.' The man looked up from beneath his hat to meet eyes with a stunned Billy.

'Mr Crankworth!' he blurted out, staring at the wide brimmed hat and black raincoat. 'It really was you at Overhang Arena! I saw you by standing Mum and Dad.'

'Yes, you did. You know, it's not very nice to tell jokes about Miss Cravity. She is a Spotter after all.'

Billy's cheeks flushed strawberry red. 'Miss Cravity is a spotter?'

'Of course. Why do you think she always happened to be there when you were performing one of your many feats? She's been keeping an eye on you for quite a while. In fact, she was the one who suggested I enrol you in the tournament early. I'm rather pleased she did. She chose wisely, wouldn't you say?'

'I … but if Miss Cravity is a spotter and she works with you… then you must be—?'

'The Space-Time President,' Mr Crankworth said, finishing Billy's sentence.

'But why didn't you say anything?'

'Perhaps you should think about what school would be like if your friend Dean thought I was showing you favouritism. You were competing with him already. That's why I've been trying to get you to stop.' He looked over at Billy's dad. 'It hasn't been all that easy,' he said, giving Tom a wink. 'It's good to see you again my friend. I do hope that we can meet for coffee some—' His phone shrilled loudly in his pocket cutting his words off. Looking awkward, he turned his back to them before answering. 'I told you not to call me on this number unless—' This time it was Mr Crankworth's turn to look like he'd been doused in ice-cold water when a look of shock filled his face. 'What? No, don't do anything. No, I mean it!' He hung up without another word and turned to leave.

'Robert? Is everything okay?' asked Tom.

'Sorry Tom, I don't have time to explain.' He looked at Billy. 'Good luck young man.' Before another word could be said, he left.

'What was that about?' Sue asked.

Tom frowned. 'I have no idea. But it seemed urgent, whatever it was.'

Tom had no idea how much he'd underestimated the importance of the call that took Mr Crankworth away with such urgency. If he'd known what the caller had reported, then maybe things in Billy's future would have turned out differently.

'You didn't say you were friends with the Space-Time President!' Billy complained. 'Why didn't you tell me?'

'Sorry Billy, we don't have time to talk about that right now. You'll be getting called down to the start soon.'

As if on cue, Schrader's voice surged from the speakers. 'Would all competitors for the Mount Everest Challenge make their way to the starting grid, I repeat, all competitors to the starting grid.'

Tom was hit with a sudden flash of déjà vu. His entire life had been thrown into turmoil only moments after starting his own final all those years ago. But this time he wasn't the one competing – it was his son.

In a flash of panic, he didn't want Billy to leave; something just felt wrong. Why had Robert randomly visited and then rushed off like his world was going to end? *You're just being paranoid,* he said to himself. *Bad memories, that's all it is.* Dismissing his fears as foolish emotion, he uttered the words he would soon give anything to take back. 'Come on then Billy, let's get your bike and head down to the start.'

59

Billy wheeled his Magbike across the starting grid and stopped at the line that marked the beginning of his final event. 'Dad, this place looks like Cheddar gorge when it snowed last year.'

Tom looked up at the steep snowy cliffs. 'It does. Although we don't have any wooden boxes filled with people back in Cheddar.'

Billy looked at the spectator stands that made Neverthaw Ravine so colourful. In a funny way they reminded him of the favelas of Brazil, looking like a disorderly staircase climbing the cliffs, all tied together with Tibetan prayer flags fluttering in the breeze. *I wish you were here to see this place*, he thought when Katie came to his mind. If there was one part of the tournament she'd been excited about, it was seeing the prayer flags. To Katie they held the hopes and dreams of the people who'd put them there.

Having not spoken to her since their visit to Peddleton's, Billy assumed that Katie would be watching in her bedroom, or maybe even the Vault, but he was wrong. Instead, she was locked in Fletch's secret showroom, powerless to stop the events that were about to unfold.

'That's my queue to leave,' Tom said, pointing to Schrader who was approaching. He gave Billy a pat on the arm. 'Good luck Billy-boy.'

'Thanks Dad. See you later.'

Left to his own devices, Billy sat on his bike and stared along the ravine toward the first chasm. Flanked by two large spurs of rock, it looked ready to swallow him whole. An unexpected bout of nerves forced a shiver down his spine as if he were frozen to the core.

'What's the matter Weeweeler?' Dean asked. 'Scared?' Not waiting for an answer, he smiled mockingly and took his place in front of Billy.

Ahead of Dean, Billy could see Louise already sitting on her bike and giving her black hair a flick before putting on her helmet. Next to her, Anderson was just milling around smiling. Billy looked on in utter disbelief when Anderson made a fresh snowball and launched it into the crowd.

Billy watched in disbelief. *You've got to be kidding me. Only a cheat could be confident enough to mess around like that!*

Behind Billy, the last competitor on the grid was Alisha. When he glanced behind and saw her staring at the ground and kicking awkwardly at the snow, it gave him some amount of comfort; at least someone else appeared to be nervous.

'Ladies and Gentlemen, please welcome our competitors to the grid. They've shown courage, they've demonstrated commitment and they've earned their place in the final. So, shake the ground with noise and show your appreciation.'

Billy looked up to the stands and spotted his parents waving and cheering. He'd expected to see Mr Crankworth with them like he had done at the Grand Canyon, but there was no sign him. What could have been so important to take him away from the final?

'Competitors, in this event there are no Focuses to find and there are no riddles to solve. There is only Everest and each other. To start your event, you must race past Base Camp before arriving at Khumbu Icefall. There, you will leave the comfort of your Magbike and climb Grivel's Chasm before skydiving from Khumbu Outpost to be reunited with your bike. From there it's a flat-out race to the finish line here. As is customary for the final event, for crossing the finish line first we will award fifty Time-Credits. Everything is to play for, so I say to all of you. Never give up!'

With the bright sparkle of the first starting light, the competitors readied themselves for the start. Dean gripped his handlebars ever harder, while behind him, Billy hunched down into his seat. Anderson squeezed his heels into the sides of his bike and Alisha stared at the lights not daring to blink. At the back of the gird, Louise watched the lights begin to sparkle one by one and rubbed her robotic arm. Nothing could stop her now.

60

'Please let me go. We can still stop the race,' Katie begged as Fletch sat motionless opposite her. 'Just because something is done, it doesn't mean it can't be un-done.'

'No, it's too late,' he said, robotically.

'But it's not too late, you can change things. You only need to make a phone call.'

Fletch snapped into life from his apparent trance. 'Didn't you listen to what I said, girl? I sold her a Hologram laser with a shockwave generator inside it.'

'Why would you do that?' Katie asked, trying to find a way of convincing him to let her go.

'She said she needed to be an achiever so she could finally make her dad proud. Believe me girl, I know how that feels. I thought she was going to use it at the first or second event, not at Mount Everest. I wouldn't have sold it to her otherwise!'

Katie thought she saw glimpse of regret sweep across Fletch's face, but it quickly disappeared.

'Anyway, the race already started,' he continued. 'What's done is done. I would have been fine if you hadn't interfered. But now you've come along and ruined it!'

'Ruined what, Fletch?'

Fletch's expression changed from contempt to one of shocked fear. 'Dad? What are you doing here?'

'Mr Crankworth!' Katie said, gasping in surprise.

'What have you done?' Mr Crankworth shouted. 'Didn't I make myself clear when we last spoke? His voice bristled with anger. 'What have you done? Tell me!'

Fletch looked utterly stunned. 'But how—'

'I've had someone watching you since my last visit. I got a call telling me you were keeping someone captive. I couldn't bring myself to believe it, but now I can see it for myself. What on earth do you think you are you doing?'

'He sold a shockwave generator to Louise,' Katie said, interrupting. 'I think she's going to use it in the race.'

Mr Crankworth almost stumbled in shock. 'You fool, Fletch. Didn't you learn anything after what happened to Tom?'

'You know about Fletch and Tom?' Katie asked, stunned.

'That doesn't matter right now, Katie. We have to stop the race.'

'You know I didn't mean to hurt him like that!' Fletch argued. 'But you always treated me like a disappointment. Like I was never good enough. All I wanted to do was make you proud, and all you did was disown me. Do you know how humiliating that was? It destroyed me.'

Katie thought she spotted a hint of guilt show in Mr Crankworth's expression before it snapped back to anger.

'I don't want to hear another word, Fletch. You're coming with me. Katie, you can come too. We're going to Everest. I can only hope that we can stop—'

Mr Crankworth trailed off at the sight of his son's expression.

'It's too late,' Fletch whispered. 'She's used it.'

Mr Crankworth and Katie turned to look at the Holo-Tab. They could only watch in disbelief as drone cameras broadcast the devastating avalanche. Smothered by a wall of ice and snow, Khumbu Icefall disappeared in front of their eyes. Anyone inside had no hope of escape.

'NO!' Katie screamed. 'No, no, no!'

***

Tom was the first to spot Katie as she ran toward the Demountable. 'Katie? What are you doing here?'

'I'll explain later,' she said, rushing the words out. 'Where's Billy?'

Tom's voice filled with gloom. 'We don't know. There's been an avalanche. Three of them made it to the finish, but Billy and Dean … they're … missing.'

Katie's heart sank. What if Billy had been hurt in the avalanche? What if she never got to say how she really felt about him?

Mr Crankworth stepped forward and put his hand on Tom's shoulder. 'We'll find them, I promise. Where's Sue?'

'She's inside with Kurt. He came over as soon as he knew they were missing. The man's inconsolable.'

'I'm going to find them,' Mr Crankworth promised. 'Both of them.' He sighed and looked at Katie. 'I need to go. Will you … explain?'

'I'll try.' She turned to Tom. 'You'd better come inside.'

61

Oh, my head … Why is it so dark? A hundred questions rattled through Billy's mind before it all came flooding back: he was standing at the bottom of Grivel's chasm when a burst of energy battered his suit. He'd barely had a chance to turn his back on the snow when his whole world turned dark. Fear began to rush through his body and threatened to drive him crazy, but then he heard a distracting voice.

'Urgh, what's happening?'

'Who's that?' Billy asked, staring into complete darkness.

'I can't move,' the voice responded. 'I don't like it. My leg hurts.'

'Hold on. I'll try and get to you.'

'Hurry up. Please.'

'Dean? Is that you?'

'Yeah. Who's that?'

I shouldn't bother helping you, Billy thought. *After how you've treated me.* But something inside him said no. He thought back to seeing Dean get a whack on the head from his dad and imagined what he must have felt after the Grand Canyon mistake; he'd momentarily looked terrified. Was he scared of his own dad? Was he ever shown any care at all? Guilt filled Billy's stomach like a giant meal eaten too quickly. No matter what Dean had done, he didn't deserve to be left alone.

'I'm on my way,' he replied. 'You need to keep talking so I know where you are. I can only see snow.'

He tried to move and was promptly reminded that he couldn't; the snow had packed tightly around him like he'd jumped in a vat of quick drying concrete. *What am I going to do? I'm stuck.* He closed his eyes and thought about Katie – she'd know what would do. The first thing of course, would be to do that hand-on-hips look of hers. Then she'd come up with something simple but genius.

'Maybe you should try your Gadget, Billy-boy,' she said.

Billy's eyes popped open. 'Thank you, K,' he whispered. 'You're the best!' He clenched his hands into fists and activated his Gadget, triggering a wonderful noise to fill his ears. His arms then began to vibrate as two Ice-pick Chisels extended from his wrists. They were supposed to help with climbing, but they did an even better to job pulverising and melting the packed snow in front of him. 'Dean. I need to know where you are,' Billy repeated.

'I'm over here,' Dean said, obligingly.

Chiselling and melting the snow ahead of him, Billy crawled along a short tunnel. With every inch gained, Dean's voice grew louder and clearer until finally he hit something hard.

'Hey, that's my head!' Dean complained.

Billy stopped and wiped the snow from Dean's visor.

'Weeweeler? What are you doing here?'

'It's nice to see you too,' Billy said, sarcastically.

Dean looked away defiantly. 'I can't move my leg.'

'Don't worry, I'll get you out.' He worked his way around Dean's body, chiselling and melting the snow as he went, but when he got to the bottom of his leg, he found a boulder pinning it down. 'There's a massive piece of ice,' Billy explained. 'If I carry on, I might hurt you. I'm going to get help instead.'

Dean's face filled with fear. 'No! Don't leave me, Wee—' He stopped, realising he was about to use that ridiculous nickname for the boy who'd come to help him. 'Please Billy, don't leave me.'

Billy stopped still, utterly stunned by Dean's vulnerability. 'Okay, but if you don't want me to go and get help then I'll need to chisel the ice away. What if I hurt you?'

'I don't care,' Dean replied. 'I tell you what. I challenge you to get me out!'

Billy frowned. 'A challenge … Really?' He thought back to last challenge that Dean had set; the day he'd split his trousers in school, showing his underwear to everyone. It had turned out to be horrendously embarrassing and got him in trouble. 'Okay, a challenge. But you've got to make me a promise.'

'A promise? What promise?'

'You remember the last challenge I did when I ripped my trousers and showed my underwear to everyone? Well, you have to promise you'll wear a pair of pants on your head for first lesson at next week.'

'Fine … Just get me out!'

Billy smiled. 'I was joking you know, but now you promised.'

'Oh, very funny,' Dean said, before a hint of a smile touched his lips; it was the closest they'd come to getting along since they'd met.

When Billy started chiselling, Dean felt a powerful vibration shudder through his entire body. Small shards of ice began to ping off his visor making him flinch. Frankly, he was scared.

Billy worked at the ice boulder, chiselling, and chipping away for what felt like eternity when without warning, a violent shudder forced him to turn away and wince in fear.

'Ow!' Dean cried. 'Hurry up, it's crushing my foot.'

Billy looked back at the boulder to see it had started sinking into the hole he'd dug. He began chiselling again, forcing himself to ignore Dean's complaints of pain, but every time he chipped the ice, it sank even further. If he didn't get Dean's foot out soon it would be crushed.

'I've got an idea,' he said, pausing. 'I'm going to carry on chipping it away, but when I shout, you've got to pull your leg as fast as you can!'

'Okay, okay. Just hurry … please!'

Billy began to chisel the ice again. He was concentrating all his effort on a large crack in the icy boulder, when suddenly, it splintered like a shattering piece of glass.

'Now!' he yelled.

Dean pulled with all his might and with a grinding jolt, his foot came free. 'You did it!' Dean said, elated. 'Come on, let's go! I can't stand it in here.' He tried to move but panic gripped him once more. 'My legs won't move! I'm going to be stuck here forever.'

'Oh, don't be a dramatic Doris,' Billy said, teasingly. 'I'll take you with me. I promise.'

'Dramatic Doris?' Dean replied, in a high-pitched voice. 'Quite the comedian, aren't you!'

'Comes from trying to keep out of trouble at school,' Billy said, making eye contact.

Dean looked away. 'I'm sorry … you know … for all of it.'

'Oh, don't worry about it, Doris.' As it turned out, an apology was all Billy had needed. He held his fists up to show Dean the Ice-pick Chisels. 'Come on, let's get out of here.'

62

Despite being filled with people, the Wheeler's Demountable remained utterly silent. Katie had done her best to explain what she'd learned during her investigation, and it had rendered everybody speechless. Nobody knew what to say to Kurt, and he didn't know what to say to anyone else. The silence was only broken when the door burst open, and Mr Crankworth came barrelling inside.

'We've got them!' he said. 'A rescue drone found them sitting on Khumbu Icefall. They'll be on their way back any moment.'

Sue burst into tears of relief and slumped back in her chair.

Kurt touched her shoulder. 'They're okay Sue.' He looked at Mr Crankworth but didn't have the energy to be angry; it had been washed away by his tears. 'I think you have some explaining to do.'

'I suppose I do,' Mr Crankworth said. Looking like a man standing in front of a court jury, he sat down in front of them and starting with Tom, his story began. 'For too many years I've been living with the guilt of what happened to you, Tom. My son Fletch, he cheated you out of the life you deserved. He was the one who'd disconnected the power pack from your suit. He didn't expect you to make it to the start, but when you did, he used a Disruptor to try and win the tournament instead. Well ... you know the rest. When I found out what happened, I panicked. If anybody had found out what he'd done it would have destroyed his future, so I sent him away and covered up the truth. I've tried to make it up to you since, but I fear I've failed you. I would have given you everything I ever had, but it would have raised impossible questions. I'm so sorry.'

He looked at the ground before turning to Kurt. 'I don't have enough words to apologise to you, either. I thought letting you take the blame and paying you to leave the tournament was the answer, but

I never imagined your family would break up because of it. I don't know how I can ever—' his voice broke, no more words would come.

Feeling sorry for Mr Crankworth, Katie continued the story. 'Ever since he was sent away, Fletch has wanted to ruin the tournament. He's been helping Louise Kelley with a Disruptor of her own. When he found out, Mr Crankworth told Fletch to stop or be exposed, but instead of coming clean when he had the chance, he kept quiet about the shockwave generator he'd sold her. That's what caused the avalanche today. She set it off to try and win the event.'

With the end of her words, came silent shock. Nobody really knew what to say. But then breaking the silence like a jackhammer smashing concrete, the Demountable door banged open.

'I think we're a bit late,' Billy remarked, tumbling through the door. 'Does this mean I didn't win?'

'I think it means neither of us did,' Dean added.

'BILLY!' Katie yelled, running across the room and throwing her arms around him. 'You're okay.'

'Of course,' he said, hugging her back. Before he knew it, Sue was there too, and then Tom. 'I love you,' he said, hugging them all, but looking at Katie.

Dean turned to his dad and found immense guilt filling his eyes.

'Dean, I'm so sorry. I thought I'd lost everything, but I was wrong, I still had you. It was never your fault. It was always mine.' The guilt in his eyes was replaced with fresh tears. 'I've been a terrible father. I'll make it up to you somehow, I promise.'

Forgetting all those around him, Dean ran over and hugged his dad for the first time in as long as he could remember. In the peace of the moment Mr Crankworth slipped away.

'Who won then?' asked Billy, struggling to hide his disappointment.

'That's a bit complicated,' Tom replied. 'Strictly speaking, Louise Kelley crossed the line first, then Anderson and Alisha. But if what Katie tells us is right, then Louise will be disqualified, which means the true winner is Anderson.'

'What did Louise do?' Billy asked, looking at Katie.

'She was the Shocker. She used a shockwave generator to trigger the avalanche you were trapped in.'

'She was the shocker?' Billy repeated in disbelief. 'But why would she want to do that?'

'I know why,' Dean said. 'Her parent-monster. She was trying not to be a disappointment to her dad. She was desperate to win.'

Billy grabbed his head in panic. 'Oh No! I thought Anderson was the Shocker. I was horrible to him. I've got to find him and say sorry.'

'What's the Shocker?' Sue asked, with her, what have you been hiding from me, look.

'Oh, um, don't worry, Mum. I'll tell you when I get back.' He grabbed the door handle to leave when for the final time, a deep and powerful voice boomed over the speakers, stopping him in his tracks.

'Ladies and gentlemen, I am relieved to tell you that the two competitors trapped by today's avalanche have managed to escape and are now with their families. However, it is with tremendous sadness that I must confirm the avalanche was not caused by mother nature, but by the reckless actions of a competitor who has now been disqualified. Despite the extraordinary circumstances, we must of course have our winner. As such, the competitor's positions will remain as they were after the Grand Canyon event, and I invite you to celebrate their success with us at the presentation.'

Billy turned to his dad. 'Is he for real?'

'I … I think so,' Tom stuttered. 'I'm sorry Billy. I know how much it meant to you.'

Billy just stared at him blankly. *I can't go back and change things,* he thought, miserably.

Tom turned to Kurt. 'Come on, you can push me to the presentation. I think we probably have some talking to do, wouldn't you say?'

'I think we probably do,' Kurt agreed.

***

Despite his sadness at losing the tournament and the chance to change the past, Billy stood below the presentation podium and stared in awe. A complicated jigsaw of granite boulders formed the pyramid-like monument reaching towards the sky. In some ways, it looked like it could collapse at any moment, but to Billy, it looked like it had existed for as long as Mount Everest itself. Tibetan prayer flags stretched from the highest boulder, hanging in sweeping loops like a corridor to the top.

Anderson was stood on the top-most step, flanked by Dean and Alisha. Despite Dean being on the podium, Billy could see the sadness that lingered between him and his dad; they had a long road ahead of them. He looked at Anderson, whose parents weren't even there on the most important day of his life; despite being surrounded by hundreds of people, he looked lonelier than a lost child. In the distance, he could see Mr Crankworth and his son. They both stood out of the way, alone with only their shame for company.

Finally, he settled on his parents. Together, they beamed at him with love and pride. That was the moment when he realised despite his dad being in a wheelchair, and for all the challenges it had brought them, they'd always shared a love and happiness that the others had lost a long time ago. In all of this, it felt like they were the lucky ones. He couldn't help but see things in a new light. His big idea had been to change the past and save his dad from injury, but now, given the chance, he would have gone back to change their lives instead.

'Ladies and Gentlemen,' Schrader began. 'In recognition of his achievement, it gives me great pleasure to award Anderson Toms with a Mount Everest Insignia and a scholarship in the Space-Time Programme.' He pressed an Everest shaped Insignia to Anderson's chest like rare honourable medal. Made of pure silver and topped in diamond dust like snow-capped peaks, it was the most precious Insignia that anyone could own. 'Congratulations young man. What a remarkable achievement. Ladies and Gentlemen, I present to you our incredible Tournament Winner!'

Anderson threw his arms in the air and began jumping around like he was dancing on hot coals. Above him, Laser fireworks streaked across the sky and confetti canons billowed enormous plumes of multi-coloured confetti into the air. After an extraordinary final event, the Space-Time Tournament had its winner.

Watching from beneath the multi-coloured paper storm, Billy tried to absorb every single detail. Throughout his entire life he'd dreamed of being in the tournament, never believing that it could ever really happen. He closed his eyes and framed the image in his mind. Forever and beyond, he would never forget this moment.

63

Katie walked into Bristol International Travel Station and promptly dashed to the nearest shop to get the latest edition of Space-Time magazine. By the time she left the store, Billy had only just caught up.

'Did you talk to him?' she asked.

'Yeah. But it doesn't matter.'

'Of course it does. What did you say?'

'I said I was sorry for thinking he could have been the Shocker and that I was an idiot. But it doesn't matter.' He beamed at her, beginning to jig around.

'What are you doing? Stop acting funny.'

'I can't help it,' he said, almost dancing in front of her.

'What? What is it?'

Billy held his hand out and showed her. Sitting in the middle of his palm was a Black Insignia. 'Anderson gave it to me. He said it's from Mr Crankworth. It's his way of saying sorry for what happened to Dad. It's a Time-Ticket. He gave me it so we can sell it.'

Katie narrowed her eyes. 'You're trying to prank me! There's no way he's given you a Time-Ticket. They're too valuable.'

Billy didn't say anything, he simply shook the Insignia. Sure enough, a holographic image popped out of the top and hovered in the air. The Space-Time logo floated in front of her eyes, with a Time-Ticket crest underneath.

'No way!'

'I'm not going to sell it though. I can still finish my big idea.'

Katie's smile disappeared instantly.

'I'm sorry K, but I have to try. I can fix things.'

She handed him the copy of Space-Time Magazine. Mr Crankworth and his son were plastered across the front page under the dramatic headline: Can Time Really Heal All Wounds? 'I know you do,' she said, 'but I can't pretend to be happy about it.'

'Come on you two,' Sue shouted from across the station. 'We've got to get going!'

'What are you going to tell your parents?' Katie asked.

'I don't know yet. I need to think about it. Meet me at the Vault tomorrow?'

'Sure … why not.' She gave him a brief hug before leaving to meet her own parents. She would barely sleep that night, knowing that the boy she'd come to fall for was about to risk everything because he loved his dad. How could she argue with that?

***

Katie arrived at the Vault to find Billy sitting in his wonky chair and reading his copy of Space-Time magazine. He looked up and offered a generous smile.

'Morning K,' he said, happily.

'Hi Billy,' she replied, glumly. 'Enjoying the magazine?'

'More than you'd think!'

'That's great,' she replied, her voice not even sounding close to what the word meant.

Undeterred, Billy continued. 'Well, it says that Louise Kelley was disqualified, and that nobody in her family can ever compete again.'

'Sounds fair to me!' Katie replied.

'It also talks about the final event and what happened, explaining about the Shockwave thingy. Dean said I was a hero.'

'Maybe I should take it back?' Dean said, standing in the doorway and sporting a surprisingly nervous smile.

'Doris! I wasn't sure you'd come,' Billy said.

'I said I would, didn't I!' Dean replied. 'Although I'm not coming with you to see Mr Crankworth. Dad decided we should move away and start over. He thinks it'll be easier for us. We're leaving today.'

'What … like, actually today?' Billy asked.

'Yeah, I just came to say sorry again. You know, for making things hard for you.'

'So, no more challenges then!' Billy said, a little disappointed. 'I think I'll miss them.'

'Yeah, me too. I'd have liked to beat the … oh, what was it? The Ginger biscuit?' Dean began to smile. It seemed he had a sense of humour after all.

'It beats Dramatic Doris,' Billy replied, smiling easily. 'Well, I hope it works out,' he said, sincerely.

Dean held his hand out for a fist pump. 'I guess I'll see you around. Bye Katie.'

Katie offered an awkward smile as he left: she couldn't get used to him being, well … nice.

'Looks like it's just you and me then, K. Come on, Mr Crankworth is expecting us.'

'Why are we going to see Mr Crankworth? I'm surprised you want to see him after everything he did!'

'You'll see,' Billy said, mysteriously.

Hardly able to think of anything other than losing her best friend – her more-than-best-friend, Katie arrived at Peregrine Heights to find Mr Crankworth waiting at the gate. Frankly, he looked awful.

'Billy, Katie,' he said with a nod. 'Listen, I'll keep this simple for you.' He held his hand out and gave Billy a Memory Trace. 'Everything you asked for is on there. Everyone that was involved in this year's tournament, I've linked them to that Memory Trace. I've enabled your Time Ticket too. It should be on your Profiler. I imagine you'll get rather a lot of money,' he said, with a weak smile.

Billy held his hand out and took the Trace. 'Mr Crankworth, can I ask you a question?'

'Of course.'

'Why did you never go back in time and change things?'

'Oh Billy, I wish I could have, but time travel wasn't even possible when your dad's accident happened. It was years later. When the time came that it was possible, your mum and dad had met, and you were born. If I'd changed the past, you'd never have happened.'

'Well … the thing is … Katie and I have an idea.'

'We do?' Katie asked.

'Yeah, we do.'

Mr Crankworth looked at Billy feeling more than a little puzzled. What kind of idea had they come up with if Katie didn't know anything about it? Little did he know that the young couple standing in front of him were about to change his life forever.

64

It was twenty-past eight in the morning when Billy crept into his parent's bedroom. 'Dad,' he whispered. 'Dad … wake up.'

A groggy Tom Wheeler opened his eyes. 'Uh, Billy,' he mumbled. 'Are you okay?'

'I need to tell you something, but you just need to listen!'

Tom rubbed his bleary eyes. 'Uh, okay.'

'I'm leaving for a bit. I'm going to a Time Port.'

'You're what?' Asked Tom, suddenly wide awake. 'A Time Port?'

'Yeah. Mr Crankworth gave me a Time-Ticket. He's letting me use it straight away.'

'Use it? What do you mean, use it?'

'I can change things … I can go back and fix the past.'

'Oh, Billy. No … you can't. The past is the past. Oh, that man has gone too far this time, giving you these crazy ideas. Why would he give you a Time-Ticket?'

'He gave it to me so we could sell it. But I'm going to use it instead. I can fix things.'

'I don't need fixing, Billy. I'm happy as I am, and I have everything I need. Besides, you can't just go to a Time Port. You're our son. What on earth makes you think we'd just let you leave?'

'But that's the point Dad. I won't be leaving. If everything goes to plan, I'll still be here. And it's not really about us anymore. It's about Fletch and Mr Crankworth, and Dean and his dad. Even Louise. I can stop all that bad stuff from ever happening.' He held out a letter. 'Just read this. It explains everything.'

Despite his many doubts, the more that Tom read, the more he understood why Billy wanted to try and fix things. Every time he tried to think of a reason that they shouldn't go ahead with the plan, there was another paragraph to justify it. Sometimes it was to do with Time-Travel itself and how Billy and Katie thought it all worked, but the one thing that Tom understood the most was the heart-breaking truth of Dean's mum leaving them. Would he ever have coped without Sue?

'Katie's a bright girl,' Tom concluded, finishing the letter.

'I know,' Billy replied, proudly.

'What about your mum? You know she won't go for it.'

Billy felt quite horrible about not telling his mum, but he knew she'd want to stop him –maybe she'd even lock him in his room so he couldn't leave. But the undeniable truth was that he had to try. Part of it was for her too!

'If it all goes to plan, she'll never know,' he said.

'And if it doesn't?'

'Then I guess nothing will get fixed.' Billy responded, flatly.

Tom stared into his son's deep green eyes. 'You really need to do this, don't you!'

'More than you know.'

'Then I supposed you should try. Come here Billy-boy.' Tom put his arms out. 'I'm so proud of you,' he said, his eyes glazing over.

'Thanks Dad. I Love you.'

'I Love you too. Now hurry up and get going before I change my mind.' He hugged his son feeling of both pride and fear; Billy could have been selfish with his Time-Ticket and lived an easy life, but instead he'd chosen to fix the lives of others. In the end he'd had no choice but to let him go.

***

Billy arrived at the Vault, puffing like a steam train: he'd run the entire distance from his house to the park without stopping once. Katie was already waiting inside the Vault and pacing the floor; her nerves were in tatters.

'Are you sure about this?' she asked, hoping that he'd changed his mind overnight.

'Are you bad at telling jokes?' Billy replied.

Katie's eyes glistened with tears, but she smiled awkwardly and hugged him, placing a gentle kiss on his lips. It might be the last time they'd ever be together, and she'd wanted to do that forever.

'What was that for?' Billy asked, a flush of pink filling his pale skin.
'It was for me,' she whispered.

He hugged her that little bit tighter. He could feel himself doubting his decision. Did he really want to give up this life … with her in it?

'Mr Crankworth will be waiting for us,' he said, letting her go and pushing the doubts away. There was no getting away from it. For the sake of everyone, things needed to be different. It was time to go.

***

Wearing his long black raincoat and wide brimmed hat, Mr Crankworth paced impatiently between the gates of Peregrine Heights. It was five past nine and neither Billy nor Katie had arrived. Unauthorised use of the Time Port would create awkward questions that he didn't have the answer to.

'Mr Crankworth,' Billy shouted, waving from down the road.

The sight of them filled him with relief. He'd half expected a very angry Sue Wheeler to arrive, but the fact Billy was there as agreed meant they'd accepted with what he was going to do. It was strange that they wouldn't be there, but Billy had insisted that he and Katie should come alone.

'Billy, Katie, I wasn't sure you were coming.'

'Sorry Mr Crankworth, I had to explain things to my dad.'

'There's no need to explain, Billy. I'd rather not waste any more time if I'm honest.' He placed a small metal ring on the floor and swiped his Profiler across the top.

'What's that?' asked Billy.

'It's a Micro-Port. We can jump to the Time Port.'

The three of them watched as a small rainbow smeared bubble began to grow from the ring. Once big enough, they all held hands and stepped inside. That same strange pressure pressed on their bodies before POP! The bubble and it's occupants were gone.

***

Katie opened her eyes to find she was gripping Billy's hand so tightly it had gone white. When she looked at her surroundings, she found herself standing in a very clinical looking room. The walls were completely smooth and featureless with nothing but the outline of a door and a simple handle. In front of her stood a large, stepped platform with what looked like a giant silver Polo perched in the middle.

'Is that where you stand?' Billy asked, pointing at the ring.

'Yes. Right there, Billy.'

Mr Crankworth wanted it done before he could talk himself out of going through with Billy's big idea. 'Okay, we shouldn't hang around. Let's get on with it.' He pointed to a red button on the Time Port. 'Stand there, Billy. When you're ready, scan your Profiler. Then, when the green light flashes, press the button.'

'Wait … that's it?' Billy asked, suddenly feeling incredibly nervous.

'Yes. That's it.'

Hesitantly, and feeling a little weak at the knees, Billy took his place on the platform. He turned to face Katie – even from the other side of the room she could see his bottom lip wobble. He took a deep breath and scanned his Profiler.

A gentle buzzing sound came from within the giant metal ring before it quickly built into a powerful electric crackle. Static electricity began to suffocate his skin, making his hairs stand on end as if they'd been rubbed with a balloon. Beside his head, a green light began to blink. The Time Port was ready.

'I … I guess this is it,' Billy stuttered, staring at Mr Crankworth.

'Yes, I guess it is.'

Billy placed his trembling hand on the red button. 'Goodbye Mr Crankworth.'

'Goodbye Billy.'

'Good luck Mr Crankworth,' Katie whispered.

Billy closed his eyes and pressed the red button. Unable to watch anymore, Katie closed hers too.

The metal ring began to spin, rotating faster and faster until it blurred like a giant Catherine Wheel. Bright blue sparks reached out like electric fingers clawing at the air, noisily snapping like whip cracks. Looking at Billy and Katie from within the chaos, Mr Crankworth could only hope that in a different time, he wouldn't let them down.

65

The Memory Trace finished and evaporated from his vision leaving a dazed boy sitting on his bed. At first, he was confused; had he been dreaming? His thoughts were blurred, as if he was viewing them through a thick morning fog. Weak legged, he walked to his VR-Wall and pulled the Trace from the dock. It all began to make sense. It felt like hours ago that he'd picked up the Insignia from the door mat, but like time passing in a dream, it had only been minutes. He'd been living another life through a Memory Trace – his own, alternative life. Now filled with clear understanding, everything held a new and immeasurable value.

'Morning Billy,' Tom said, walking into his bedroom. 'Ready for the final?'

Billy span around and awkwardly hid the Trace behind his back like a child who'd been caught stealing cake.

'Are you okay?' Tom asked, seeing his son's odd expression.

'I … yeah … I think I'm just a bit tired,' Billy replied. He stared at his dad, feeling a little shocked. He'd just spent an unknown amount of time living a different life in which his dad wouldn't have been able to walk into his room.

'Well, I'm not surprised, you were up early enough. I thought I heard someone at the door earlier. Did you see anyone?'

'Um, no.' Billy replied, not being entirely truthful. He wasn't sure if he should say anything about the Memory Trace just yet; he didn't know how his parents would react. Besides, he hadn't actually seen anyone, he just knew someone had been there, so he hadn't really lied either.

Tom shrugged. 'I must have been hearing things. Anyway, I came up to say that Dean and Kurt are going to meet us after we port.

They've got to pick something up on the way. You have an extra ten minutes before we need to leave.'

'Cool,' Billy replied, shuffling a little awkwardly.

Tom began to leave the room but then suspicion took over. 'Are you sure you're okay?'

Billy nodded. 'Yeah, I'm good.'

'Okay, good. You need to be a hundred percent if you're going to beat Dean and make it father and son, Space-Time champions.'

'The fearless Wheelers,' Billy whispered, for the first time in this life.

Billy had experienced several stark realisations in few the minutes that followed the Memory Trace ending, but there were two things that that stood out above all others. The first was that his dad was a Space-Time champion, and not restricted to a wheelchair – he always had been of course; in this life, that's all Billy had ever known. The second was that Dean and Kurt Tuffnell were their friends, not enemies. They were nothing like the ones he'd met in the Trace.

Lost in thought, he turned to cross his room and noticed a folded piece of paper lying on the floor. In his haste to pull the Memory Trace from the envelope he'd hadn't seen it fall out. He picked it up and unfolded it. It was a letter ... from himself!

Hi Billy,

I'm ... well ... I'm Billy. This feels a bit weird because I'm writing this letter to myself, in the past. In theory, I don't even know about it!

I hope I haven't freaked you out too much, showing you my own life. There were quite a lot of things that didn't deserve to be the way they were, so Katie and I wrote some letters and sent them back in time to try and fix things. They must be a lot older than you by now. We sent them back to 2053!

I guess the first thing to say is that if you're reading this, then Mr Crankworth must have arranged for Mum and Dad to meet. In my life they only met because of Dad's accident, so I asked him to arrange for them to meet at the tournament dinner. Maybe you should ask them how they met ... just for fun?

In total we wrote three letters: one to Mr Crankworth, one to you, and one to Katie. The problem we had was that whenever anyone time-travelled from my life, nothing seemed to change. Katie said she thinks it's because whatever they did meant that our lives had already become what they were. So, changing the past had already made our life what it was. Weird, right! In the end, instead of me travelling back and trying to change things, Mr Crankworth agreed to deliver the letters in the hope that they would work. Confused yet?

It could be that my life is same as yours, and that we didn't change anything, but I really hope that things are different. One thing I can be certain of is that I did live my life, even if it's only a memory now.

So anyway, the letters. Firstly, we sent them all to your Mr Crankworth, asking him to deliver yours and Katie's on the day of the Everest challenge. He'll have had his own letter for years. It explained about his son Fletch, and what he did to Dad. I bet that wasn't nice to read! I do hope your Mr Crankworth managed stop Fletch making his mistake. You'll already know if he changed things, because Dad is either in a wheelchair or he isn't.

I wrote to Katie and told her about us in my life. She's the best friend I ever had, so I hope she might be yours too. If Mr Crankworth delivered her letter like we asked, then she should be at the Everest challenge to meet you. I asked her to make a sign that says 'Fearless Wheeler's No.1 Fan' so you can recognise her. After everything that's happened the last few weeks, I've realised that I more than like her ... you know ... like that. The letter she's reading today tells her how I feel. I couldn't tell her to her face, I was too embarrassed. Don't be a wuss like me if you meet her.

I'm also hoping that you and Dean aren't still enemies and that Dad and Kurt get on too. That was the worst part of it in my life. Both Dad and Kurt hated each other for years, when neither of them should have.

I suppose you might be wondering why I asked Mr Crankworth to deliver this letter when you could have been perfectly happy without knowing about us, but it's very simple. It's K. She's the only real friend I ever had, and we only met because Mr Crankworth arranged for me to attend Peregrine Heights. I couldn't bear the thought of you never meeting in her in your life, so I had to tell you! If you do end up meeting at her Everest, it won't take long to see how amazing she is. Seriously, she's like the only red Pop Rocket in the box.

Billy.

66

Billy walked into the kitchen where his parents were eating breakfast.

'Morning Billy,' Sue said.

'Morning,' he replied, before leaning over and giving his mum a hug. He didn't normally do such a thing, but then his morning hadn't exactly been normal, had it.

'What was that for?' she asked.

'No reason, I just wanted to.'

'Are you feeling alright?'

'That's what I said,' Tom remarked, from behind his newspaper.

'Yeah, I'm fine. You know ... big day.' He emphasised the words with finger quotes as if to make his point. 'So anyway, listen. We're doing a project at school on family history, and one of the things we need to do is ask our parents how they met to see if any of them are weird or interesting.' It might have been his second white lie of the day, but this felt important.

'Well, it was a bit funny, come to think of it,' Sue replied. 'We met at your dad's tournament dinner. I'd just started a new job as a tournament medic, when a man passed out next to your dad's dinner table. I remember it because even though we were inside and it was warm and dry, he was wearing a raincoat and a big black hat. Your dad and I bumped into each other trying to help him up and I knocked your dad over. As they say, the rest is history.'

Billy grinned from ear to ear. 'The tournament dinner ... awesome! Right, I'm going to get ready. Hurry up, we've got to get going.'

Sue looked at Tom who'd gone back to his paper. 'That was odd.'

'Teenagers,' was all Tom had to offer.

Billy didn't care that his parents thought he was acting strangely; he had somewhere to be. At first it had felt impossible, that an alternative

Billy had lived a different life. But then not only had he just been living within the Memory Trace, but his mum had described an undercover Mr Crankworth at the tournament dinner. The letter had been right about how they'd met, which meant that Katie might be waiting for him at Mount Everest.

Running into the bathroom, he splashed soap and water everywhere except for on his face and considered himself done. Instead of drying himself with the towel, which would take far too long, he simply ran around his bedroom – wind dried! He might have been living a different life, but he was the same old Billy.

***

Less than an hour had passed when Billy watched the dark bubble of his Deca-Port brighten to reveal Mount Everest towering high above him. The familiar Port squeeze pressed against his body before the bubble split and popped.

Leaving the Port and his parents behind, Billy had been so utterly lost in thought that he hadn't even told them what he was doing. Instead, he'd just left them behind, heading towards Neverthaw Ravine in a daydream. If the letter in his hand was right, then surely someone was waiting for him.

'Where are you going?' Dean asked, leaping in front of him; he was already wearing his Kinetic suit.

'Dean! Oh, hi. I was just um … going for a walk.' He hid the letter behind his back; he couldn't explain that just now.

Dean looked at him, one eyebrow raised. 'A walk? What for?'

'I … uh … I was—'

'Spit it out Mumble Mary.'

Billy didn't want to make himself look crazy by telling the truth, so instead he just stood there looking a little daft.

'Oh, it doesn't matter,' Dean said, not waiting for an answer. 'Listen, they've pulled the race forward. Something about a blizzard. We won't even get a change to practice. We start in fifteen minutes.' He turned and ran a few feet, shouting over his shoulder. 'Good luck by the way. You're gonna need it!'

Billy coughed out a comedy laugh. 'Ha! You always were the joker.'

Dean threw a double thumbs up without even turning around. He didn't need to see that Billy was smiling. He could hear it in his voice.

Above Dean's head, Billy could see ominous looking clouds in the distance, all grey and heavy with their cargo of snow. Reluctantly, he turned away from Neverthaw Ravine and headed for his Demountable – his potential visitor would have to wait.

Billy arrived at the Demountable just as the first few flakes of snow began to settle on his jacket. Inside, he found his dad and Mr Peddleton huddled around his Magbike. Unable to resist the temptation, the first thing that they knew about his presence was when a snowball exploded on the back of his dad's head.

'Got ya!' Billy shouted, proudly.

'Oh, not again!' Tom complained, scraping snow from around his neck. 'Kurt got me with one five minutes ago.'

At the sound of his voice, Sue appeared from the bedroom. 'Billy! Thank goodness you're here. You disappeared after we ported, and we didn't have a clue where you were.'

'Sorry Mum, I was going—'

'I'm afraid there's no time for explanations,' Mr Peddleton said, saving Billy from the chore of an excuse. 'I've finished fitting your Gadget, but you don't have time to test it. You've got eight minutes to get to the start.'

Billy smiled. 'Don't worry, Mr Peddleton. It'll be awesome!'

'I can only hope you're right, Billy. I've never seen anyone use this Gadget at Everest before!'

'We'll find out soon enough,' Tom said. 'Seven minutes Billy. Go!'

***

With the letter tucked safely into his suit and only two minutes spare Billy arrived at the starting grid. The snow had become heavy enough for the distant peaks of the Himalayas to disappear. Helped by the odd gust of wind, the occasional white Snownado threatened to appear before blinking out of life again.

'Ladies and Gentlemen,' Schrader began. 'Please accept my apologies for the hasty beginning to our final event. I don't think it needs too much explanation,' he said, holding his hand out and catching a handful of snow. 'So, without further delay, please welcome your final five contestants. Leading the way, Anderson Toms, followed by Dean Tuffnell, Billy Wheeler, Louise Kelley and Alisha May.'

In response Schrader's introduction, the spectators launched into enthusiastic cheers and applause. Amongst the crowd, Mr Crankworth and Fletch stood side by side revelling in the atmosphere of the tournament they'd built together.

'What do you think?' Fletch asked, looking at the crowd that filled Neverthaw Ravine.

'I think it's the finest tournament we've ever had,' Mr Crankworth replied. 'You've outdone yourself yet again.' He raised his hand to acknowledge Billy who was sitting on his bike. *How you ever managed it Billy, I'll never know, but I'm more grateful than you could ever believe. I got my son back.*

Billy gave a slightly awkward wave. *Which Mr Crankworth are you?* he wondered.

'Competitors, in this shortened event you must race straight to Khumbu Icefall. Once there you must climb Grivel's Chasm and collect a Focus before rappelling back down to your bike. From there it's a flat-out race to the finish. As it has always been for the final event, if you cross the finish line first you will earn fifty Time-Credits. More than ever before I encourage you to never … give … up!'

Billy looked for his parents in the crowd eager to give them a wave, but instead found a blonde-haired girl holding up a sign. His mind began to drift back the Memory Trace and the thought of his potential visitor, but it was promptly yanked back when the first starting light began to sparkle. For now, at least, daydreams and visitors would have to wait – his final event was about to begin.

67

Billy lifted his feet and felt the instant magnetic bond as his boots clamped onto the sides of the bike. Beneath him, it trembled like a caged animal ready to take flight. *Was that her?* he thought again, just as the second light began to glow. *It could be her!* With every glowing light, his heart rate jumped ten beats. Three lights lit, then four, then … go!

Still distracted by the sight of the blonde-haired girl, Billy opened the throttle to maximum. He'd expected to launch off the start line and charge straight into a race with Dean, but instead found himself bucking wildly from side to side as if riding an untamed rodeo horse. If it wasn't for the magnetic bond, he would have been thrown clean off. Instead, in a kind twist of fate, when his hands flew into the air and he let go of the throttle, the bike slowed to a crawl.

Seizing their opportunity, Louise and Alisha shot past him throwing rooster tails of snow into the air. By the time Billy got himself back under control, all that stood in front of him was a white wall of powdered snow.

Further along the track and leaving Billy far behind, Dean and Anderson were already locked into a fierce battle of bravery; the first chasm jump was approaching fast, and with only one perfect approach, both needed to get there first.

Dean tucked in behind Anderson and got ready to slingshot past but quickly realised that he'd made a mistake. Freshly powdered snow flicked from Anderson's wheels and bombarded his visor like a thousand miniature snowballs all being thrown at once. He tried to react, but it was hopeless. Unsighted and out of control, Dean swerved across the track, and disappeared.

'Ladies and Gentlemen, we've had our first incident,' Schrader declared. 'Unfortunately for Dean Tuffnell, he's now enjoying the close embrace of a rather large snow drift.'

The initial reaction of the crowd was to gasp in shock, but it was quickly followed by a roar of cheers and humorous approval when Dean clambered out of the snow looking like a long-lost Yeti. Filled with fresh determination, he jumped back on his bike and gave chase. He was almost up to speed when a flat-out Billy shot past.

'Lost your way?' Billy joked as he flew past. He looked in his mirror and watched Dean disappear into the snow cloud behind. *One down, three to go,* he thought. Dismissing Dean, he looked ahead and spotted the first chasm jump, its steep snow kicker rising several meters into the air.

'How slow can you go?' Dean yelled, swerving into view beside him.

Billy almost fell off in surprise. 'How did you do that?'

'Back Thruster Caught you up easy! Bet *you* can't keep up!'

For the next fifty meters Dean and Billy yo-yoed back and forth, each taking the lead before falling behind again. Locked into a fierce battle, they were so obsessed with each other, it was only when they hit the chasm jump that they realised how fast they were going. Before either could react, they were air-born. Below them, threatening fingers of granite pointed up at the sky as if surprised to see flying contraptions overhead.

'Oh No!' Billy shouted, seeing the nose the bike dropping. He stared at Dean, his eyes filling with concern. 'There's nothing I can do!' With no other option, he held on tight and waited.

***

Further ahead and out of sight, Anderson made his final approach to arrive at the foot of Khumbu Icefall. Seeing it up close, his first thought was that it looked like a colossal white dried-up riverbed, all cracked and chaotic. Huge crevices in the ice formed wonky Seracs that were infinitely bigger than his house. Built over centuries, the ice columns were more vertical and threatening than ever before. It was one of these that he had to climb.

He looked up at the towering Serac in front of him. Its deep blue heart had been smothered by fresh snowfall hiding the few climbing routes that existed. Undeterred, he took a deep breath and triggered his Gadget. Instinct claws extended from his fingers and toes, glistening in the light like diamond cut blades. He reached up, buried his hand into the fresh snow and began to climb.

Several meters up, Anderson arrived at his first obstacle. Above him, an ice overhang loomed over him like an older brother trying to tell him what's what. Defiantly, he rammed his hand into the ice, hoping to find grip, but instead it broke away in pieces, tapping on his visor as it fell. With no way to continue upward, he began to climb sideways in the hope of finding another route. That's when the high-pitched whir invaded his ears. To the side of him he could see a fine cable. He looked down to find its source and saw Louise in her black widow suit. She was walking up the ice as if she were on an afternoon stroll. Before he could move over and get in her way, she was already passing him.

'Hyper-wind grappling hook,' she said, answering the question that was written all over his face.

Then a more worrying sound arrived. It was quiet at first, but it quickly built into the familiar roar of a Magbike. Anderson looked back and spotted the approaching rider just as they threw their bike into a slide. A tall wave of snow swelled into the air before cresting below his feet. For the briefest of moments, it felt like he could have surfed on it, but then it fizzled out to reveal Billy at the bottom of the Serac. Alarm bells began to ring in his ears; at this rate he'd end up being last. He turned away and clambered across the ice, clawing at the surface with much less caution. He'd only made it another few steps when he rammed one hand into the snow and let go with the other.

Unfortunately for Alisha, she was right beneath Anderson when he fell. Unable to move fast enough she took the full force of his fall. For a moment she managed to hang on, her own instinct claws digging into the ice. She dared to imagine they might make it, but then her grip broke free from the ice, and they both fell to the ground. Neither would win the tournament.

'It's beginning to look a one-horse race,' Schrader announced to the spectators of Neverthaw Ravine. 'Alisha May and Anderson Tom's have fallen behind, not to mention Dean Tuffnell and his disastrous final. Although we do still have a challenger,' he added, enthusiastically. 'A certain Billy Wheeler is still in the hunt and not giving up. Who will be our new Space-Time Champion? Will it be Billy? Or will it be Louise? It won't be long before we find out!'

Billy was half-way up the Serac when Louise dropped past him.

'Shouldn't bother if I were you,' she said. *Please don't beat me,* she thought. *My dad will never forgive me if I fail now.*

Still angry at her for using a Disruptor and cheating, Billy ignored her and climbed with even more determination. Reaching the top, he looked over his shoulder, expecting to see Louise riding away on her Magbike, but he didn't. Instead, she was still at the foot of the Serac, frantically battling with her grappling hook. *I can still beat you,* he thought. He climbed onto his knees and linked his Profiler with the Focus. Then, summoning all his bravery he, stood on the very edge of the cliff, straightened up and closed his eyes.

'What's he doing?' Schrader said, asking the question that only Billy could answer. 'He's not attached to the rappel rope. Surely, he's not going to jump?'

Standing in Neverthaw Ravine, Sue covered her eyes. 'I can't watch!' she said, fearfully.

Schrader had asked the question. Billy gave the answer.

68

With no rope attached, Billy jumped from the Serac. Snow flashed past his visor so fast it felt like he was driving in a blizzard at a hundred miles an hour. He looked at the ground racing towards him forcing his pulse to rocket like he'd been given the biggest jump scare. If he got this wrong, he wouldn't be meeting his visitor whether she was there or not!

'Your son is one clever young man,' Harvey said, giving Sue a reassuring pat on the shoulder. 'He chose an Airshield as his Gadget.'

'What will that do?' she asked, peering out from between her fingers.

'You'll see,' Harvey replied confidently.

Inside his suit, Billy counted down. 'Three … two … one … now!' He activated the Airshield and punched his fists toward the ground creating a huge plume of snow that billowed outward as if the ground had been struck by a meteor. When the white cloud cleared, Billy's snow smothered figure was revealed. With one knee on ground and a fist to the floor, he'd nailed it – Iron Man style.

'Yes!' Harvey said, doing a mini fist pump with himself. 'That's one brave boy you've got there.'

'He'll need to be when I get hold of him. He just about gave me a heart attack!'

Back at the foot of Khumbu icefall, Louise was still frantically trying to unclip from her grappling hook. 'You cheated!' she said accusingly, staring at Billy.

'No, I didn't. You did!'

'Who told you that?'

'My friend,' he replied. 'And cheats shouldn't win!' Without waiting for a reply, he turned his back on Louise and jumped on his Magbike, but not before seeing utter devastation flash across her eyes. Hesitating only for a moment, he opened the throttle and sped away into the snow.

***

Half-way back to the start, Billy spotted the lonely looking black suit that belonged to Dean. He was sat on the floor with his head in his hands like his entire world had come to an end. Drawing closer, he saw Dean's Magbike, the front wheel smashed to pieces, its race over. He slowed to a crawl and looked behind. Finding only snow, he pulled over and came to a stop. 'Hop on. I'll give you a lift.'

Dean looked up. 'Are you for real? You're in a race!'

'Louise is still messing with her rope. She's miles—' He hadn't even got the last word out when the roar of a Magbike filled the air. He looked at Dean, his eyes wide in disbelief. 'She was miles back!' he said, regretfully.

Dean leapt up and jumped on the back of Billy's bike just as Louise shot past. 'Go!' he shouted. 'I'll use my Backthruster I've got one charge left. We can still catch her.'

Needing no further invitation, Billy opened the throttle to maximum and gave chase like a tournament Hunter pursuing its prey.

Huddled down onto her bike and tearing along the track, Louise looked in her mirror. When she'd passed him, Billy had been but a small dot, but now he took up half the mirror. To try and slow him down she began to swerve from side-to-side, carving fresh waves of snow that swallowed him like a surfer riding the tube of a giant wave. Frustratingly, after he disappeared inside each one, he re-appeared even closer.

'Can you believe it?' Schrader asked, his voice booming across Neverthaw Ravine. 'I thought it was all over, but Billy and Dean look like they're going to catch Louise before the finish line. It's all up for grabs. Who will be crowned the new Space-Time champion? We'll soon find out!'

Fifty meters from the finish, Louise tried to lose Billy in another wave of snow, but it was too late; he was alongside. He looked at her, expecting to see defiance, but instead he found tears.

'I didn't cheat!' she shouted.

'That's not what Katie said.'

'Who's Katie?'

When the question reached his ears, Billy's thought was immediate. *Oh, I'm such an idiot! Katie didn't tell me Louise cheated. I've never even met her.*

Guilt smothered his misplaced annoyance; he'd seen the sadness in Louise's eyes when he'd left her behind at the Serac – it was all because of her dad, and it was horrible.

'I can't do it,' Billy said, letting go of the throttle and slowing down.

'What are you doing?' Dean asked. 'You're going to lose.'

'You're doing the right thing,' Katie whispered in his mind.

Billy turned and looked at Dean. 'It doesn't matter. She needs it more than me.'

'Of course it matters! You're going to lose the race!'

'It doesn't,' Billy repeated. 'Besides, I have something else I need to do.' *Someone I want to meet,* he thought.

'What can be important than winning the tournament?' Dean asked.

'I can't explain right now, but I will,' he said, turning away.

Overflowing with relief, Louise watched Billy fall away in her rear-view mirror. *Why did you do that?* she thought. *Won't your parents be angry?* For a moment she planned on asking him that exact question, but she quickly gave up on the idea; her dad wouldn't let her hang around with someone who was willing to give up on a win like that and she knew it.

'Ladies and Gentlemen, I can barely believe my eyes.' Schrader said, his voice booming across Neverthaw Ravine. 'Billy Wheeler has a problem and is slowing down just meters from the finish. It's all over. We have our new Space-Time champion. Please welcome her as she crosses the finish line. It's … Louise Kelley!'

When Louise crossed the line, confetti canons exploded blasting their vast cargo of multi-coloured paper high into the air. Filled to the brim with relief she thrust her arms skyward as if trying to catch every piece of paper and never let it go – maybe in her dad's eyes she'd be an achiever at last.

A few moments later and hidden within the mass of paper strips, Billy and Dean rolled over the finish line. 'Can you do me a favour?' Billy said, having to shout over the crackle and thump of the laser firework display. 'I need you to stall my parents. I need to go and do something.'

'You are acting weird! You've just finished in second place … on purpose … and now you have to go and do something? What could be so important?'

'If things turn out how I think they will I'll tell you after, I promise. I'll be back in a bit.'

Dean gave him a quizzical look, but Billy didn't respond. 'Okay, fine. Whatever it is, it better be good, Billy-boy!'

When Dean left in search of Tom and Sue, Billy ran toward the spectator stands. He'd just given up winning the tournament because a girl he'd never met told him it was the right thing to do. If he had any hope of explaining himself, he had to know if she was real. Above him, the colourful favela-like buildings were teaming with people watching the firework display. His eyes scanned the horde of bodies looking for the girl with blonde hair when, at the edge of his sight a sign caught his eye. The voices and fireworks faded away as each painted word came to him. 'Fearless Wheeler's number one fan.' His heart began to thump in his chest. Could she really be there? Waiting for him?

He grabbed the letter he'd hidden in his suit and made his way to the sign. A bubble of doubt began to swell into his stomach. Surely it was all just a coincidence, wasn't it? Or maybe somebody had played a blinder of a joke on him? Everything he'd experienced in the Memory Trace came into question. Had there really been another version of him? Had his dad ever needed a wheelchair in another life? Surely it couldn't be true. But when he stopped in front of the sign, all his doubt flowed away like sand through an egg timer. Having spent several weeks in her company, he recognised the girl instantly. He'd never met her in his own life, but the close bond he felt made his heart skip a beat.

'Um … hi,' he said, stuttering foolishly. 'I'm … um … Billy.'

The girl with the soft blonde curls glanced at the letter he was holding, and then held hers up to meet it. She smiled brightly and gave him the truth he was looking for.

'It's nice to meet you. I'm Katie.'

Printed in Great Britain
by Amazon